SOUTHERN CROSS

SOUTHERN CROSS

VAUGHN A. JACKSON

Charlotte, NC

FALSTAFF
BOOKS
WWW.FALSTAFFBOOKS.COM

For my wife, who was also confused why Confederate vampires were always the heroes.

Ezekiel rode into the burning town at dusk, the repeating rifle draped across his lap. Shattered remains of wagons and buildings littered the street, each piece threatening to trip his iron-colored stallion as he cautiously guided it through the desolation. He pulled his scarf up over his nose to ward against the smoke and dust.

A slight tug on the reins brought the horse to a stop and he slid from his saddle to the ash-blackened dirt below. He surveyed the charred corpse of the town from beneath his wide-brimmed hat and sucked in a breath. Even through the thick fabric, it stung his throat. Only one building remained intact amidst the smoldering town—the saloon. The wood was warped and blackened from the fire, but still it stood, sign dangling from a broken chain. He took a cautious step towards it.

Something moved in the darkness of the structure's open portal, whose once-swinging doors lay splintered at his feet.

"If you're alive in there, come out now." His voice was gravelly and muffled by the makeshift mask.

He stared at the swirling smoke that filled the doorway. There was no response, save another flicker of movement so slight it could have been a trick of the fading light playing on the dancing smoke.

"Last chance." Ezekiel fired a warning shot into the sky. It cracked like thunder in the empty silence that had once been Natchitoches, Louisiana. Quick as he could, he pulled the rifle's lever, ejecting the spent cartridge to the ground below and loading the next one. "Next time, I ask with this."

"We're coming out," a voice called. It was young, carrying the last vestiges of a falsetto and cracking on the last word. "Don't shoot."

Ezekiel aimed at the door, his finger a hairbreadth off the trigger. Two figures stumbled down the crumbling steps of the saloon. The first was a boy no more than nineteen. He had the beginnings of facial hair sprouting awkwardly on his upper lip and chin, and sandy blond hair dusted black with ash. The second figure hung limp, arm around the shoulders of the first. He was older, with a full grey beard and crumpled features. A bloody gunshot wound leaked blackish red from his side.

Their uniforms were different colors.

The boy wore a tattered blue wool jacket, but the older man's was grey. Ezekiel adjusted his aim to focus on the Greycoat.

"You're Union." Ezekiel's eyes narrowed and shifted between the two of them. "Why're you helping him?"

"His battalion left him after…" The boy hesitated. "They abandoned him when the city caught fire. He's been shot and I couldn't just leave him. Will you help us?"

Ezekiel sucked his teeth behind his crimson scarf. "Him dying is his business, not yours."

The boy's face steeled with resolve, though dark-rimmed eyes revealed his exhaustion. "I'm not leaving him to die."

The older man's grip tightened, ragged nails pressing into the thick blue wool of the boy's overcoat. His voice was raspy and harsh, punctuated by a phlegmy gurgle. "Please, don't leave me."

"I won't," the boy said. He patted the old man's hand and tried to give him a reassuring smile. "Don't worry."

"I'm so…thirsty." The man licked his dry, cracking lips.

The boy turned pleading eyes to Ezekiel's face. "Sir, please, help us."

Ezekiel growled through gritted teeth. "Move your ass, boy, I'm not asking again."

The boy stood his ground, light blue eyes piercing into Ezekiel.

"Fine." Ezekiel spat, and relaxed a bit, beginning to lower the rifle.

"Thank you, sir, I knew—"

His sentence was cut off by the report of the rifle as Ezekiel kicked it back up and fired. The slug made a wet *thwack* as it tore through the older man's chest, sending him sprawling to the ground a few feet behind the boy, whose face paled with shock. He turned, trembling, to look at the old man splayed out behind him in a puddle of blood.

The boy rounded on Ezekiel, fury dancing like firelight in his eyes. "What the hell is wrong with you? He was a *wounded* old man." His fists clenched tight at his sides. "You gonna shoot me next?"

Ezekiel reloaded and hoisted the rifle up over his shoulder. "Not unless I have to."

The boy threw his arms out wide and took a single step forward. "Go on then, shoot me you fucking bastard."

"Please..." The old man's voice came out wet and sucking like the hole in his chest. He rose to his feet and stood hunched over, arms dangling down to his feet. Blood dripped from the wound in his chest, watering the black-stained sand in front of the burnt-out saloon. He raised his head and smiled, revealing a mouth of razor-sharp fangs that glinted in the last light of the setting sun. "I'm *so thirsty.*"

"Damn it all." Ezekiel dropped to a knee and took aim again. "Move!"

"What the hell?" The boy turned and stumbled away from the old man, tripping over a charred board that had come loose from the crumbling building. He landed on the ash covered ground and scrambled backward toward Ezekiel, never taking his eyes off the old man. "How is he—?"

Ezekiel fired, the shell splintering the doorframe and tearing a hole through the grey Confederate coat. But the man was no longer there. His gnarled body slammed into Ezekiel before he could react, knocking the rifle from his hands. Both men grappled for dominance, but the savage Confederate won the struggle. Ragged claws ripped through the thick leather of Ezekiel's coat, drawing bright blood to the surface of his dark skin. The old man threw Ezekiel to the ground, tearing the scarf from his face in the process, and revealing his neck to the open air. The slip of fabric blew away as a gust of wind swept through the smoldering town.

The old man stood over Ezekiel, cocked his head to the side, and cackled. He tossed a glance over his shoulder to look at the boy. "Well, lookie here, we got ourselves a runaway slave what thinks he's a soldier." His gaze snapped back to Ezekiel, and his lips pulled back into a menacing grin. "You got a horse, and a gun, but you still ain't nothing but my next meal."

"And you're nothing but a fucking mosquito." Ezekiel kicked the heels of his boots up into the man's gut. Air rushed from ravaged lungs as he staggered, giving Ezekiel a chance to scramble back and roll to his feet. He stripped off his duster, revealing a torn white undershirt. Glimpses of ebony skin decorated with cross shaped burn marks peered out through the ragged openings. "Still thirsty? Come and get me."

The man roared, a deep basso from the back of his throat, and charged, fangs bared like a wolf. Ezekiel was ready this time. He dodged and launched a punch that caught the man square in the jaw. Ezekiel felt it shatter beneath his fist. He followed through with a kick to the chest and sent the old man sprawling to the ground. The skin on the old man's face hissed and smoked. The man began to shriek and writhe, clawing at his face until it bled. Ezekiel cracked his knuckles, each bearing the same cross-shaped scars as his chest.

The old man began to laugh, a wheezy gurgling sound that made blood spurt from the cavity in his chest. Fury bubbled over inside of Ezekiel, and he fell on the old man, fists pounding into his face over and over. Bones cracked, shark-like teeth dislodged beneath his knuckles, and his vision blurred a bloody red.

The old man's laugh choked into a wet bark and eventually he fell silent. His eyes glinted gold despite the sun having disappeared from the sky. Ezekiel's chest heaved as he came out of his rage. The first thing he saw was his own blood-stained knuckles. He swallowed hard.

"Boy, my rifle." His breath was labored, exhausted. He extended a hand behind him, to where the boy still sat.

The old man gurgled and twitched on the ground. "I'll rip out your intestines and lap up your insides." He reached a clawed hand up, but Ezekiel pounded into it, shattering the bone.

"I doubt it." Ezekiel turned to the boy and shouted. "Today!" The injuries would last longer, because of the crosses, but he could already hear the man's body stitching itself back together, a slurping, hissing sound like a snake choking on a frog.

The boy scrambled over to the rifle and tossed it to Ezekiel. His eyes were still fixed on the bloodied old man. Ezekiel caught it and ejected all the cartridges in a smooth, repeated motion. He dug a single slug from his pocket and slipped it into the chamber.

"You can't kill me with that." The old man giggled. "You already tried. And those burns of yours hurt, but they can't finish the job either. Soon, I'll get back up and there's not a thing you can do to stop me."

"The first shot didn't kill you because it was a regular bullet. But I know what you are now, and more importantly, I know what kills you." Ezekiel cocked the rifle and forced the barrel into the old man's mouth. "You ever wondered what silver tastes like?"

The old man's eyes widened with fear, a bright amber glow in the full, inky darkness that had settled over the town. "No, wait. Don't kill me. I can…I can make you like me! You could be immortal, all powerful, all—"

Ezekiel scowled in disgust and pulled the trigger. The rifle's sound was muffled by the old man's head, and the dirt beneath it. The recoil sent a shock of pain through Ezekiel's shoulder as red and grey brain matter splattered onto parched ground that greedily sucked it down into the depths of the Earth. Ezekiel stood and backed away; he knew what came next.

The old man began to decompose at a rapid pace. His hair and fingernails grew as his skin dried and tightened over his skeleton. And then he caught fire like a match on sandpaper. The corpse burned with a sound like crackling bacon, and within seconds, it was gone, crumbled into nothing but grey ash that smoldered orange in the dark.

"Funny, you don't look immortal to me." Ezekiel staggered away from the old man's remains and toward the boy who was still staring at him, speechless. He loaded another silver slug in the rifle. "I'm going to ask you this once: were you bitten?"

The boy frowned. "What?"

Ezekiel took aim.

The boy's hands shot up, covering his face. "No. No! Why would I let him bite me? I didn't even *touch* him until you came along."

Ezekiel held the boy in his sights a moment longer, waiting for a trick or sudden attack. Nothing came. He lowered the gun. "You got a name?"

It took a minute for the boy to realize Ezekiel hadn't shot him.

"W-Will Taylor." His eyes flicked between Ezekiel and the pile of ash that had once been the old man. "Who are you?"

"You got lucky, Will Taylor. That one was young. Strong, but stupid."

The blank mask of shock crumbled away from Will's face, finally replaced with panic and terror. "He was sixty-three! How could he do...any of that? What the hell was that?"

Ezekiel whistled for his horse and climbed into the saddle. "That *was* a vampire."

2

The scorched black earth of the town gave way to soft, swampy ground as they trekked through the Louisiana wilds. Ezekiel kept them close to the western shore of the Red River as they traveled. The rising sun glinted off it like the glimmer on the edge of a knife.

Will walked quickly to keep pace with Ezekiel's horse's long, slow strides.

"Vampires aren't real." He plucked a reed from the bank of the river and clamped it between his teeth, chewing it nervously as he spoke. This was the most recent of his attempts to convince himself of the fact. "They're a spooky story for kids."

Ezekiel scoffed. "That kid's story wanted to drink you like a damn canteen."

Will shoved his hands into the pockets of his tattered blue coat.

"You know what you saw." Ezekiel took off his hat and fanned himself with it. "Why try to convince yourself otherwise?"

Will stopped and threw his hands to the sky, the full extent of his mid-Atlantic lilt revealing itself when he shouted. "Because how could that be real? People would know, people would—"

"Die." Ezekiel kept his horse moving, leaving a flustered Will to fall behind. The drone of insects and bullfrogs that carried from the cypress choked swamplands filled the silence. He gave the reins a gentle tug, giving the boy a chance to catch up. "I know. Now you know, too. I'm sure other people have found out. Not so sure they lived to tell the tale."

"You mean…"

"I *mean* your ass wouldn't have survived if it weren't for me showing up." Ezekiel sniffed.

Will sheepishly assessed the mud-stained boots on his feet. "Thanks for that."

Ezekiel grunted in reply.

They moved in silence, the sun slowly reaching its peak as they traveled. After a while, Will's brow tightened and relaxed as if he were always on the verge of saying something. More than once, he glanced up at Ezekiel, then quickly looked away.

"Spit it out before you burst like an overfull tick." Ezekiel didn't look at Will when he spoke. He stared out across the river, letting his horse forge its own path.

"Oh." Will's voice was startled at first, then hesitant, but at last he asked, "Are you a slave?"

"Not anymore."

"But those marks…the crosses…did your master—?"

Ezekiel glared down at Will. "No."

"I didn't mean offense, I just…" Will trailed off. He went back to scrutinizing his boots as he walked. His nervousness had worried the reed down to nothing but a small bit. "I heard rumors they branded your people…like cattle. Is that true?"

"Cattle got fed better." Ezekiel made no effort to disguise the bitterness in his voice.

Will nodded solemnly. "I didn't know if what I'd heard was true. Lots of wild rumors. The older folk don't talk about it too much. I think it offends their sensibilities." He spat a pasty green glob to the ground.

"Where're you from, boy?" Ezekiel's hand instinctively went to his gun belt.

"Pennsylvania." Will shrugged. "Family were Quakers originally, but that bit trickled off. Never left the area though. Dad said it was too pretty to leave behind."

Ezekiel placed his hand back on the other rein. "I did the crosses myself. It hurts them because they view the cross as a holy thing." His expression darkened, and he revealed a burn on the side of his neck: a capital 'P' set inside the curve of a horseshoe. "*This* one was a gift from my late master." Sarcasm dripped from his voice like acid.

"My God," Will said, aghast. "That ain't right."

"Might be the first smart thing you said since I saved your ass."

Around the time the sun began its descent, they crested a small hill and saw a war horse grazing in a patch of overgrown swamp grass. Its saddle and saddlebag were still attached, but there was no one around.

Ezekiel looked over his shoulder at Will and jerked a thumb at the horse. "Bad luck for them, good luck for you."

Will crept towards the horse. He held his hands up in a placating manner while making reassuring noises. The animal lifted its head and perked its ears, watching him approach with a single shining eye. It snorted softly as Will placed a calming hand on its side, stroking it.

He spent a few more minutes soothing the horse before he finally climbed into the saddle. He gripped the reins tight as the horse started and bucked before settling back into the feeling of having a rider.

Will rode past Ezekiel, then pulled up alongside him. "I signed up because of them rumors, you know? Had to see for myself and stop it if it were true."

Ezekiel side-eyed him. "Truly, you are a hero."

Will's face went red. "Hey! People are fighting—dying—for your sake. You could at least show a little bit of gratitude."

"My master used to tell me to be grateful for my beatings, because it meant he wasn't gonna kill me. You blue boys ain't fighting for me. Y'all just mad cause half the country tried to cut and run. No moral high road there, just politicking."

"Now come on, that ain't fair. We got morals too!"

"Fair says you can ride along 'til we hit Alexandria. Hear some of your blue boys are stationed in the town. You can get right back to having morals."

Will scowled. "And what are you gonna do, sulk away into the sunset?"

"I got business to attend to."

The sun reached the horizon, tinging the sky with the slightest bands of purple and red. Shadows of trees stretched across land and water like talons, clawing and reaching to spread their inky darkness. Ezekiel spurred his horse faster; night was *their* time.

"Seems to me we have time. Might as well tell your tale." Will leaned forward in his saddle, trying to gauge Ezekiel's expression from beneath his hat.

"I don't know you; you don't know me. Let's keep it that way."

"It'll be a mighty long ride, if I have to sit here and talk to myself the whole time."

"Then shut up."

"Doesn't really solve the problem of me being bored."

Ezekiel sighed heavily. "I could just shoot you, save us both the frustration."

Will gave a crooked smile. "Can't see you saving me just to kill me now. You don't seem like that kind of man to me."

Ezekiel brushed back his coat, revealing a six-shooter at his waist.

Will's smile faltered in the fading light.

Ezekiel let the coat fall back into place and shook his head. "Ezekiel."

"Like from the Bible?"

Ezekiel shrugged. "Probably. Bible's the only book we had. My wife gave it to me after Pickett's late wife taught her to read. First word she taught me…"

"What's your wife's name?"

"Her name was,"—Ezekiel sucked in a harsh breath—"*is* Anna Marie. She's the reason I'm down here."

Will gave him a 'keep going' look, eyes wide and pleading. It was a puppy-dog face on a boy too old to truly make it work. Ezekiel kneaded his forehead. He pulled his horse out in front of Will's and stopped in its path. Will tugged at the reins and brought his horse to a gentle stop. The blood red of twilight had given way to the last vestiges of violet waiting to be consumed by night.

"My life story ain't pretty boy. It'll leave you questioning both your God and your fellow man." Ezekiel's features were hidden in shadow beneath the brim of his hat as he spoke. "I don't hunt these things for fun. Hell, I'd quit right now if I could…but I can't."

Will's expression became serious. "Tell me. I'll listen."

"Go get wood for a fire." Ezekiel hung his head. "I'll talk once it's good and burning. I can't stand the dark. Not anymore."

3

Ezekiel sat with his back to the river, silent as an ancient grave as Will prepped the fire, and when the golden glow of its flames illuminated the muddy field around them, he stared into its crackling depths for a long while. Then he spoke. "I'm not a slave…but I was."

"Get up, boy!"

The bullwhip burned across his back like a tongue of fire, leaving a raw and bloody gash in its wake. He clenched his jaw so tight he swore his teeth would break under the pressure.

He refused to let them hear him scream.

Anticipation tensed his muscles, straining against the rope that bound his arms to the whipping post. The blood-stained gravel beneath him bit into his knees, and every breath of air that touched him set all his nerves alight with agony.

"I said, get up."

The whip cracked again. More pain, like fire, surged in a line across his back. His eyes stung from the tears that streamed down his sweat-soaked face. Dizzy from exhaustion and blood loss, Ezekiel struggled his way onto unsteady feet. "I'm up."

"Good boy."

Ezekiel couldn't see the man who stood behind him, but he knew the voice, and the slow, sensual pace with which each lash was delivered. Josiah Pickett was a hard, unfeeling man who only seemed pleased when he was causing pain, either to one of his many slaves or any other person with the misfortune to cross him.

"Old Caesar tells me you were thinking about running away, cheating the man who homes you." He brought the whip back down across Ezekiel's back. "The man who feeds you." The leather of the whip came away from the sticky wet of his blood-soaked back with a sick slurping sound. "The God-fearing man who gave you a damn purpose in this world."

Ezekiel choked back the scream rising in his throat and heaved as though he was going to vomit. His eyes rolled aimlessly until they landed on the woman quivering in the corner of the shed: Anna Marie.

"It's okay." Ezekiel struggled to mouth the words. "I'm gonna be... okay."

Pickett continued his rant. "Now then, what *is* your purpose?"

Ezekiel screwed his eyes shut and took a deep breath. "To serve."

"And would you running away serve me any good?"

"No, sir."

"No. It. Wouldn't." Each word was punctuated by the crack of the whip and another white-hot streak of pain. Pickett stepped around to Ezekiel's front and lifted his head by the jaw.

Ezekiel glared at him, exhausted, but defiant.

"So why'd you want to do it?" Pickett's face was a contorted mockery of concern. "Don't I treat you well, boy?"

"Yes, sir,"—Ezekiel sucked a stinging breath—"of course you do, sir."

"Of course, I do." Pickett let Ezekiel's head drop. "Well, seems you've learned your lesson."

"I have, sir."

"Good." Pickett drew out the word like a man in thought as a smile slowly warped his sunburned face. "Better make sure the bitch learns too."

Ezekiel's screams grew incoherent as he wrenched at his bonds. Pickett swaggered over to Anna Marie and hoisted her from the ground by the arm.

"It's like I always tell my boys,"—Pickett hung her up by her wrists so that she could just barely stand on the tips of her toes—"ain't no lesson really learned without a little old fashioned corporal punishment." He sounded the word 'corporal' out in three distinct syllables.

"Don't you touch her!" Ezekiel shouted.

Pickett paused, the whip raised above his head. His face turned an apoplectic red. "Don't you give me orders about what I do with my property." Spittle flew from his mouth as he seethed. He brought the whip down with a sickening crack.

Anna Marie screamed.

Ezekiel winced as the flesh was stripped from his wife's back, and her blood mixed with his on the black leather of the whip. He etched every scar she received onto the tablet of his heart and set it ablaze with fury.

Night had fallen, and Ezekiel hurried about, stuffing their meager belongings and a few supplies stolen over the last few months into an old potato sack.

"Don't do it." Anna Marie laid on her side, her back bare and still tacky with blood and sweat; a dark stain sullied the white cloth beneath her. "If he catches you, he'll kill you this time for sure."

"He won't catch us." Ezekiel spat the words. "He thinks he's broken us, but we're still strong. We can get away."

Anna Marie was silent for a moment. "I'm not going."

The words were barely a whisper.

Ezekiel stopped mid-movement. "What?"

He dropped the sack to the dirt floor of their tiny shack. An apple fell out and rolled under the rickety cot that was meant to be their bed. Anna Marie reached down, gasping at the pain in her back, and picked it up. She held it out to him.

"I won't—*can't*—stop you, but Ezekiel, I'm scared. He did this just over a rumor." She stood and touched a hand gently against his back. He sucked in a pained breath. "If he catches us actually running…he'll kill us for sure."

"But he won't catch us." Ezekiel knelt down and took her hands in his own. "We've been preparing. By the time he knows we're gone, we'll be down in Mexico. We'll be free!"

"You don't know that." She pulled her hands away and wrapped her arms around herself, shaking with quiet sobs.

"I know we'll die if we stay here. He'll beat us over and over, and we'll die like dogs!" He caught his rising voice and forced himself back down to a whisper. "If there's even the smallest chance we can get out of this torment…shouldn't we take it?"

"I don't know," she snapped at him. "I just don't want to hurt anymore."

"We've endured this long enough." He took her head in his hands and kissed her on the forehead. "We have to go. Trust me."

She looked into his eyes, fear etched into the tired lines of her face. Her whole body shuddered, and she struggled to catch her breath. "All right."

The plantation was dark as a slaver's heart and still as a fresh dug grave as they crept through the neat rows of sprouting tobacco. Ezekiel stayed ahead, keeping to the shadows and signaling to Anna Marie when he saw that the way was clear. They made it to the edge of the forest, and just as Ezekiel started to relax, the alarm bell began to ring. The dogs woke, their barks and howls like a chorus of tormented souls gnawing for the opportunity to drag someone down to hell. Torches sprang to life in front of the main house, and Ezekiel heard voices rise up in the night: Pickett's and at least one of his three sons. He hesitated, struggling with whether to run, or stay put and hide. Behind him, Anna Marie's breath grew quick and shallow with terror.

The hound's cacophony grew closer. He grabbed Anna Marie by her arm and pulled her deeper into the forest that framed the plantation. As they ran, he looked to the sky, catching a glimpse of the North Star through the canopy.

He turned his back to it and ran harder than he'd ever run in his life. Mexico was south, and closer than the Canada whispered of in stories of the great Harriet Tubman.

It wasn't long before Anna Marie's shallow breaths turned to gasps of pain. "I can't keep running. My back...the world...spinning."

"We have to keep going." Ezekiel didn't want to admit it, but he was feeling faint as well. The wounds on his back were open again, and the blood that wasn't gluing his shirt to his back was pouring down to the grass below. He hadn't expected to have to run so soon. "If those dogs catch us..."

As if on cue, a great black hound leapt from the bushes, its muzzle a snarling twist of slobber and foam. It howled in triumph and all the other hounds frenzied in the distance.

They weren't that far behind.

The black hound leapt at his throat, but Ezekiel managed to catch it by the jaws. He brought it to the ground, wrestling with it as it growled and thrashed, trying to escape his hold. The two of them toppled to the ground in a violent struggle. He managed to pin the hound's head to the ground but knew it would come after them both the minute he let go. The others were drawing closer now too.

He looked up at Anna Marie, who wielded a decent sized tree branch in her trembling hands. The hound's teeth pierced the palms of his hands. "Go! Don't stop until you *know* you're free."

"But I won't make it without you."

"Just keep running that way." He tried his best to give a reassuring smile. "You'll be in Mexico before you know it."

Anna Marie lingered, conflict playing across her face like a dark dancer.

"I said *go!*"

The tone of his voice made her jump. She gave him one last heart-broken look, then turned and ran. Ezekiel kept the hound pinned until she disappeared amongst the trees.

"Just you and me now." He got his feet up under him and lifted the thrashing dog above his head. His back felt like it was tearing apart at the seams. Before the hound could struggle free, he tossed it. It slammed into the nearest tree with a sharp yelp, but the pain only served to disorient and enrage it.

Ezekiel began to sprint. He flailed his hands and shouted, "Follow me."

Outpacing and outlasting the dogs would be impossible, especially as the solid dirt ground beneath his feet gave way to swampy mud the nearer he drew to Hunter's Thicket. Even though he couldn't see them the hounds' cries seemed to come from right at his heels. He rummaged through the potato sack as he ran and pulled out a small tin container. Black pepper scattered as he shook it out behind him. The particles burned his nostrils and stung his eyes, bringing forth a stream of tears. He hoped a nose full of the spice would mess with the dogs' heightened sense of smell and deter them —at least for a bit.

Ahead, a cypress tree had toppled almost entirely over, leaving a wide pit in the thick mud, half-covered by the tree's wide and tangled roots. Ezekiel dove into the pit, sliding briefly before sticking in the mud. He stripped out of his shirt and pants, and scrubbed his body with the clothes, trying to soak up all the sweat and scent. When done, he balled up both articles and tossed them as far out as he could, in opposite directions.

Sinking back into the pit, he dug as deep as he could with his hands and covered himself with mud and brush and leaves. He huddled up against the roots of the tree and hid amongst the shadows and compost. The night breeze blew in between the roots of the tree, and he shivered.

It didn't take long for the hounds to find his pepper trap. He could hear their startled and disgruntled yelps, followed by a resurgence of angry barking. Torches illuminated three figures arriving on horse-back as the hounds struggled to regroup.

Pickett had a wild, furious look in his eyes, made all the more manic by the flickering of the torchlight. "God damn that black son of a bitch," he spat, "leading us on this wild goose chase."

One of the hounds pointed, not exactly in Ezekiel's direction, but close enough that his whole body tensed, and he inched farther into the shadows as quietly as he could. A spider tickled its way across Ezekiel's face, disturbed by his sudden appearance. He tightened his jaw and fought the urge to swat at it.

"What'd you find, boy?" Pickett's younger son, Collin, hopped down from his saddle, and the hound led him out of sight. "Something in the bushes?"

Ezekiel allowed himself to relax a small amount. The hounds hadn't discovered him yet.

Collin tossed Ezekiel's shirt at his brother Thomas. "Just his damn shirt. The bastard's smart. Bet you we'll find his pants round here somewhere too, right?"

Thomas remained unsettlingly silent.

The hounds were tracking around in circles, sniffing at the ground. Their fervor had died out and been replaced with confusion, and a hint of disappointment.

"Dogs can't find his scent again," Pickett said. "And damn if it ain't black as pitch out here."

"Blacker than him," Collin said with a laugh. His father's glare silenced him.

"We headin' back?" Thomas sounded bored as he spoke, with the smallest flicker of irritation.

"Yeah," Pickett said. "Let him go. At least we got back one of our slaves today."

"Silva got the bitch?" Collin asked, doing his best to sound tough and disinterested.

Ezekiel's heart froze in his chest.

"Had the dogs run her down just before she got to the river," Pickett said. "If we're lucky, he'll come back looking for her. Let's go."

"Actually," Collin said, "I ain't too tired, Daddy, so I was thinkin' I could keep lookin' a bit, see if I could catch the trail again." The desperate appeal for approval hung thick in his voice.

Pickett was silent for a moment. Ezekiel could picture him rubbing his chin as he thought. "You go right on ahead with that," he said finally. "Just don't come back so late you worry your mother."

"I won't," Collin said, nodding slightly.

Pickett and Thomas spurred their horses back towards the main house, taking the dogs with them. The sound of hooves faded into the night, and the patch of illumination grew dimmer with the light of just Collin's single torch. Silence fell thick over the night for what seemed like hours. Finally, Collin spoke as though he were having a regular conversation.

"My daddy and my brother ain't the best trackers," he said. "They're impatient and miss the obvious." He paused. "Like a pair of muddy tracks leading to a nearby tree."

Ezekiel wanted to run, but his body was rooted to the spot. He cursed himself for forgetting to hide his footprints. Of course, the mud would give him away. How could he be so stupid?

"It's dark, so you have to forgive them a bit I suppose. So, come on out, ain't no sense in hiding since I know where you are." When Ezekiel didn't respond he said: "Get your black ass out of that hole right now, boy, before I come down in there and drag you out."

The voice was strikingly similar to his father's, and it made Ezekiel's blood turn to ice. He scrambled to his feet and came out of his hiding place.

"Holy shit, that worked." Collin grinned slyly. "Figured you weren't too smart. Ain't no damn footprints out here I can see." He gestured around at the muddy ground. "It's all slop."

Ezekiel's face grew hot with embarrassment and rage.

Collin laughed, but there was no mirth in him, only cruelty. "You really are buck-ass naked. That's got to be uncomfortable. Mud and gunk all up on your sack. Cold too." He angled the torch down and quirked an eyebrow. "Guess even you folk don't all go around swinging an Arkansas Toothpick."

"Why'd you send them off if you knew I was here?" Ezekiel asked, biting back the fury burning as it spread through his chest and rose up his throat.

"Daddy's always picking favorites." Collin sneered and shook his head in disapproval. "And I think Thomas has held that spot for too long. Figure it's my turn." His eyes flashed towards Ezekiel. "Figure handing him back your black ass may just be the ticket to that. Now, I'd love to just drag you back to my daddy and let him handle you, but if I don't rough you up here, he might just beat my ass for being too merciful. You understand."

"Please," Ezekiel said, his throat dry and sticky with drying mud. "Anna Marie practically raised you."

Collin scowled. "It ain't personal, you know, us coming after you two. Just protecting our investment. You weren't cheap." He put on a sympathetic face. "And this is better anyway. You and the missus back together." The look of sympathy twisted into a malevolent grin. "I'm sure Thomas will leave her mostly intact for you. Maybe a bit looser in places."

Ezekiel was on Collin before his brain realized he'd moved. He dragged the smug young man from his horse, sending the frightened beast galloping away with a scream as the muddy ground doused the torch. His hands clamped around Collin's pale throat. In the dark, Ezekiel could see the wet shine in Collin's panicked eyes, the gaping, fish-like movements of his mouth as he struggled for breath. The other man's hands grabbed at his own, slipping off from the mud and sweat that coated Ezekiel's body. Collin's movements became slower and twitchier, until finally they stopped. Ezekiel's hands throbbed as he pulled them away from the young man's throat. He put his ear to Collin's mouth. The faintest rattle of breath whispered from the boy's mouth. He stripped Collin of his clothes and his revolver before dragging his body and leaving it slumped against a nearby tree stump. The clothes were too small and tore as Ezekiel moved, but he wasn't completely naked anymore.

For a minute, he angled the barrel of the revolver at the unconscious body. He pulled back the hammer as he'd seen others do so many times before. Times Pickett or one of his three sons shot one of his people, just for the crime of being a negro they no longer needed. Times shots were fired, and the hot metal of the barrel pressed against flesh as punishment. Times he'd imagined turning the weapon on his captors. The desire to pull the trigger bubbled up from his core, bursting as white spots before his eyes.

"Anna Marie always had a soft spot for you; said you were good as a kid." His hand trembled. "Said you'd have turned out alright, weren't for your dad. If you were her son.

"I don't know about that. I seen what you do." His finger tightened around the cold metal trigger. He tucked the pistol in the belt that now hung at his waist and delivered a swift kick to Collin's unconscious body.

"I ain't gonna kill today. For Anna Marie's sake. *She* wouldn't want you dead." He slid the gun into its holster. He tried to mount the horse. He failed the first two times, but on the third was able to get atop the saddle and squeeze his legs tight enough not to fall off. He looked down at the unconscious young man. "You best pray to your God she don't ever change her mind."

With the reins in hand, he urged the horse back to the plantation.

Ezekiel half expected Josiah and Thomas Pickett to be up, waiting to catch and beat him as he rode onto the plantation grounds.

He didn't expect the fire.

The wind kept the smoke blowing in the opposite direction. It wasn't until he reached the tobacco fields that the acrid burn overwhelmed his senses. He coughed, sputtered, and shielded his eyes.

It was like riding into a furnace.

Or Hell.

The main house burned a brilliant scarlet orange, and the flames leapt from the once white structure to the trees and all the way to the slave quarters. Ezekiel spurred his horse forward, rushing to the place where he and Anna Marie were kept. The roof of the shack burned as

Ezekiel leapt from the horse and kicked open the door. Empty. The shack collapsed in on itself as he ran to the next one over and bolted inside. A single black man, the oldest on the plantation, huddled in the corner, nearly blending with the shadows.

"Caesar." Ezekiel addressed the man slowly, his voice guttural, almost a growl. "Have you seen Anna Marie?"

Caesar's wide, jaundiced eyes stared at him in terror. Ezekiel had avoided him since the incident, afraid of what he might do if he caught the man alone. Fury at the older slave's betrayal bubbled at the back of Ezekiel's throat, and his hand twitched towards the revolver, but he choked the acid feeling down like bile and stayed his hand.

"You did this!" Caesar hooked a crooked finger at Ezekiel. "You angered the master and now he's punishing us all."

Ezekiel reached down and grabbed the man by the remains of his ragged clothes and lifted him into the air. Flames licked at the man's back as Ezekiel leaned in close enough to smell his sour breath over the infernal heat. Smoke began to choke the air. "Have. You. Seen. Her?"

Caesar shook his head, eyes bulging as he trembled in Ezekiel's grasp. He croaked out the word, "No," and then, "I'm sorry." Tears welled in his eyes, only to evaporate in moments from the oppressive heat. "I shouldn't have told. I shouldn't have. But Master..."

Ezekiel scowled in disgust and dropped him. Caesar landed on the dirt-caked floor of the shack. The rotted wooden planks groaned in protest as he sat up.

He quivered at Ezekiel's feet. "I'm sorry."

"What happened here?"

Caesar blinked and looked around. "Someone came—didn't see who—threw a torch at the place. Everyone ran..."

"Why're you still here, old man?" Ezekiel asked. "Do you want to be punished?"

"I... I want...to be free?" Caesar spoke as if he wasn't sure about the words he was saying. As if freedom was a foreign concept to him, and perhaps it was. It had been for Ezekiel until the first time Pickett savaged his wife; until he realized he had to protect Anna Marie.

Fire ate its way through the roof, slowed only by the wet mold that infested the building. The windows cracked and shattered from the heat. Ezekiel choked on the black smoke flooding into the one-room building. It would collapse soon.

Ezekiel hoisted the old man back to his feet, and dragged him outside. "Then go."

"Go where?" Caesar glanced about as if the answer lay somewhere amongst the burning wreckage of the shack.

"South to Mexico, north to Canada, somewhere not on fire, or somewhere that is, I don't care," Ezekiel stared up at the glowing conflagration that was the main house. "You're free. That means you get to choose."

He didn't look back as the old man climbed to his feet and hurried out into the night.

The flames inside the house licked at him, threatening to sear the flesh from his bones. Ezekiel was almost thankful for the smoke that filled his lungs. It kept him from smelling the burning, bubbling flesh of the people, slaves and white folk alike, that hadn't escaped in time. Bodies littered the manor house, crackling like bacon fat under the intense heat. Ezekiel grinned at the sight of Pickett's wife, recognizable only by her dress, still burning as it stuck to her charred flesh. Somewhere, a bone shattered like a gunshot.

None of the bodies were Anna Marie, but something about them still sent a chill racing down his spine, despite the heat. He'd seen corpses beaten, bloody, and even burned, but these all shared a common, primal wound. Their throats were torn open, blood boiling as it pooled from the savage wound. Several bodies had angry, blistering gashes cut across them, as though a wolf or bear had run loose through the building.

Fire didn't tear men apart. It didn't leave them holding their intestines in their hands.

Ezekiel slipped and fell to the floor. When he looked, he saw the now stomped remains of a human heart. His stomach lurched.

"Anna Marie!" he called, but the roaring fire swallowed the noise.

Someone coughed behind a door to his right.

Ezekiel grabbed the doorknob and immediately pulled away with a shout. The palm of his hand reddened from the burn. He clenched his fist tight to stymie the pain, casting about, searching for a way to open the door.

One of the bodies still clutched an ax in its charred hands. Ezekiel ignored the fact that the head was stained with blood.

It took more force than expected to pry the ax from the dead man's hands. Three of the corpse's charred fingers snapped like twigs in the process, and burned skin clung to the wooden handle as it came free. Ezekiel wiped his hands on the torn shirt he wore and turned the ax on the door, ignoring the melted flesh that squelched beneath his palms.

The first strike of the ax cracked the solid oak door, and the second made a hole that breathed fire with a force that sent Ezekiel stumbling backwards. He recovered, drew his gun, and threw his shoulder into the door with his full weight, crashing into the burning room and narrowly avoiding being impaled on an exposed rod of burning wood. The leg of an upturned chair splintered and jagged. Ax in one hand, revolver in the other, he searched the room. He nearly passed it off for empty, but then someone coughed again, and spoke in a voice he knew by hate.

"Who's there?" Josiah Pickett said before giving in to a coughing fit.

Ezekiel aimed the revolver in the direction of the man's voice. The ax hung loose at his side.

Pickett came out from behind the sofa, brandishing his rifle. When he saw Ezekiel, a grin stretched across his face. When he saw what Ezekiel wore, the grin evaporated like water in a flame. He pointed the rifle at Ezekiel's head. "You kill my boy, nigger?"

Ezekiel remained expressionless. "Maybe I did."

"You ain't fool enough to kill Collin and then come back here."

Pickett half-cackled, half-coughed. His eyes betrayed the worry he might be wrong.

"Where's Anna Marie?" Ezekiel asked.

"Dunno," Pickett said with a grin. "All chewed up in a steaming pile of dogshit."

"Where is she?" Ezekiel shouted, threatening with the gun.

"I got more pressing issues to attend to than a slave bitch," Pickett growled. "Some bastard lit my house on fire and killed all my property. I owe him a bullet. Now be a good boy and drop them things before you hurt someone." He fired a warning shot. "I'm not too keen on killing my property, but that's the only warning you'll get."

Ezekiel dropped the ax. As Pickett's eyes followed it to the ground, Ezekiel fired. The red bloomed like a rose on Pickett's chest, staining his yellow jacket. He grasped at his chest, bared his teeth, and tried to return Ezekiel's shot, but the pain finally registered, the rifle falling from his hand as it spasmed.

"I'll...kill...you." Pickett dropped to his knees, then fell face first into the burning carpet.

"No, you won't." The rage that had roiled inside Ezekiel for so long breached his control. He fired again. And again. And again. He fired until all bullets were spent, and the gun only responded with an empty, tired, clicking sound. "But I'd kill you again, if I could."

A shadow crept up the wall in front of Ezekiel, growing large, tendrils unfurling like bat wings in the flickering light. Behind him, someone clapped, a slow, mocking sound. Ezekiel turned. Thomas leaned on the burned-out doorframe, a curious look gleaming in his eyes. He waved his hand, and the air went cold like ice.

The fires dimmed and flickered out, plunging everything in darkness. Ezekiel looked around in terror. The flames weren't doused as if by water—no smoke drifted in their wake, no embers glimmered amongst the charred remains—it was as if they had never been. Out in the hall, the dancing light of the flames died as well, letting shadow consume the space behind the leaning man.

The room seemed to hold its breath.

"I didn't think you had it in you." Thomas's accent was wrong—not the lazy drawl Ezekiel knew. It was foreign and filled the air like the stink of an open grave. "To kill the miserable old bastard."

Ezekiel suddenly regretted the empty gun in his hand. This *thing*—his brain refused to acknowledge him as a man, as if some veil had parted and whisked away an illusion—radiated danger more fiercely than any predator. Ezekiel searched for an escape, but Thomas blocked the room's only exit. He tried to remember any of the prayers Anna Marie had taught him, but they all flitted out of his mind the second he grasped for the words. He doubted they would do anything anyway.

"Saved me the trouble of doing it," Thomas continued, disinterestedly, as though he were discussing the weather. "Personally, I thought the fire would get him. The slaves would get blamed, and I would just…disappear." A wolf-like grin curled his lips, revealing teeth that seemed impossibly sharp. "After claiming a nice insurance payout of course."

"You'd kill your own daddy?" Ezekiel tightened his fist around the empty gun. It was the only safe thing in the room with him. His eyes wandered to the ax on the floor, its head gleaming in the moonlight that poured through the burnt-out roof. He tensed his muscles, waiting for the opportune moment to grab it and chop his way free. Thomas laughed, a deep, rumbling sound that shook the whole room with its force. Ezekiel clamped his hands over his ears and hunched over trying to block out the sound.

"My real father's been dead for six hundred years. Pickett merely *thought* he was my father, and I played along," Thomas sneered, "but the centuries have not made me more tolerant."

"No man can live that long." The words left Ezekiel's mouth, and their falsity weighed on his tongue like the words he spoke to himself so often, just to keep himself alive. The ax was only a few feet away, but in his head the distance was insurmountable.

"No man, indeed." Thomas's face scrunched into the semblance of a smile. "I'll admit it was nice while it lasted, having a family. Humans never last as long as you'd think."

Ezekiel shook his head, trying to ignore Thomas's rambling, but keeping his eyes locked forward even as he made slow progress towards the weapon. It was almost in reach. "Where is Anna Marie?"

Thomas shrugged. "Maybe she burned."

Ezekiel's jaw tightened, his anger flaring as it had with Pickett's response. He heard the rapid sound of hooves come to a sudden stop outside. Silva grunted, something dragged across the ground, and then Anna Marie gasped in pain.

"Collin! Thomas!" Silva's voice sounded harsh with worry. "Y'all alright? Is Pa with you?"

"Oh." Thomas waved a disinterested hand. "Guess she didn't burn after all." Thomas's drawl returned for the moment. "Up here, Silva. I don't know what happened, but Dad's hurt. Come help me." He grinned at Ezekiel and turned to wait for his brother.

Ezekiel snatched up the ax and swung it, cleaving into the man's head. The blade sank deep, nearly splitting his face in two. Thomas turned to face Ezekiel again, the wide grin twisting into an animalistic snarl that showed his blood-encrusted teeth, sharp and serrated like the edge of a saw. Ezekiel tried to back away, but Thomas caught him by the throat.

"That bites," he growled, pulling the ax from his head. "But so do I."

His mouth began to stretch wide—too wide—like a snake's.

"Thomas?"

Thomas's mouth snapped shut at the sound of his brother's voice. He tossed Ezekiel to the ground like a child discarding a broken toy. Not wanting to be caught off guard, he scrambled to his feet and pressed his back against the nearest wall.

Silva stared at the visceral chasm in his brother's head. The wound was knitting itself back together, tendrils of flesh creeping across the ragged gash and hooking, pulling, mending.

Silva led Anna Marie on a chain linked to a shackle around her neck. Her skin was raw from where she'd stumbled and been dragged along the ground trying to keep up with her captor's horse—Silva's favorite punishment. Ezekiel's blood boiled, replacing the horror of what he just saw.

"Silva, come closer," Thomas's voice was now a raspy whisper. "I need help. He tried to kill me with an ax. He shot Dad. I think he's dead…"

Silva dropped the leash he was holding and rushed to his brother's side. Thomas dropped into his arms and stared up at him as his face continued to repair itself.

"Lean down, I have something to tell you."

Silva did, tears in his eyes, oblivious to what was happening to his brother's face. Ezekiel almost wanted to tell him to stop, that whatever Thomas was, he'd done this: the burning, the torn throats, the heart freshly carved from some poor man's chest. But he didn't because Silva wouldn't have done it for him.

"I'm not your brother." Thomas shark-like teeth pushed further out from his gums. His face sealed back together with a wet, sucking sound, and he clamped down on Silva's throat.

Thomas's whole face had changed. Gone was the younger image of Josiah Pickett. Instead, a man in his fifties suckled on Silva's bleeding neck with a sound like a babe at the breast. Golden eyes replaced blue ones and gleamed even in the absolute darkness. Blond hair darkened until it was black as the night around them.

Silva blinked in shock, barely processing the turn of events. Finally, his eyes went wide, and he tried to scream, something impossible with the human leech slurping at his pulsing jugular. Ezekiel's mind blanked in the face of the horrific attack, he couldn't fight or flee—fear rooted him to the spot.

Thomas jerked his head back, tearing out Silva's throat and spitting the chunk to the side. The blood splattered like ink in the darkness. Thomas licked the open wound with a worm-like tongue, savoring the taste with a cold lust. He moaned in pleasure as panic wrinkled Silva's face. The dying brother gurgled and choked on the blood that filled the ragged hole where his throat had once been.

"Don't worry." Thomas stroked his brother's face. "I'm not going to let you die."

He pushed Silva over and loomed above him, hands on either side of his head, mouth dripping blood on his face. Thomas's jaw unhinged with a click, stretching open his mouth in a silent wail. He made a harsh barking sound, like a bone had caught in the back of his throat and he desperately sought to dislodge it. A torrent of green vomit poured into Silva's gaping mouth, trickling to a stop as Thomas's mouth slowly began to close. His face returned to normal, and he cocked his head to the side like a vulture checking to see if its prey was truly dead. He stood and brushed himself off, then wiped his mouth, smearing blood and sick across the side of his face.

Ezekiel wanted to run to Anna Marie, who stood, frozen in terror, just like him. Their eyes met, but neither could move. He tried to mouth, "Don't worry," but his jaw was locked open in shock. Her eyes slid from him to the horrific scene before them, then up to the monstrous man standing over his dead brother.

"Now," Thomas licked the blood from his lips and smiled. "You did me a favor here, killing that old fool, and I'm old enough to have a sense of respect, unlike the rest of you flies. So I'll do two things." He held up two fingers, the nails of which grew into iron black talons as he did. "One, I'll give you my name since I consider you of note for the moment. And two, I'll give you a chance to survive the night."

"I don't need your name," Ezekiel managed to croak out. "But please, let us go. We just want to leave."

"My name is Palaiologos." The man scowled, and his voice took on an irritated sharpness. "And this will go as I say it goes."

Ezekiel flinched and waited to feel those shark-like teeth dig into his throat. The feeling never came. He eyed Palaiologos warily. The man's face had returned to one of relative placidity.

"Now, your chance."

"Both of us, right?" Ezekiel asked.

"*You* did me the favor," Palaiologos's eyes slowly rolled in the direction of Anna Marie, then snapped back to Ezekiel. "So, *you* get a chance to live."

He kicked the ax towards Ezekiel, who picked it up, eyes still locked on Palaiologos. Movement drew his gaze away and the blood in his veins pricked like icy crystals.

Silva rose to an uneasy standing position behind Palaiologos. He rocked back and forth, blood still dripping to the ground at his feet.

His head rose, and Anna Marie screamed. The man's face contorted and shifted like clay in a rough worker's hands. The crunch and pops of bones cracking and reshaping themselves filled the air. Silva tore at the blond hair on his head, ripping it out along with chunks of bloody skin until nothing remained but a raw, bloody scalp.

Razor sharp teeth forced their way out of his gums as he hissed and choked and spasmed. He lurched backwards as his spine cracked and twisted, leaving him with a hump that caused his knuckles to drag on the floor below. Finally, everything stopped. The creature that had been Silva heaved with ragged, primal breath, and stepped forward.

"Ah, just in time, Silva." Palaiologos cast a glance over his shoulder. "I've got a task for you." He turned back to Ezekiel. "Kill him, and you're free."

Ezekiel swallowed hard. His hands shook as he clung to the ax, and his knees wobbled at the sight of the lurching, lurking thing. "And Anna Marie?"

"Worry about yourself." Palaiologos snapped his fingers.

The Silva creature shrieked so loud Ezekiel's eardrums strained like they might burst. Palaiologos vanished, leaving nothing but a cloud of smoke. He appeared seconds later by Anna Marie's side and stroked her face. She shuddered at his touch.

"Leave her alone," Ezekiel shouted.

The Silva creature leapt at him, faster than Ezekiel had ever seen something move. He barely managed to catch its claws with the ax, and the wood creaked from the strain. With a grunt, he shoved the creature back, staggering it.

"Maybe I was trying to have the wrong type of family. After all, it's been just as long since I've had a lover." He held Anna Marie's face and made her look at him. Palaiologos's eyes flashed a bloody red, and Anna Marie fell limp in his arms.

"No!" Ezekiel swung the ax, cleaving through the air where the creature had been.

Palaiologos's grin turned cruel. "Even longer since I've taken one. I hope you don't mind."

And they were gone. Nothing but a cloud of grey smoke remained.

Ezekiel roared in frustration and ran towards the lingering wisps. A clawed hand caught him upside the head and sent him sprawling to the floor. The creature loomed over him, bile-colored drool dripping down to the floor below. Fear spread through Ezekiel's limbs, a poisonous fatigue trying to drain his strength. But something else burned at the back of his throat, coarse like the moonshine the slaves would sneak from the kitchen. Like fire and coal oil. He tightened his grip on the ax and swung it with a shout. It bit deep into the creature's collarbone and stuck. The creature screamed and stumbled away, yanking the ax from Ezekiel's grasp. It pulled the ax from its flesh and hurled it at Ezekiel, howling like the wind in a storm. The ax handle shattered into splinters as it hit the wall behind him. The head stuck, but a thin crack ran through the grey metal.

The creature lumbered forward, a trail of brown drool drooping to the floor.

Ezekiel scrambled, searching for something else to defend himself with. Beneath a shifted piece of debris, he found one of Pickett's old decorative crosses that had hung on the walls of the house. With a frustrated grunt, he kicked it aside. It slid across the floor towards the creature.

One of the sitting room tables had survived the worst of the inferno. He pulled on one of its legs and pushed at the rest of the furnishing with his foot, straining until it cracked, and the leg splintered free, leaving him with a length of wood just under three feet long. He gripped it like a club and waited for the creature to strike again, but it didn't. It huddled away from an object that lay at its feet until its back was inches away from the charred wall of the room. Blood red eyes were locked in an intense focus, forgetting everything else. Ezekiel followed its gaze until he saw the cross he'd kicked not seconds ago. He swore it gleamed, despite its rugged, iron black surface.

Something Anna Marie had told him once surged forward from his memories, something she'd learned from her snippets of conversation with the local preacher. Reverend Walker would come under the guise of converting the slaves, but often brought them extra food, or clothing, right under Pickett's nose. It was a small kindness, and Ezekiel had always thought it was more to make the man feel good about himself, rather than to actually help them, but he'd never spoken so aloud. The reverend had given Anna Marie a Bible and pointed to the cross on the front saying that demons feared the sign of the cross. That it would protect her from evil.

Ezekiel hadn't believed in demons then, but he wasn't a man to ignore what he saw now. He took a hesitant step forward, halfway expecting a trick or feint of some kind. He waited to feel hot breath on his neck, and the cold feeling of blood sucked from his body, but it didn't come. The creature continued to shudder as Ezekiel reached down and took hold of the cross, bringing it level with the creature's face. It took a step back, back thumping against the wall and showering the floor with ash. Ezekiel thrust the cross forward. The creature shrieked and shielded its face with clawed hands.

"You don't like that, do you?" Ezekiel pulled a strip of fabric from the torn shirt still hanging ragged from his body, and wrapped it around the cross, tying the symbol to the top of the broken table leg. A final tug ensured it was sturdy and wouldn't slip free. He swung at the creature, and it flinched away in terror. Ezekiel surged with strength at the creature's fear.

He lowered the cross-headed club down towards the creature. It tried to slink away, but there was nowhere for it to go. Ezekiel smirked, raising the club above his head. With a roar he brought it down like a hammer. The creature's skull cracked, and its skin hissed where the cross touched its flesh. He squeezed his eyes shut tight and hammered at the creature until his arms gave out. The smell of burning flesh filled the air when Ezekiel finally stopped. He staggered back, staring in a contorted mix of horror and admiration at his work. The creature's head was a seared, pulpy mass. Its body still twitched, prompting Ezekiel to run it through the heart with the chair leg— nothing could survive without a heart. He raised it above his head and brought it down with all the force he could muster. The first strike cracked its chest, caving it in slightly. His next strike broke through the softened flesh and penetrated the heart almost as much as it pulped the bloody muscle.

The creature moaned as its body began to shrivel and hiss, then it burst into flames. Ezekiel toppled backwards and landed hard on his tailbone. The fire petered out as quickly as it had started, leaving nothing but ash.

"That works," he said, chest heaving from the exertion. He fell to his knees, body shaking, heart racing. He buried his face into his hands, and Ezekiel began to weep.

4

Nocturnal creatures took up the charge to fill the silence as Ezekiel finished his story. They sat still as statues in the dark, both actively avoiding making eye contact with the other, until Will broke the silence with a question.

"So, you've been looking for her for ten years?" His voice was a mixture of sympathy and incredulity. "Just you?"

"Me and this old bastard," Ezekiel said, patting the side of the horse's neck. "Ten years. Started off just avoiding white folk and killin' bloodsuckers—hopin' to fight the right one. Now I gotta deal with this damn war what got everybody on edge. As if my job weren't hard enough already."

He spat as the firelight flickered across his face. The crackling glow did little to keep the darkness at bay beyond their small circle, but it was enough. The river burbled, a slow relaxing motion amidst the night sounds. The shattered reflection of the fire danced on its mirror-like surface like fireflies.

"Is it safe to be out in the open like this?" Will glanced about. "What about the vampires?"

"Thought vampires weren't real?" There was the hint of a smirk in Ezekiel's voice.

Ezekiel reached up into the horse's pack and pulled out a bottle of brown liquid. He popped the cork from the bottle and took a long swig. He offered some to Will, but the young man waved it away.

"Well maybe I believe you now. Can't see any other reason why you'd mark yourself all up like that." Will stretched out on his side of their patch of green by the riverbank, resting his back against a log the river had spat onto its bank.

"Maybe I'm crazy." Ezekiel stared at the reflections in the water.

"Crazy is a dead man getting back up and trying to suck my blood. Not the man who saved me from him."

Ezekiel chuckled. It was a hollow sound. "Rest. I'll keep watch."

"Shouldn't you sleep too?" Will raised an eyebrow.

"Not if you want to survive the night." Ezekiel took up a position on a rock, sitting down and crossing his legs. His rifle rested across his lap as he scanned the horizon in the opposite direction of the river.

Will stared up at the night sky, shifting uncomfortably beneath its open expanse. He rolled to face the river, then flipped over on his back again. He did this a few more times before Ezekiel cleared his throat.

"None of the ones I've encountered can fly," he said. "And they can't cross running water on foot."

"Now I'm gonna have nightmares about vampires on boats."

"Drown. It'll wake you up."

"Bully for me," Will said, rolling to face the river. "Vampires and *drowning*."

The sun was high in the sky when Will awoke. He'd rolled over in his sleep, and half his face was caked in drying mud with blades of grass clinging to it like glue.

"Ezekiel?" He looked around, but the other man was nowhere to be seen. His horse still stood where the man had posted for his watch, minus the rifle that usually hung in its saddle. Will was alone with the horses, the river to his back, and several clumps of reeds rustling along the muddy bank.

His sleep-addled brain lingered in confusion for a moment before flicking into panic. Will bolted upright, scanning his surroundings more intently. He opened his mouth to call out again, but snapped it shut when he heard the sound of hooves. Not Ezekiel's single horse, but several trotting out of time with each other.

Over the slight rise of the riverbank flew a flag made up of a plain white field interrupted only in the top left corner where a red square held a blue, starry cross.

The Confederate flag.

Will scrambled to his feet. There was nowhere the horses couldn't run him down. He let his shoulders slump. He slowly worked himself to his feet, smoothing out his ragged Union blues and stood facing the approaching sound.

Moments later the horses and their riders came into view. It was a small detachment of six haggard men in a motley grey line. They stared down at him with a mixture of contempt and exasperation.

Will raised his hands above his head, showing that he was unarmed and surrendering.

A young girl, no older than thirteen, rode up beside the men on a small pony. She carried herself with the poise of a lady, but the disheveled state of her hair and the slightly-too-small dress that hadn't been mended in years spoke to the poverty prevalent in the outskirts of the wartime South. "See, Captain Beauregard. I told you there was a Bluebelly sleepin' by our river."

Beauregard's ruddy mustache bristled, and he glanced down at the girl with undisguised irritation. "So you did, Miss Katherine, so you did. Why don't you run home to your mother while we handle things here?"

"It's Kate, and nah, I'm gonna stay right here, thank ya very much." She blew a few loose brown strands out of her face and crossed her arms over her chest.

Beauregard cleared his throat, reassuming control of the situation. "Detain this man. We'll question him back at base camp." His voice was the same commanding bark every man with authority acquired over time, tinged with a slight Creole accent that decorated the end of every word. He looked Will up and down as if appraising his hound's latest excrement. "He's either very lost...or a filthy deserter. Either way, he will be dealt with."

The other men surrounded Will. One dismounted and bound his hands with rope that scraped against the skin of his wrists. He gave the other end to a different rider and climbed back into his saddle.

"I'm not a deserter," Will said. "I got separated from my unit and ended up here."

"Stupid Bluebelly." Kate made a rude gesture at him. "You should know you ain't welcome down here."

Will shrugged. "Can't know where I am if I don't got a map."

"Enough," Beauregard snapped. He took a deep breath, smoothed his ragged grey coat, and returned his attention to Will. His eyes raked over the river's bank. "Are you alone?"

"Far as I know."

Beauregard narrowed his eyes. "Yet there are two horses."

"There are." Will nodded slowly, trying to come up with a believable story. "This one" —he thumbed at Ezekiel's horse— "been following me since the mix up."

"Bring both horses." Suspicion still lingered in Beauregard's eyes, but he seemed satisfied. He turned his horse and whistled, signaling his men to fall in line. The rope jerked Will forward, and he almost fell. Kate laughed as he struggled to catch his footing and keep pace with the horse. Will said nothing, focusing instead on his feet as he walked.

The river faded into the horizon as they took him west into the open lowland of the Mississippi plains. Blue-green rivulets criss-crossed the overgrown marsh greens that made up the ground beneath them, creeks and tributaries that softened the earth and made progress slow at times. Every so often, Will would look around, hoping to see Ezekiel charging to his rescue, and every so often, he was disappointed. After a while, Kate slowed her horse and fell into step with Will and his handler.

Will cocked his head up at her. "So you're the one who outed... me?"

"If you found a rat, wouldn't you want someone to get rid of it?" She sniffed, refusing to look at him. "Same thing with Bluebellies—gotta root 'em out before they cause problems."

"That so?" Will scoffed indignantly. "You make it sound like we're the ones doing something wrong."

This time she did look at him, and sneered. "You *are*."

Without another word, she lashed her pony with the reins and sped forward, leaving Will in a spray of mud and grass.

"Charming girl," Will sputtered, spitting out bits of the debris.

His handler looked down at him. He was older, but not by much; the first embarrassing vestiges of facial hair, including sprouts of sideburns, could be seen beneath the dirt that clouded his face. His eyes held none of the contempt of his captain or the young Kate. He offered Will a drink from his canteen. The soldier then pulled a flask from his coat and—after checking that Beauregard was not looking—took a long swig.

"Union soldiers killed her older brother," he said, exhaling the burn that came with the liquor. "Can't blame her for not being too fond of your kind, huh?"

"I didn't put the bullet in him," Will grumbled.

"You think it matters if you did or didn't?"

"No." Will sighed and rolled his neck—it had gone stiff from staring at his feet. "Of course it doesn't matter. She has every right to be angry."

He stared at the back of Kate's head, wondering how old she'd been when her brother died. Kate glanced over her shoulder and caught him staring. She scowled and rode back alongside him.

"What do you want?" she snapped.

Will opened his mouth.

"If you say you're sorry for my loss, I'll yank your rope and make you fall head over ass." She smiled wryly down at him, seemingly enjoying his shock. "Ain't hard to hear you gossiping when no one else is talking."

Will composed himself with a deep breath. "Was your brother a soldier?"

Kate's smile vanished, replaced by a pained look. "He didn't want to fight, but the army said they needed him. So he went. Died in his first battle. Mortar shell they said." She wiped her eyes on her sleeve, and it came away wet.

"Will apologizing now still lead to bodily harm?"

"Why do you even care?" She scowled at him, her eyes red and damp.

"Cause I'm not the monster you think I am." Will returned his gaze to his feet, his mouth turned down in a solemn expression. "I haven't killed anybody in the war, and I haven't lost anyone either. I can't imagine what you're going through, but I am truly, terribly sorry for your loss. Were the two of you close?"

"He was my brother!" Kate snapped.

At the front of the miniature caravan, Beauregard's head whipped around, his eyes flashing with anger. "Katherine, cease this fraternization at once. Run ahead and inform your mother that there will be a prisoner in our camp. My men will stand guard, but she should take precautions as well."

"Fraternization!" Kate scoffed, and fixed Will with a hateful glare. Then she was gone, once more kicking up debris as she raced towards a modest house that rose from the flat of the land. It was a squat, blue building with what appeared to be a fresh coat of whitewash. The field to its left was abuzz with the few slaves toiling away at the marshy ground. Two white women and a male slave stood in front of the house alongside Kate, still mounted on her horse, one grey-haired and hunched, the other a middle-aged woman whose beauty had yet to fade at the grasping hands of poverty.

Several canvas tents sat adjacent to the house, though there was little movement between them. The Confederate flag hung above each tent, dusty and ragged, but flying all the same.

"Oh, thank god," Will muttered. His body ached from the endless walk. He knew his ordeal was far from over, but it was preferable to marching any further.

Beauregard ordered a soldier to escort Will to his tent, where he was placed in a chair, and the bindings that had strung him to the horse were repurposed to hold him in a seated position. Will wiggled, testing his bonds.

"Even if you were to escape," Beauregard said, taking a seat behind a large field desk, "my men have orders to shoot on sight. Should you survive that, you would be hanged as a deserter."

"Just getting comfortable." Will offered what he hoped was a relaxed smile.

Beauregard shook his head. "Now then. What were you doing down by the river, so deep in Confederate territory and all alone?"

"Like I said earlier," Will started, "I was separated from my unit. We were passing through Natchitoches—"

"So you were with the ones that burned down that fine town?"

Will shook his head. "We didn't start the fire. The people in the town tried to burn their supplies so we couldn't get them, but it burned out of control. We tried to help, but..." He trailed off, remembering the panicked screams and the final call for retreat...and then the man who wasn't a man—the vampire.

Beauregard toyed at the ruddy mustache that curled from his upper lip. "I see. But you must understand from my perspective that your story comes off as little more than a convenient excuse to disguise one's desertion."

"I have no map and no knowledge of the terrain—I was hoping to make my way to the encampment at Alexandria to resume my service."

"We found you unarmed," Beauregard drawled, "and even the most craven of deserters would know to keep their weapon. So you are a deserter *and* a fool." He paused, searching Will's face for any give. "There's also the fact that you admitted to having never killed a man. Every soldier, even the rank and file, has killed. Unless they fled before the battle."

"I'm a member of the Ambulance Corp. My job is to keep people alive until they can be properly treated. I lost my weapon in the chaos back in Natchitoches…"

"Sawbones." Beauregard grimaced.

"No, sir. I *wanted* to be a doctor before all this but…" Will smiled sadly. "From what I hear, amputation is…always an unfortunate last choice. It's just what people remember most."

Beauregard rose. "The worst things are often what we remember most clearly. Tell me, did you treat both sides? Union and Confederate?"

"An injured man deserves treatment regardless of the color of his coat." Will attempted a shrug, but his bonds made it a futile effort. "I'm Union, but as a medic, my honor dictates I aid anyone in need."

A smile—completely devoid of warmth—stretched across Beauregard's face. It made him look haggard, and frayed. "Deserter or not then, you may very well be useful to my men and I, should you be willing to…adjust…your allegiances."

Ezekiel had been washing behind some of the riverside scrub when the girl had caught his eye. He'd crouched low—practically underwater—to ensure she only saw Will, still sleeping by the dead fire. When she disappeared, he considered leaving the boy to whatever fate might come his way—maybe the girl was a Union sympathizer. He'd gotten a fair distance when he saw the Confederate troops on the march.

Staying out of sight for the duration of the young boy's prisoner march had been far more difficult than hiding in a nearby clump of reeds. Now Ezekiel kept himself obscured within a nearby copse of cypress trees at the edge of the house's land. He didn't know why he'd come back for Will, save that the thought of leaving anyone in the hands of a bunch of pro-slavery rats left him ill at ease.

He counted eight tents and scowled at the sight of the Stainless Banner flying high, but felt a hint of satisfaction at how ragged the traitor flag looked. A few sentries ambled about the encampment, but hardly spared a glance beyond that.

The main house lay nestled between the slave quarters—and fields being worked—and the Confederate tents. Will had been taken to the latter, but with one rifle and two revolvers, Ezekiel didn't stand much of a chance against a group of soldiers. His eyes flickered back to the slaves, and he wondered if—with a little push—they'd be willing to help him. There were no overseers amongst them, unless they were other slaves pressed into the position.

It was a chance he'd have to take.

The two women and the young girl entered the house, leaving the slave—a light-skinned man who looked to be around thirty—to return to his duties. Ezekiel tied his horse to a tree, pulled his scarf up over his face, and met the man as he reached the edge of the field. The man's eyes went wide at the sight of Ezekiel, who held a finger to his lips.

"I don't want no trouble. You speak English?"

The man pointed to his ear and nodded, then pressed his hand to his mouth and shook his head. He repeated these actions a second time, then cupped a hand to his ear.

Ezekiel frowned. "You understand, but can't speak it?"

Another nod. The man opened his mouth, revealing bright red tonsils, but no tongue. Rage flickered like a candle catching flame in Ezekiel's chest. "You can't speak at all." His eyes shot to the house. "They do that to you?"

A look of shock ran over the man's face, and he shook his head vehemently. Then, as if struck by a sudden realization, the man pointed to himself, then drew a series of letters in the air.

Ezekiel blinked, taken aback at the man's ability to spell. "Jeremiah? That you?"

Jeremiah nodded and smiled.

"Okay, Jeremiah." Ezekiel's anger didn't dissipate, but he was able to pull his focus away from the squat manor house and back to the task at hand. He dragged a hand down his face. "I need to speak to the slave commandeur." It was risky, and Ezekiel knew it—some slaves turned on their own kind, siding with the planters and the overseers, despite their unequal treatment—but it was his only shot at freeing Will.

Jeremiah pointed to a series of small buildings at the back corner of the field.

Ezekiel grunted, keeping a wary eye on the Confederate sentries. Up close, they seemed even less inclined to perform their duties. "Lead the way."

The slaves at work all stopped to watch as Ezekiel and Jeremiah walked by. When Ezekiel turned his head to see them, they immediately looked away and returned to their work.

They walked in silence until they came to the faded white door of one of the slave quarters. It was much nicer than the one he and Anna Marie had shared; twice the size, with fresh white paint and a distinct lack of mold-smell.

Jeremiah knocked three times. Sounds of movement, straightening up most likely, came from inside the small shack. A soft hum of displeasure followed.

"Get on in here," a woman's voice called. "Ain't got time for you to linger out on the steps. Just ignore the mess, would you, child?"

Jeremiah opened the door, gestured for Ezekiel to enter, then closed it behind them.

An older black woman busied herself amongst candles, bones, plants both growing and dead, and other strange objects. The space was filled with trinkets, save for the freshly cleaned bed that sat in one corner. She looked up and brushed off her dress as Ezekiel entered. Her coarse black hair was parted in the middle and combed back into a fraying bun. Crow's feet and smile lines ran like cracks of pure darkness across her umber skin. She gave him an unimpressed look over.

"Who're you?" she asked.

Jeremiah stepped in front of Ezekiel and made several more hand motions.

Henrietta nodded in understanding.

Ezekiel frowned. "You can understand him?"

"He's speaking ain't he? Hands, lips, eyes, they all the same once you know." She spoke in a tone both gentle and no-nonsense. "Now, Jeremiah here says you asked to speak to me. Is he talkin' true?"

Ezekiel wrinkled his brow in confusion. "You're the commandeur?"

"Don't have one of those here." The woman grimaced. "Thought of the word leaves a sour taste in my mouth. But if you're looking for the head negro that'd be me." She gestured to several chairs positioned around the space. "Sit down."

"I'd rather—"

"Did I ask? Sit so I can get a better look at you."

Ezekiel hesitated, then crossed dusty floor planks and sat in the wooden chair nearest to Henrietta. It was the only chair in the room, and it creaked with his weight as he eased himself into it. He removed his hat and unwound his scarf.

Henrietta picked up a candle, held it up to him, and studied his face intently.

"You're tired," she said, "and angry, and so very sad."

Ezekiel said nothing.

Her eyes bored into his. "You've lost something."

"I've lost a lot," Ezekiel said.

"You won't find it here."

"*Here* is not where I wanted to end up." He made to rise, but Henrietta put a soft, firm hand on his shoulder. "There's a young Union soldier over in that Confederate camp you got over there. I need your help to get him out."

Henrietta sucked her teeth. "What you want us to do?"

"If all of us band together—"

Henrietta smiled softly. "They treat us well here. Don't want to go messin' that up."

"Treat you well?" Ezekiel clenched his fists at his sides. "You're *slaves*! Don't you want to leave? You could be free!"

"And go somewhere else in this country to be a slave? Or have white folk smile in my face and tell me I'm free all the while they're lookin' down their nose at me 'cause I'm black? If I'm gonna have to weave spells to be treated right, I may as well do it here where my mother was brought. Way I figure, it's the closest thing I got to a home now." Henrietta sighed. "Look, the missus and the old lady took a bit of *intervention,*"—she gestured to a small diorama: two white clay statues surrounded by several black clay statues, all connected by a single silver thread. Ezekiel didn't know exactly what it was, but knew that some of Pickett's slaves had indulged in similar practices—"and kindness came naturally to little Kate, until her brother died. We get on as well as we like here. As for those soldiers, they'll pass, just like they always do." Her soft smile returned.

Ezekiel's anger faltered under the benevolent look. "I need to help that soldier."

"I'll do you one better. I'll help you with your soldier friend and point you where you need to go for your other task as well, *obayifo* hunter."

Ezekiel straightened in his seat. "What did you say?"

Henrietta waved her hand dismissively. "In New Orleans there is a woman with strong powers, the Eucharist, daughter of the Voodoo Queen. She excels at finding lost things. And she looks like you and me. She may not be *happy* to help, but she will, I'm sure."

"How did you know—?"

Henrietta scoffed. "She may not be the Voodoo Queen, but old Henrietta ain't no fool. I can smell them on you, like blood and death, but not the soldiering kind, the rotting kind."

"You want me to go to a witch doctor."

"A miracle worker." She shook her head at Ezekiel's skeptical look and searched through the pile of objects cluttering her small table. Despite her small height and stocky stature, she moved nimbly about the room, like a dancer moving to a song only she could hear.

"Believe it, or don't, but if I lost something that made me like you," —she turned back to him with a small leather pouch in hand—"I'd make use of whatever I could." She placed it into the palm of Ezekiel's hand.

"What's this?"

"Gris-gris," Henrietta said. "Put something of yours—blood, skin, hair—in it. It'll work until you don't need it no more."

Ezekiel frowned. "Will it actually work?"

"Will it,"—Henrietta rolled her eyes heavenward—"Lord, bless this man for a fool. He be out there huntin' vampires and have the nerve to ask me if my spell bag'll work." She waited as if expecting her prayer to be answered.

"It'll work," she said at last.

"What will it do?" He gave a wry grin as he looped it around his neck. "Make me white?"

Henrietta looked at him the way she might look at a dumb child— half annoyed, half disappointed. "No, boy, you won't be no white man. Just ain't no white folk gonna question why a negro's walking around acting all high and mighty. Now, do you want it or not?"

Ezekiel closed his hand around the small bag.

"That's what I thought." She shooed him out of the chair. "Now go on, get. Got other things to do 'sides jawin' with you all day."

"Thank you, ma'am." Ezekiel placed his hat on his head and tipped it. "For everything."

Henrietta turned her back on him. "Everybody got something they desire more than anything else. I just try to help those who are still searching for it."

Ezekiel nodded and stepped down off the porch, back into the sweltering sun that hung over the plantation. There'd been no trace of the oppressive heat inside Henrietta's cabin, as if the inside and the outside temperature didn't match up. He looked at the cabin and saw that it was the same as the other six in appearance, all of them nicer than any he'd seen before.

"Huh," he said, and strode across the field, clutching the small pouch around his neck in a fist that clenched tighter as he approached the Confederate encampment.

5

Ezekiel approached the Confederate encampment with all the confidence of a defeated general returning home. He clutched at the gris-gris looped around his neck as he walked, rolling the contents between his fingers. Instinctively his other hand went to the raw patch of his chin where he'd plucked his beard to feed the pouch.

He sucked in a deep breath, dropping his hands to the revolvers at his belt. There was no plan—he couldn't risk waiting until nightfall, for Will's sake—but to trust in Henrietta's magic. Ezekiel still wasn't sure he believed, vampires or not.

He froze.

The soldier who'd manhandled Will stepped around the corner of the nearest tent, rifle shouldered as he went about his patrol. He stared in Ezekiel's direction, brow furrowed as though he *thought* he'd seen something. The rebel rubbed his eyes with the sleeve of his grey coat and looked again. Shaking his head, he continued on his patrol. Something like a laugh started in Ezekiel's chest, but he trapped it behind gritted teeth. He didn't know if they'd be able to hear him, and it wasn't a risk he wanted to take.

Each of the camp's tents was identical—a drab, brown canvas, worn and dirtied by the elements—and Ezekiel wasn't about to pop his head into the wrong one and set the soldiers on alert. They couldn't, or at least had difficulty trying to, see him, but he doubted the voodoo or hoodoo extended to the things he touched.

He snuck around, avoiding the few soldiers patrolling. Eight tents, and three soldiers on patrol. Ezekiel couldn't tell how many men there were, just that there were enough to be a problem. Rounding a corner, he bumped into one of the men circling back along his route. The soldier recoiled and brought his rifle to bear. Ezekiel drew, his iron aiming at the man's head, his thumb easing back on the hammer. Instead of firing, the soldier glanced around warily, his reflex aggression settling into confusion.

"What in tarnation?" The Greycoat narrowed his eyes, then shook his head. "Plum losing it out here..." He shouldered his rifle and continued on his way.

Ezekiel released a held breath. He clicked the hammer back into place and slid the gun into its holster. Keeping it cocked and in hand—with his itchy trigger finger—would only lead to trouble. Movement in the corner of his eye drew his attention. The captain, Beauregard, strode from a tent, a wicked smile on his face. He crossed the camp to a tent at the edge and disappeared behind its flap.

"Better shot than any other," Ezekiel mumbled. Staying more aware of the patrol's location, he inched his way towards the recently vacated tent. He drew the flap open—trying as best he could to make it seem as though the wind had caught the fabric—and stepped inside. Will sat tied to a chair in front of a battered field desk. There were some papers scattered on it, and an unlit lantern off to one side. That, a trunk, two chairs—one of which Will occupied—and an unmade cot were the only effects in the small space. Ezekiel grunted softly. The space was not much bigger than his own slave quarters on Pickett's plantation, as if soldiering were its own kind of slavery. He shook his head. These men chose this, chose to go to war—this is what they were willing to endure to keep his people in chains. He ground his teeth as he approached Will and stood in front of him.

"Can you see me?" Ezekiel didn't whisper but kept his voice low.

Will startled in the chair. He sat up straight and cast his eyes around the tent's interior as best he could. "Ezekiel? Where? How?"

"Hush," Ezekiel hissed. "I'm right in front of you. Focus." He wasn't sure if it would help, but he hoped it would keep the young soldier from panicking.

"In front of..." Will squinted, staring directly at the space where Ezekiel stood. "My God, it's like you're there, but not...like my eyes don't want to see you. How are you doing that?"

"You'd argue with me if I told you." Ezekiel knelt by the chair and undid the ropes binding Will. The young soldier stood and rubbed the raw skin of his wrists. Ezekiel scanned the tent. "How do you not have a gun on you?"

"I lost it."

Ezekiel balked. "You what?"

"I..." Will sighed. "It wasn't as important as the lives of the wounded."

Ezekiel searched his face, trying to root out a joke, but none was forthcoming. He pulled a gun from his belt and shoved it into Will's hand despite the young soldier's protestations. "Make peace with it now, before you end up dead—killin's a part of war. Hell, I'm startin' to think maybe it's just a part of life. Time to go."

Navigating through the tents with Will—visible and clumsy as a newborn calf—proved more difficult than Ezekiel expected. He used the rope to garrot one of the soldiers and cracked another on the back of the skull before dragging him into the nearest tent.

Beauregard's voice boomed from his tent. "All on guard, the prisoner has escaped."

With that, Ezekiel ceased his attempts at sneaking. He grabbed Will by the wrist and pulled him as he sprinted to where his horse was tied. As they crossed the front yard of the house, he glimpsed the young girl—Kate—stepping out the door, staring with wide eyes. Behind them, the soldiers opened fire. Bullets struck the earth alongside them as they ran, the mosquito scream of their traversal making Ezekiel wince each time one came near.

The bullets stopped. Someone screamed, and Will jerked away from Ezekiel.

"What the…?" Ezekiel's ankle screamed as he came to an abrupt halt.

Will stood locked in place, staring back towards the camp. Beauregard had Katherine by the hair, his pistol angled at her temple. By now the other two women had exited the house. The younger of the two was screaming at Beauregard as the older one held her back. Soldiers gathered around Beauregard, eyeing each other with expressions of shock and confusion. A few had their rifles trained on Will, but most lingered awkwardly—present, but trying to remain uninvolved.

Kate scowled—more angry than afraid. Her hand shifted in the pocket of her dress. Ezekiel took a hesitant step, fully expecting the soldiers to unleash a volley of lead in his direction.

Nothing happened.

"Captain, please!" The woman Ezekiel assumed was Kate's mother shouted at Beauregard. "Let her go. We've let you stay here—"

"Let?" Red flushed from Beauregard's neck up to his cheeks. "It is your *duty* to provide shelter and succor for our men while they toil against this Northern aggression. Anything less is treason."

"Captain Beauregard." Will's voice shook. He raised his hands over his head, Ezekiel's gun noticeably absent. "Didn't you tell me your men had orders to shoot? Here I am. Kate doesn't need to be involved in this at all."

"I'd *like* to keep you alive for further questioning." Beauregard sniffed, his mustache bristling. "And having seen your bleeding heart," he tapped Katherine with his pistol, "she is involved to hasten your surrender. Make no mistake, private, I will shoot her, and then my men will gun you down as well if need be."

Ezekiel made his way beside Will. "When you can, shoot him."

Will's eyes flicked in his direction for an instant then refocused on Beauregard. Ezekiel continued to creep towards the soldiers, picking the nearest one brandishing his rifle. He placed the barrel of his remaining revolver inches away from the back of the man's head and nodded at Will. Will shook his head—almost imperceptibly—eyes wide.

"Remove your coat," Beauregard ordered. "Given the bodies left in your wake, I refuse to believe you remain unarmed."

To Ezekiel's chagrin, Will did as he was told, revealing the revolver hidden in his waistband. Beauregard motioned with his gun for Will to toss the gun aside before returning the barrel to Kate's temple. Will's hand closed around the grip, and Kate struck. Her hand—and the knife clutched within—slid from her pocket and flashed upwards raking across the hand Beauregard used to hold her hair. The captain cursed, releasing his grip. Kate dropped to the ground and scrambled away as the gun went off in his other hand, the bullet striking the ground right by her head.

Kate climbed to her feet and sprinted towards her mother.

"You filthy little brat!" Beauregard roared. He clenched his wounded fist and leveled his gun at Kate's back as she ran. The hammer clicked.

"No!" Will shouted.

Beauregard's eyes went wide, and he spun back to face the young soldier just as the report of the revolver filled the open air. The soft sound of the bullet hitting flesh followed shortly after. Beauregard staggered back a step, looking down at the bloody stain spreading through his grey uniform. His arm shook, and he clenched his jaw, raising his pistol to return fire. Will clenched his eyes shut and fired again. The center of Beauregard's forehead vanished in a spray of red, his revolver clattering to the ground.

Ezekiel pulled the gris-gris from his neck and fired into the skull of the soldier he stood behind, then quickly turned, and fired at another soldier as he turned, striking him dead in the chest. The remaining soldier stared in shock at his sudden appearance from nowhere. Ezekiel glared at them and cocked his revolver again. "Y'all down a captain and four men. Anyone else wanna try their luck?"

The last three soldiers broke into an unintelligible susurrus before responding.

"Ain't even want to be in this war," said the first, tossing his rifle to the ground and looking around nervously. "Got a farm and family to get back to."

"Just wanna go home," a second man said.

The third remained silent but nodded in agreement.

"Pack up and get." Ezekiel considered shooting them all, on the principle of them being Greycoats, but this wasn't the time or place for revenge. All it would take was one of them picking up a discarded rifle and returning fire. He glanced at Will—shocked by his own actions, gun trembling in his hand—and shook his head. Ezekiel didn't plan on dying...not here, not now. "Now!"

The soldiers shuffled awkwardly but trickled off one by one.

When they were gone—vanished into their tents—Will dropped the pistol to the ground and fell to his knees. He pressed his forehead against the cool earthy ground. A violent gag wracked his body, and he threw up into the mud.

"I shot him," he moaned.

Ezekiel sauntered over. "Where was all that back in Natchitoches?"

"How are you so calm about this?" Will screamed into the dirt. "I just killed a man!"

"Not much of one," Ezekiel grunted, "takin' a little girl hostage."

"First, do no harm." Will clutched his head in his hands. "My pop was a physician. He always made me swear..." He gave Ezekiel a pained look before returning his gaze to the ground.

"Sounds like your daddy thought the world was a better place than it is." Ezekiel crouched down beside Will. He put a hand on the young soldier's shoulder. "Take whatever time you need, but do it quick, because the hard truth is...it's a hell of a lot worse."

Will gave him a look of horror. "How do you go on, thinking like that?"

"Get up, you'll be okay. You'll get used to it." He shifted his hand and held it out for Will to grab. He did, and Ezekiel pulled him to his feet. "Now you know you can handle yourself if the moment comes down to it. That's the difference between staying alive and ending up like the captain over there."

Will blinked. "Would you have let him kill me?"

Ezekiel held him in a silent gaze for a moment, then stood.

Kate's mother ran over, avoiding the sprays of blood that decorated the ground. She fell to her knees and wrapped her arms around Will. "Thank you, sir, thank you so much!" Tears stained her cheeks as she squeezed the young soldier tight.

The woman rose and turned to embrace Ezekiel. Ezekiel took a step back and she froze.

"Thank you," she said quietly.

"We should be on our way," Ezekiel said.

"Please," the woman said. "After everything, I feel like you deserve hospitality without pretense. We'd be happy to provide…"

"No." Ezekiel spoke brusquely, still keeping his distance from the woman. He eyed Will, waiting for the youth to agree. "I'll get the horses."

"He's right." Will stood, brushing his hands off on his pants and then brushing off his pants in turn. "I need to report back to my unit, and any time we spend down here" —he cast a glance at the Confederate encampment— "runs the risk of *this* happening again."

The woman nodded and offered a solemn smile. "Of course." She rose, and turned to Kate, who was buried under her grandmother's smothering embrace, the back to Will. "I doubt she'd thank you, even if I made her—"

"It's fine," Will said. "I understand." He gave a slight bow. "We'll be on our way, now."

It hadn't been an hour of riding when Ezekiel brought his horse to a stop. Will slowed beside him, casting a curious glance. Ezekiel turned his horse and stared back the way they'd come.

"What is it?"

Ezekiel unslung his rifle and stared down the iron sight at the horizon. "Someone's following us." A mixture of rage and vindication filled him as he expected to see one or more of the remaining Confederates cresting over the brief rise they'd just surmounted. He growled. "Come on, you Greycoat bastards."

Instead of angry rebels, a lone horse crested the hill, galloping quickly, and urged on by a small figure standing in her stirrups. She didn't wave or call out, but Kate rode towards them like a woman pursued by Hell itself.

"This can't be happening." Ezekiel lowered his rifle.

Kate came to a stop in front of them, kicking up a spray of trodden earth. Both her and the horse panted with exhaustion, but Kate's was clearly mixed with a spur of adrenaline—her mouth was curved in a triumphant grin.

"What are you doing here?" Will asked.

"I'm coming with you!"

"No." Ezekiel turned his horse. When Will didn't do the same, he glanced over his shoulder at him. "You coming?"

Will's hands were on his hips, and he looked for all the world like someone's bedraggled mother. "Your ma and gran'll be worried sick about you."

"Nah." Kate shrugged. "Least not for a while. I asked Henrietta to keep them busy. So they won't miss me until at least tomorrow."

"But after your brother—"

"*After my brother*," Kate snapped, "they both didn't even want me to leave the house. I know it's dangerous, I know they're scared, but if I stay there I'll" —she paused, and lowered her voice— "I'm right pissed, and I wanna wallop *something*. Y'all look like trouble, and I want in."

"Work out your anger problems somewhere else," Ezekiel said. "I'm not a goddamn nanny."

Kate cut her eyes at Will. "He's not much older than me."

"Him and I are done after Alexandria. There's—" He caught himself from finishing the thought, but Kate did it for him.

"Strength in numbers?"

Ezekiel cursed under his breath.

Kate gave a mischievous grin. "Besides, I've been riding horses since before I could walk proper. If you leave me, I'll be right there alongside you next time you look. You *can't* get rid of me."

"We'll see about that." Ezekiel spurred his horse.

After a few moments, Will followed suit. He called back to Kate. "Go home."

Kate was true to her word, keeping pace just behind them as they galloped, searching for the army road that ran towards Alexandria. The sun began its descent from high noon, and none of the horses could run any farther without the risk of their hearts bursting. The three came to a stop. Kate was soaked in sweat and seemed about ready to slip from her saddle. Will rode up to her and reached out a hand to steady her. She swatted his hand away.

"I'm fine," she snapped.

Ezekiel kneaded his fist against his forehead. "Why are you following us?"

"I'm not." Kate gasped between each word and pointed at Will. "I'm following *him.*"

Will's eyebrows shot up. "Me? Why?"

"Because you..." Kate sucked in a deep breath and straightened herself in the saddle. She looked at Will with a strange cross between scowl and a smile—like she was in pain. "Every other Bluebelly—hell even most of the Confederates I've met—didn't care about my dead brother. But not you. You asked about him, and said you were sorry he died. You cared about how I felt." She looked away.

"Oh." Will looked to Ezekiel for help. "That's..."

Ezekiel grunted. "If she slows us down, I'm leaving both of you behind."

6

It was dusk by the time they found their way back to the main road that ran from Natchitoches down to Alexandria. The soft marshland clung to the horses' feet and made all progress slow and tedious. Ezekiel scanned the treetops for signs of movement as they proceeded, while Will and Kate hung behind and talked.

"Whoa," Ezekiel said. He held up a hand to bring their small company to a halt.

"What's wrong?" Will rode up beside him and peered into the growing darkness.

Ezekiel pointed. "Wagon up ahead with a small fire."

"How can you see anything in this dark?" Will squinted. "I don't see any light."

"I learned the hard way."

"We should go introduce ourselves, so they don't think we're bandits," Kate said, starting to ride past them. "I'd hate to not get shot this morning, only to get shot tonight."

Ezekiel made a sharp noise, stopping Kate in her tracks. "Not yet."

Kate frowned. "We're not bandits...are we?"

"*He'd* make a terrible bandit." Ezekiel jerked his thumb at Will. "I want to make sure *they* aren't dangerous.

"If they aren't, maybe we can borrow a fire," Will said cautiously.

Ezekiel turned his horse off the road and into the adjacent woods. He hopped down and tied his mount to a thick, low tree branch. "Stay here."

Will threw up his hands in exasperation.

Ezekiel crept toward the dim light of the campfire, trudging silently through calf-deep muck, careful not to disturb any of the brush or branches that might alert those ahead. He reached the edge of the forest and crawled, quiet as he could, into a thick bush and waited. There was no one around the fire at first, and no one seemed to move inside the covered wagon. After a few minutes, a woman in a nightgown stepped off the back of the wagon, followed by two little boys. They sat around the fire while the woman placed a cast iron skillet in the fire, laying out strips of bacon and pouring a can of beans that sizzled and filled the night air with a warm and comforting smell. Ezekiel waited to see if anyone else would exit the wagon. The two boys giggled alongside their mother.

There was no one else.

After a minute, Ezekiel stood up and exited the bush, hands above his head in a placating manner. The woman gasped and gathered the children up into her arms, a look of fear etched on her face.

"I don't mean you no harm," Ezekiel said, "so long as you don't mean me none. Name's Ezekiel."

"Hard to believe that from a man showing up out of the woods at night," the woman said. The two boys' eyes were wide with fear, and they huddled closer to their mother. "Especially one as dark as you."

Ezekiel's clutched at the gris-gris around his neck with a bitter grimace. He was no longer on Elizabeth's land. He yanked it off and stared at it a moment before tossing it into the fire. He worked his face into a smile. "My companions and I were passing along and saw your fire. I just wanted to make sure you weren't a threat."

"And are we? Me and my children?" The woman's tone bit with each word she spoke. "What about you, dressed like an outlaw with those guns at your waist?"

The two boys perked up. "Guns?" they asked. "You have guns?"

"Glenn, Gene, hush," the woman hissed.

"I do have guns," Ezekiel said slowly. "A man's got to protect himself out here."

"So does a woman," the mother said. She was quick and in the seconds before Ezekiel could react, a small silver revolver pointed itself at him, held in the woman's trembling hands.

Ezekiel scoffed. "Smart lady. But really, you don't need to do that. I just came to see what kind of people you were and if maybe we could share your fire. It's been a long day for us, and we were hoping for some…"

"No." The woman motioned with the gun. "Go."

"…hospitality." Ezekiel fidgeted under the black eye of the silver revolver. "We're a little short on supplies and—"

"I don't care about your kids," the woman said. "I have mine to worry about."

Ezekiel dropped his hands. "Alright. We'll pass on, soon as you lower that gun."

The woman didn't move.

Ezekiel rolled his eyes, then whistled. After a few moments, Will and Kate arrived with his horse in tow.

"We're moving on," he said as they approached.

Will looked at the woman and her two boys.

"Are they dangerous?" A tinge of confusion warbled in his voice.

"Nope." Ezekiel jutted his chin at the revolver in the woman's hands. "I've just gotten pretty good at knowing when I'm not welcome."

"Wait, *these* are your kids?"

"Never said they were mine," Ezekiel said. "Said I had two kids with me."

The woman's face crinkled as she worked to process the situation. She waved Will and Kate over. "They can stay. The poor things look worn half to death."

Ezekiel opened his mouth, but Kate spoke first. "We travel together. That's that."

The woman was taken aback. "What's your name?"

"Kate."

"Hi, Kate." The woman offered an awkward smile. "I'm Jennifer. Can you tell me what two good kids like you are doing with a guy like him?"

"What are you talking about?" Irritation twisted Kate's face. "I chose to."

"Kate," Ezekiel said darkly. "Let's go."

"No," Kate snapped. "Why can't we stay?"

"Because…" Jennifer's attention snapped back to Ezekiel. "You're a runaway, I know it. And there are rewards for returning runaways to their masters. Where's yours?" Her eyes widened. "Did you kill him?"

"Yes." Ezekiel's voice frosted over. "Shot him six times, to make sure he stayed dead."

The woman fell silent.

Kate looked at Ezekiel in astonishment. She blinked away the last effects of the gris-gris, the luster leaving her eyes, and she saw Ezekiel's true face for the first time.

"You killed him?" she asked.

Jennifer hissed. "We brought you over from that dark continent, gave you shelter, food and God, in exchange for work, but you do nothing but complain and run away and kill us out of spite. This whole war is because you folk just couldn't learn your place."

"You give us…" Ezekiel mulled the words over, tasting each one like the poison of a lead bullet. Silently, he stripped off his coat and set to unbuttoning the shirt he wore beneath it. He tossed both articles of the clothing to the ground and revealed the jagged spider web of old scars that decorated his back to the firelight.

"Ezekiel—" Will gasped.

Jennifer jerked away with a sharp cry and covered Glenn and Gene's eyes with her hands, dropping the gun in the process.

"This," Ezekiel growled, "is all you give us. I could sit here and tell you why I got each and every one of these, and not a damn one was for being ungrateful."

Kate's face dropped as her eyes scanned the raised, cracking lines that made up most of Ezekiel's back skin. Fury broke out in dark lines on her face in the orange glow of the fire. She rounded on Jennifer.

"What the hell is this?" Her voice was shrill in the night and Ezekiel flinched, looking around for any sign of disturbance in the darkness that surrounded them. "Is this what you do to your slaves?"

"I never—"

"Our slaves were like our family back home. Why would you do this?"

"I didn't." Jennifer stammered. "His master did. It was his choice to make."

"Slaves, soldiers, statesmen," Kate continued, "each one is what they are, but we should treat everyone with respect. That's what makes the South special. But uppity gallinippers like you ruin it for everyone."

Ezekiel fumed in silence as Kate carried on her tirade.

He'd heard the argument a thousand times. *Well as long as the slaves are well treated...*

In the past Ezekiel's response had always been simply, "They're still a slave." Usually followed by the report of his rifle or twin revolvers. Kate's logic was little more than the blind acceptance of youth—ingrained in her for most of her life—regurgitated here, in his defense. Something about that last bit—the fact that she thought her statements absolved the horror he'd seen *and* was being used to justify why he deserved kindness—only served to stoke his anger.

Will awkwardly went to put a hand on his shoulder but retracted it when he saw the look on Ezekiel's face. The firelight warped the black man's features into something from a nightmare as he glared down at the woman. And then, in an instant, it was gone. Ezekiel looked at Will, and the darkness had vanished.

"Just go." Jennifer choked out the words through a sob. Her sons shared confused looks, not understanding what was happening around them. "Leave us alone."

Kate snorted derisively. "Let us take a coal then, so we can make our own fire far away from you."

"No," Jennifer said, then hurriedly added, "and we used our last match to start this fire."

"Shame," Kate turned her horse around and tugged on the reins with the tiniest amount of force. The horse kicked its feet behind it, spraying dirt onto the small fire until it went out completely. She turned back around with a smile on her face.

The woman's pale face reflected the moonlight, revealing the horror etched on her face.

"Oops." Kate gestured to Ezekiel and Will. "We really should get going, you two. We aren't wanted here."

"She's evil," Will mumbled.

"She's something," Ezekiel said. "Come on, let's find a safe place to settle."

"Thank you, for showing me what Southern hospitality really is," Kate spat bitterly as they rode off into the night.

They'd traveled about less than fifteen minutes down the road from the family's wagon—keeping their horses at a slow trot on the uneven ground—when a blood-curdling scream pierced the night. The wind kicked up into a furious howl that matched the shriek. Moments later, two more cries rose up to join in the terrifying chorus—children. Quick as it started, the darkness fell silent.

Will turned to Ezekiel with a look of panic on his face.

"No." Ezekiel's voice was stone.

"We have to go help them." Will kicked his horse into a quick gallop, cutting off Ezekiel's horse and making it rear back in shock. "They're in danger."

"She's armed." Ezekiel glowered. "A few midnight bandits aren't our problem."

"Ezekiel," Will said, "some of the other soldiers used to tell stories about it. They didn't mean anything to me then, but now..."

"There are stories about every road," Ezekiel said. "What do they matter?"

Will lowered his voice to a whisper. "The stories talk about a forest watered by blood, and a creature that stalks in the dark...what does that sound like to you?"

Ezekiel stared into Will's eyes, searching for a lie that wasn't there. "Fuck."

"We left them *in the dark*," Will pleaded with Ezekiel. "We have to go back."

"What about her?" Ezekiel barely tried to hide his irritation. His eyes slid over to Kate, who appraised them with suspicion.

"I'm fine, thank you." Kate crossed her arms. She sniffed. "Though I don't see why we should help them."

"Even they don't deserve this," Will said. "Trust me."

"You have no idea what we're up against," Ezekiel warned.

"Then I'll learn." She held him in a serious stare. "Henrietta said you're hunting bigger game than just Greycoats. I can handle blood and guts."

Ezekiel eyed her with a grim frown. "Okay then, girl. Hope you're right."

The remains of the fire were scattered over the makeshift campsite, logs and kindling stomped and crushed. Far more damage than Kate's horse could have kicked up. Jennifer's revolver lay, unfired, near the smoldering pit. The cover of the family's wagon was ragged, torn by something sharp and crooked, and bloodstains dotted the white cloth, culminating in a bloody streak that led down to Jennifer's body. She lay slumped against a splintered wheel; her nightgown had been ripped to shreds, and something had clawed trenches across her face and chest. The wounds poured red blood down over her body and into a pool that muddied the ground beneath her. She could barely raise her head to look at them when they arrived.

"My boys." Every breath wheezed painfully from her throat. "He took them."

"Who took them?" Ezekiel searched their surroundings. "Where did he go?"

"My husband, Jonathan. He came out of the forest like you and… Oh, God, he was a monster!" Her sobs turned to choking pain as her salty tears ran into the open wounds on her face. "I was trying to get them away from him—all of us away from him—but he took them." She pointed a trembling finger at the woods, then dropped it back to her side.

Will practically fell from his horse in his rush to kneel down and assess her. "Okay, okay, don't try to move anymore."

"Stay here. Help." Ezekiel pulled his rifle down from his saddle bag. "Try not to let her die."

"What about me?" Kate asked.

"Help Will. Entertain yourself. Whatever. I'll be back."

"Give me a gun."

Ezekiel scoffed. "I don't think so."

"Stop treating me like a child!" Kate leapt down from her horse and stomped twice, her foot sinking deep into the mud. "I know how to shoot a gun."

"That's great," Ezekiel said. "It won't do you any good trying to save a woman's life."

Kate turned to Will. "Do you have a gun?"

He shook his head without looking back at her.

"What if he comes back?" she asked. "What'll we do then?"

Ezekiel held her defiant gaze for a second, then walked over to where Jennifer's revolver lay on the ground. He checked to see if it was loaded and saw that it wasn't.

"Where's the ammo?" he asked.

Jennifer shook her head. "Never had any."

Ezekiel sucked his teeth and reached into the pockets of his duster. He pulled out six silver bullets and slid them into place one by one. He clicked the cylinder shut and tossed the revolver into the grass near Kate's feet.

"If you miss, you won't get a second chance."

"If it moves, I'll shoot it, and I *won't* miss." Kate picked up the gun and double-checked Ezekiel's work. "Mama said I'm a crack-shot, so you don't need to worry."

"I'm not."

Ezekiel cocked his rifle and waded into the swampy forest. Behind him, Kate threw some debris from the wagon into the makeshift fire pit and doused it with the moonshine.

She held up a single match and glared at Jennifer. "Look who was lying, Will."

"Doesn't matter now," Will shook his head. "I need that fire."

Kate struck the match and flicked it into the pile of wood and alcohol. It crackled to life. The darkness behind him receded as a new orange glow roared to life. Jennifer's groan grew higher pitched as Will poured the moonshine onto her wounds. She thrashed and Will struggled to hold her down until the pain relented.

"Kate." Will's voice muffled as Ezekiel waded into the woods. "Bring me the skillet."

Ezekiel winced at the hiss of heated metal against flesh and the woman's piercing scream cutting through the night. The sounds of nature fell silent, allowing the high-pitched agony to fill every inch of the silent air. As the scream died out, the buzz of mosquitoes and the rhythmic croaking of bullfrogs returned, bringing life back to the darkness.

"Keep her quiet," Ezekiel hissed to himself. "Bring every damn creature in the woods down on you like that." He spat at the ground and flicked the lever on his rifle.

Something moved in the trees overhead. Ezekiel dove to the side, sliding in grime, just as the figure slammed into the ground where he'd been standing. The figure stood up and cocked its head to the side, his ginger mutton chops brushing against the shoulder of his wool coat.

"Jonathan?"

"You're fast." Jonathan's voice rumbled like a landslide.

"Have to be." Ezekiel aimed at the figure. "Don't want to get your ugly all over me."

The man snarled, a wet, throaty sound, like a man drowning in the dark.

"Where are the kids, Jonathan?" Ezekiel struggled to keep his voice even.

"*The* kids?" Jonathan bared his teeth and growled. His gums receded, revealing multiple rows of shark-like teeth. Dirty, ragged fingernails stretched out into raptor-like claws that gleamed with blood in the pale moonlight. He circled Ezekiel in the dark, like a tiger in a cage. "You mean *my* kids?"

"Funny, I was with your wife earlier and, well, it was just her, the kids. Oh, and me." Ezekiel kept the rifle trained on the slow-moving target. "Some father you turned out to be."

"*You* were with my wife?" Jonathan's teeth shredded his gums to bloody pulp as he spoke, slurring his words. He gnashed and foamed, twitching like a rabid dog.

He charged, and Ezekiel pulled the trigger. The rifle cracked like thunder, and the impact of the slug launched the man backwards into the nearest tree, splintering it against his body.

"Don't get too upset, she didn't like it much either." He ejected the shell and slid another silver shell into place. "That was a warning. Nothing vital. This next one won't be. Now tell me where the kids are."

Jonathan cracked a pained laugh as he rose to his feet. He dug the bullet out of the wound in his shoulder, fingers sizzling as they gripped it. He dropped it to the muddy ground. "Silver," he hissed. "You know what you're doing?"

"Be dead if I didn't," Ezekiel said.

"You'll be dead regardless." Jonathan cracked his neck and pointed above Ezekiel. "And I'll have my kids."

Ezekiel glanced at the branches overhead.

Nothing. He'd been played.

The quick look was all the vampire needed. Ezekiel wasn't fast enough to dodge the furious assault. The man's talons raked along his ribs, tearing strips of flesh from his body as he rolled out of the way. Ezekiel's teeth clacked as he hit the ground, and his hand instinctively cupped the wound in his side. He gasped at the burning pain that raced through his side. His hand came away slick and red.

Jonathan sucked the blood from his steaming fingernails and grinned. "Got ya."

"Where are they?" Ezekiel barked.

"Dad," one of the boy's small voices called from a nearby bush. "I'm itchy."

"Glenn, Gene!" Ezekiel struggled to his feet. "Your momma's worried sick about you. Head on back to her now."

The bushes rustled with movement as the two boys emerged.

"Dad, can we go back?" The boys spoke in unison.

"No! They're mine." Jonathan screamed as he charged the boys, and their eyes went wide with fear. "I'll make them like me, and that bitch will never take them from me again."

"Got ya." Ezekiel fired. The silver bullet caught Jonathan in the leg, ripping through the limb and severing it at the knee. Jonathan howled in pain as he crashed to the ground, clutching at the ragged, bloody stump that had been his knee.

"Fuckin' Christ," Jonathon shouted. He glared at Ezekiel with bloodshot eyes. "Do you know what you've cost me?"

"Looks like a leg to me," Ezekiel said, reloading. "I was aiming for your head, but it's dark."

"You're gonna wish you'd made that headshot, you bastard!"

"Don't worry, I plan to rectify my mistake."

Jonathan cackled and plunged his fangs into his own arm. Black blood burst from the limb like a squashed tick, spraying both his face and the ground around him. Bile green venom poured from his gums and into the wound. The blood vessels in his eyes burst, darkening his eyes, and sending blood pouring down his face like corrupted tears. He released his arm and let it fall limp to his side. The surface of his skin began to bubble and hiss, melting around the bone like candle wax.

Horror dawned on Ezekiel as the severed limb began to grow back, but it wasn't a human foot that returned. Grey, rotten flesh with chunks of missing skin that revealed necrotic black muscle extended down to a clawed foot. The rest of Jonathan's body followed suit, flesh stretching and sizzling and tearing. His human form melted away, revealing the blackened, rotting corpse beneath. Solid black eyes stared out from a hairless, bat-like face. Ribs cracked and protruded upward, stretching the remains of Jonathan's original skin into two blood-filled membranes: wings on the creature's back. Clawed hands dragged in the mud as the creature that was Jonathan lumbered to his feet. A ragged howl tore from his throat, and he flapped his fleshy wings, rustling the leaves on the surrounding trees as he launched into the night sky and vanished into the shadows.

"That's new." A chill ran down Ezekiel's spine, carried by the sweat that broke out all over his skin. He steeled himself against the fear that wormed its way into his racing heart.

"What?" Jonathan barked out a haunting laugh that seemed to come from everywhere all at once. "Never seen a *real* vampire before?"

"I've killed plenty of you." Ezekiel searched the sky.

"Plenty of ghouls, I bet," Jonathan replied. "But none like me, boy. Nothing like a gargoyle. We're the real deal."

"Well ain't you cocksure," Ezekiel said dryly. "Especially since you're actin' like a yaller dog, hiding from me in the dark. But I guess I'll get to add killing a gargoyle to my growing list of exploits."

"Hiding?"

Ezekiel whirled around, following the direction of the voice.

"From what, an empty rifle?"

Fear erupted like stars behind Ezekiel's eyes. He'd been so caught up in the horror of Jonathan's metamorphosis, he hadn't reloaded. He cranked the lever, ejecting the spent shell, and fished in his pocket for a replacement.

Too slow.

The gargoyle descended on him, plunging jagged claws into the space around his collarbone with a satisfied snarl. Ezekiel's rifle dropped into the mud, and Jonathan kicked it away into the brush. Ezekiel screamed as Jonathan's claws wrapped around his collarbone like it was a handle and lifted him into the air.

"I can see the course your blood takes through your body," Jonathan growled. "I'm deep enough to cause you *agony*, but don't worry, this won't kill you." He hurled Ezekiel aside, letting go of his collarbone at the last second. Pain exploded across Ezekiel's back as he crashed through a tree and hit the ground in an uncoordinated sprawl.

He rolled over onto his stomach, feeling ribs and vertebrae grinding, sliding in and out of place, and forced himself to stand despite the screams of every muscle and bone in his body. Pain was the only thing that kept him from passing out. It raced through him like lightning and spurred him to action. He drew his six-shooters.

Twelve bullets left.

"You're still standing?" Jonathan's head twitched left, then right; a predator scenting the air. "I could have sworn that I broke your back. That's a shame, it really is, because now you'll feel what happens next."

With a single beat of his heavy wings, the gargoyle launched himself at Ezekiel, only to receive a hail of silver bullets. Three tore through his wings, and one lodged itself directly in his eye socket. He veered off course as the metal burned inside his flesh, slamming into the mud to Ezekiel's left. Ezekiel turned and unloaded the rest of the bullets into the vampire's body, each one leaving a steaming pool of black blood in its wake. He dropped the guns, and his arms fell limp. He staggered over to where Jonathan's body lay sizzling on the ground.

He spat a congealed clot of blood to the ground. "Fuck y—"

Jonathan's hand shot up and clamped around Ezekiel's throat. "It'll take a lot more silver than that to send me to hell. But I can give you a free one-way trip, with just a little squeeze." His voice was low and throaty, wracked with pain.

Ezekiel kicked at the air, panic tingling through his body like pinpricks. He beat his fists against the gargoyle's arm, but his arms were useless. His vision swam, slowly constricting into a narrow black tunnel. His lungs burned like hot coals in his chest. The crosses on his fists scorched Jonathan's flesh as Ezekiel pounded away, but the pain only made the vampire squeeze tighter.

"All those cross-shaped burns and you didn't have the damn sense to wear one around your neck," Jonathan mocked. "Not that it would've saved you."

The crack of a rifle echoed through the night. Jonathan screamed as the bullet tore through his arm, releasing Ezekiel from his grasp. Dazed, Ezekiel pounded his fists into the gargoyle's face, focusing on his eyes, trying to burn them out of their sockets.

He painted a bloody cross on Jonathan's chest and slammed his fist into it. Something cracked, and he hoped it wasn't his skull. He couldn't tell; all the pain blended together.

Ezekiel staggered backward and collapsed to the mud. His eyes scanned the forest floor; his rifle was nowhere to be seen. Movement in one of the bushes told him where the two boys were hiding.

Jonathan thrashed as he struggled to catch his breath.

"Show yourself so I can rip your head off and suck the marrow from your bones," Jonathan shouted into the darkness as he clutched his bloody, steaming face. The reply came in the form of another shot, tearing one of his wings off at the joint. The gurgling cry was worse than anything Ezekiel had ever heard.

"No thank you," Kate's voice said from the shadows. It seemed to come from all around. "See Ezekiel, I learned something," she went on. "I *always* learn something." Her voice dropped, becoming as low and menacing as a thirteen-year-old's voice could be. "I know how your power works."

"Cute." The gargoyle turned in the direction of the shot. "And what good does that do you, little girl? I can hear the fear in your voice. The little tremor—

The rifle thundered again, this time from the opposite side of the forest. Silver embedded itself in the creature's back. Ezekiel mustered a weak smirk at the creature's suffering. Its tantrum kicked up mud and grass and filled the night with its howling.

"I don't know," Kate continued, "I probably could kill you. But if not, I'll be damned sure to make you suffer."

"You can't hide forever," Jonathan hissed.

"No," Kate replied, "I can't. So let's make a deal."

"Kate," Ezekiel's voice was barely more than a whisper, "just kill it!"

Every painful breath threatened to send him plummeting into unconsciousness. His whole body grew cold, and it struck him that he had yet to stop bleeding. This needed to end fast.

"Are the kids safe?" Kate asked.

"Bushes," Ezekiel mumbled weakly.

"Okay then," Kate snapped, "shut up and try not to bleed out. Now, whatever the hell you are, let's talk."

The gargoyle hissed out a cloud of steamy breath. "I'll listen…until I figure out where you are. Then I'll flay the flesh from your bones and—"

"Stop being gross," Kate chided. "Just take your kids and go."

"What?" Ezekiel stirred. The effort sent him into an excruciating coughing fit that made his head spin. Anna Marie's face flashed in the glimpses of darkness that veiled his eyes. She was so disappointed that he couldn't save the kids. "Kate, no."

"Their mother's dead." Kate's tone was flat. "We tried to save her, but she wouldn't stop bleeding. There was *a lot* of blood." Ezekiel could hear the shrug in her voice. "The boys have nowhere else to go."

Jonathan paused. "You're lying."

"Can you hear her?" Kate asked. "Smell her?"

Jonathan put his deformed snout to the air and sniffed. Once. Then a second time, deeper. He took one final deep breath that seemed to suck in all the air around him before exhaling in a panicked gasp. "It's just…burning…"

"The wounds were too deep," Kate continued, "and we had to burn her, so she didn't end up like you. So, take your kids and lie to them. It would be bad if they found out their mom was dead. Oh…Ezekiel, did you mean *these* bushes? Oops."

The boys in the bush spoke. "Momma's…dead?"

There was hesitation in the first voice, but the second fell straight into a snotty sob.

"Boys?" Jonathan shrank in size, bones snapping and cracking back into place until Jonathan stood, completely human in appearance once more, in the center of a bubbling pile of flesh, head hung low.

His body was covered in scars where Ezekiel had injured him, but they looked days old, weeks even. "I didn't mean to. I didn't mean—"

His words were cut off by the rifle's final report. The bullet blasted a gaping hole in Jonathan's skull; he blinked twice and touched at the gaping space before his entire head burst in a burning spray of black blood and brain matter. His body collapsed, igniting the small patch of ground around him, only for it to be doused in seconds by the blood-soaked earth. Ezekiel stared in shock.

"Boys." Kate emerged from a bush to Ezekiel's left. "I lied, your mom is fine, go back to the campsite."

The crying faded to a whimper as both boys stumbled out of hiding. They looked at Kate and Ezekiel with wide, wet eyes—on the verge of breaking down again. Ezekiel blocked their view of their father's corpse, and Kate snapped her fingers before pointing back towards the flickering light nearly obscured by the brush. "Get moving."

But boys nodded solemnly and mumbled their thanks as they began the trek back to their demolished wagon.

"How did you know?" Ezekiel asked.

Kate's face was covered in sweat and dirt. "I didn't, so I'm glad it worked." She gave a tired grin. "He just really made it seem like you'd regret missing his head." Her eyes went wide, and shock ran down her body like a tremor as the gravity of the situation caught up with her. She stared at Ezekiel, mouth gaping in horror. "What the fuck *was* that?"

"A problem," Ezekiel groaned. "Definitely a problem."

7

Kate struggled to half-help, half-drag Ezekiel back to camp. Will sat next to Jennifer, whose chest rose and fell slowly. Her face and torso were wrapped in blood-stained strips of clothing from the wagon that obscured most of her features. Both boys lay curled up against her, dead asleep. The heavy scent of moonshine and burned flesh filled the air.

"She really is alive," Ezekiel said in slight disbelief.

Kate helped him settle down so that he was laying on his back next to the fire. He grunted with discomfort, adjusted a little, then sighed with relief.

Will gave him a confused look. "Of course, why would you think—?"

"It's a long story," Kate said. "I did a bit of lying earlier."

"Oh."

Ezekiel spasmed, clutching the angry gashes on his chest. Will sprang into action wielding the half empty bottle of moonshine in one hand and the iron skillet in the other.

"How the hell did you keep her from screaming?" Ezekiel looked between the two items.

Will held up a hand wrapped in bloody cloth. "No bullets here to bite." He offered the hand to Ezekiel. "You might need it."

"Pass." Ezekiel pushed Will's hand away. "Just wrap the cuts up and let me rest."

"They're too deep. You'll bleed out if we don't cauterize the wounds." He reheated the skillet over the fire and held out the bottle of moonshine to Ezekiel. "You'll probably want a drink."

"No," Ezekiel said. "You're not doing this."

"I'm trying to save your life." Will brandished his skillet like an angry cook.

Ezekiel bolted up quickly for a man covered in deep gashes. He caught Will by the lapels of his coat and pulled him close until their faces were barely inches apart. The skillet dropped into the fire, spraying ashes, and embers up to the sky. "I will not let another white man brand me, ever again. If that kills me, so be it."

With the last of his strength, Ezekiel shoved Will away and collapsed back into his supine position. He stared up at the stars, partially obscured by the rising smoke from the fire. His breathing grew shallow and laborious. Will and Kate were talking, arguing maybe, but couldn't make out what they were saying. A moan escaped his lips, and they turned to look at him before resuming their conversation. Darkness crept into his vision, causing the stars to dim before vanishing entirely, swallowed up in the blackness of unconsciousness.

Ezekiel woke to the blinding rays of the sun beaming down onto him. The nausea hit him first, making him retch violently into the dirt at his side. This in turn brought with it a burning pain that dragged its way across his chest, back, and abdomen. He hissed at the sensation and looked down. The claw marks on his front had scabbed over with burned flesh. He reached around to his back, and touched the wounds, finding similar damage. His collar was pocked with cauterized flesh in place of the deep holes Jonathan's claws had left. He sat up, an act that started up a new round of retching and vomiting. With a frustrated groan, he wiped his mouth with the back of his hand.

"I respected your wishes," Will poked the fire with a stick, then pointed it at Ezekiel without looking, "as much as I could while still saving your life."

"What did you do?" Ezekiel croaked.

"I traced each laceration as closely as possible with a smaller heated instrument—he held up a tent spike—when your blood started pooling up around you in your sleep. It won't look like a brand...just new scars." He turned to Ezekiel. "I couldn't let you die."

Anger bubbled up inside of Ezekiel for a moment, then cooled as he saw the dark circles under Will's eyes, almost black as night in the clear morning light. "Did you sleep?"

Will scoffed. "I have two patients who could have died overnight if I didn't stay up to tend to them."

"I wasn't gonna die."

"You almost did."

"I told you not—"

Will's eyes flashed, and his exhausted placidity broke. He tossed the stick into the fire and rose to his feet, looming over Ezekiel and shading him from the sun. "Look I get that you had things done to you that I don't...that I could *never* understand, but there's a difference between taking a moral stand and being so damn stubborn your friends have to watch you bleed to death." His voice trickled off at the end, and he sank to a sitting position beside Ezekiel.

Ezekiel raised an eyebrow. "Didn't realize we were friends."

"I like you," Will said, "and you saved my life, so I owe you. But you, sir, are an ass."

"I know. That's why I don't have friends." Ezekiel paused to catch his breath. "How's the lady?"

"Kate's—"

"The other one."

"Surprised you care."

"Just want to make sure I didn't almost die for nothing."

"She's fine. Unhappy about her burns now that she's out of immediate danger. Spent most of this morning griping about how she'll never be beautiful again now that she's been branded like cattle. But she'll live, and that's what matters."

"I suppose so." Ezekiel cast a sour glance at the sleeping form of the woman on the other side of the campfire. "And Kate?"

"Asleep in the wagon. The dirt was a bit much for her high standards of living." He cracked a slight smile. "You know I just realized something."

"What's that?"

"You just asked about all of us, woman who harassed you included."

"You just realized that?" Ezekiel scowled. "You slow on the uptake or something?"

"Nah, but I realized that you do care about other people even if you act like you don't."

"Then you also realize that I'll probably put a bullet in you to keep that secret." Ezekiel let a dark smirk cut across his face.

"You'd have to do both of us then." Kate stretched with a yawn as she emerged from the wagon. "Because you two are loud and I'm a light sleeper." She plopped down next to Will and warmed her hands on the fire.

They all sat in silence, listening to the morning birds sing their songs.

"So, vampires?" Kate asked finally.

Ezekiel grimaced. "Yeah."

"And you're both...?"

"Just me."

Will shrugged. "I'm picking up what I can along the way."

"But yesterday you were caught off guard by that demon or whatever it was—" she gestured about herself to indicate Jonathan's transformation, "—and you were clearly outmatched. How have you survived this long?"

Ezekiel stared into the fire mulling his thoughts before he spoke. "I always thought Palaiologos was the only vampire like him. He turned other people into...ghouls, Jonathan called them. Rabid, nearly mindless things with an insatiable lust for blood." He made eye contact with Will. "Like the man in Natchitoches. They'd tear you apart to make sure they could lap up every last drop. But they were weak enough, and I could handle them. I've never had an issue handling a vampire..."

"Until last night," Kate finished.

"If there are more like him..."

"Which there probably are," Kate said. "Lots."

Will shook his head. "Probably a fair amount, but not a lot."

Ezekiel coughed loudly, pain shooting through his extremities. "What do you mean?"

"Well, it's like this: Sherman is the Lieutenant General of the Union, and he'll have some Lieutenant Colonels—aides-de-camp— and a Brigadier General directly under him, to help with logistics and issuing commands to different components of the army. So, if this Pala...Pali...Pa—"

"Palaiologos."

"Right, if he's like a general, he wouldn't want too many people directly under him, not just to streamline the chains of command, but also in case of a mutiny. The ghouls would make up the majority—the troops, so to speak." Will scratched his head. "Not to mention that you've been doing this for ten years and Jonathan was the first of his kind that you've encountered."

"Well, that's much better than the alternative," Kate said, rolling her eyes. "Need I remind you that *one* of them almost turned Zeke here into a prime cut of meat?"

Ezekiel adjusted so he was staring at the blue, cloudless sky over- head. "I just can't believe I haven't come across one like him in ten years of searching."

"Actually," Will said, "given what you've said about ghouls being mostly feral, I think the old man may have been an aide-de-camp...a different kind perhaps, but still."

Ezekiel frowned. "Now that you mention it, he was the first vamp I met that could talk and plan. I didn't think much of it at the time because he went down just as easy as any ghoul, but..."

"But it makes sense, right?"

"But this guy was on a whole different level." Ezekiel clenched his fists until the pain of digging his nails into his palms made them tremble. He wanted to scream but kept quiet for fear of reopening his wounds. "I couldn't even begin to handle him."

"Alone and unprepared," Kate said, standing up and crossing her arms.

"What?"

"You couldn't handle him because you went in alone and were completely unprepared," she continued. "But together, we killed him."

Ezekiel sneered, all of his anger finally boiling over. "Why would you help me again? Shouldn't I still be a slave? Isn't that my place? Like a soldier or a statesman? Aren't I breaking the natural order of things?" His voice rose in volume, his tension pulling at the seared scabs as he spoke.

Kate recoiled, a look of hurt confusion twisting her face. "You're upset about that?"

"You think I am supposed to be a slave," Ezekiel said slowly, "and I'm supposed to be okay with that?"

"Our slaves were always treated kindly. They had shelter, food, clothes, and respect. We treated them like family. What happened to you *can't* be normal."

"Normal?!" Ezekiel bolted upright and a rush of nausea surged into a wave of lightheadedness that almost made him topple over. He groaned. Henrietta's words drifted into his head, warm with her knowing smile. *The missus and the old lady took a bit of* intervention, *but kindness came naturally to little Kate.*

Ezekiel screwed his eyes shut and forced himself to breath deep, slow breaths. He opened them again and looked at Kate. Tears had welled up in the corners of her eyes. She was just a kid. His treatment hadn't been her fault, and of course she didn't understand. Ezekiel bit down on his tongue until the taste of blood filled his mouth. He gasped, unclenching his teeth when the pain became unbearable.

"Not all slaves are treated like your family's." Ezekiel's tone was bitter and harsh. "Most are overworked, beaten...tortured, and made to live like animals in their own filth. Hell, I've seen kids younger than you take the whip. Ain't surprising to me at all that you'd be all for the 'great institution' of slavery." He paused, remembering young Collin's face, staring up at Anna Marie when she was his nursemaid. The image shifted to a mockery of that same childlike innocence as the boy had grown. Cruelty warped everything around it, if given free rein. "Get this straight, being a slave is no normal thing…it's an atrocity."

"Really?" Kate frowned at Will. The young man nodded his head solemnly.

"It's what this whole war is about," he said. "Freeing the slaves from slavery."

"But I thought,"—her frown deepened—"we're fighting for *our* freedom?"

Will shook his head. "The South just can't stand to have all its free labor stripped away."

"My brother… Is that what he died for?" Kate's tears ran freely, leaving clean streaks through the dirt that covered her face. "But he went off to be a hero. To save us." She pointed a finger at Will. "From you."

Will shrugged and gave her a sad smile. "I don't know what your brother really believed, so I can't say. But this war is about the slaves, no matter how you look at it." He glanced at Ezekiel. "Even if it's just politicking, slavery is evil. This war is evil. We know that the law is made for the lawbreakers and rebels, among them slave traders, liars, and perjurers." The Bible verse rolled off his tongue like honey-wine.

"Slaves, submit to your masters, be they good and equitable or perverse." Kate snapped back, reciting another biblical quote with acrid bitterness.

"But we're also taught that in God's eyes there's neither slave nor free, because we're all one in Christ."

"That can't be true! Because we're all_supposed to be slaves to righteousness."

Ezekiel's voice rumbled darkly, ending the theological back and forth. "If God intended for us to be slaves, then I hope he chokes to death on the corpses of every negro who died by white hands."

Will gave Ezekiel a horrified look before turning back to Kate.

"God didn't make people slaves. He gave everyone free will, and some people *choose* to enslave other people. And as far as what they could do, some of them might be farmers, merchants, or soldiers,"—he gestured at Ezekiel—"or some of them might be vampire hunters. No man should get to decide another man's fate."

Kate stood, her body trembling. She looked from Ezekiel to the fire then back. Her mouth opened and closed as if she were about to speak, but no words came out. After several moments, she finally spoke.

"I'm sorry that I upset you, Ezekiel," she blinked away tears, "I don't…think I understand completely. It's a different…story than I was raised with. But I swear I meant no harm, and I certainly don't think you are beneath me. Different, sure, but…"

Ezekiel grunted. "Will, when's the earliest you think we'll be able to get moving?"

"I thought I was standing up for you." Kate wiped away the tears that continued to roll down her cheek, smearing their cleanliness across her dusty face.

"Ezekiel," Will said softly, "she just apologized…"

"And?" Ezekiel asked in an icy tone. "You want me to tell her that it's okay, that it's fine that she's thought my people were meant to be slaves, or that it's fine she's been ignorant of the suffering going on just outside her little homestead? It's not, and an apology doesn't just make it okay."

"She's just a kid."

Kate opened her mouth to protest, but Will held up a hand to quiet her.

Ezekiel stared at Kate. He saw Anna Marie, kneeling down in front of the crying girl and holding her close, trying to comfort her. Tears began to form in his eyes, and he looked away, forcing the rest of his anger out in deep, powerful breaths. He clenched and unclenched his fists until the feelings subsided and he could look Kate in the eye again. "You saved me last night, and that's more than what I'd ever expect from white folk 'round here. But you're wrong, and what you believe ain't better than any of these other Confederate sons of bitches. Might be worse—least they just don't view us as people—you view us as people that are born to be beneath you."

Kate wiped fresh tears with her sleeves and stared at the ground. "I—"

"But I talked to Henrietta," Ezekiel continued, "and she said you're a good kid. I want to believe her—Lord knows I need to believe in some good, with things the way they are—but everything in me tells me I should hate you just as much as I hate anyone else keepin' slaves." He dragged a hand down his face and sighed. "But it's been a long time for me, dealing with this shit. Maybe I'm too tired to hate…"

"Does that mean you forgive me?" Kate asked.

"It means you have the opportunity to prove Henrietta right." Ezekiel's eyes flicked between Kate and his rifle sitting by her side. "Keep the gun; for now, at least, you're with us. Maybe forgiveness will come along, maybe it won't."

Will blew out a low whistle. "What's next?"

"I'm still going after the vampire that took Anna Marie," Ezekiel shifted his focus from Kate, and locked eyes with Will, "but I think there's something down in New Orleans, and it looks like I'm going to need all the help I can get it."

"Count me in," Kate said.

Ezekiel raised an eyebrow.

"You're not terrified?" Will asked.

"Of course I am." Kate looked Will up and down. "But you know what's scarier than knowing there are vampires out there?"

"What?"

"Knowing vampires are out there and not doing anything about it." Her smile turned to a sly smirk, and she elbowed Will in the ribs. "You're not too scared, are you? You gonna ditch us, Bluebelly?"

"I was already planning on staying before we even met you," Will grumbled. "Just wanted to wait until he couldn't ditch me on the side of the road."

Ezekiel kept his expression blank despite his confusion, and the small spark of happiness he felt. "Why would you guys want to be a part of this? It's all blood and death."

"So's war, and I signed up for that," Will said. "Besides, you saved my life. I owe you."

"And I honestly enjoyed sending that demon back to hell." Kate grinned at Will and mimed firing with the rifle. "Got me all tingly inside!"

"Those are dark words for a thirteen-year-old," Will said, eyeing her nervously.

"Well one of us has to be the tough one."

"Will," Ezekiel said, "if you ride with me, you're going to have to kill. There's no way around it. If you don't, you will die."

Will scuffed out the fire with the heel of his boot. "Only in self-defense."

"I don't want your blood on my conscience," Ezekiel said.

"It's my choice. None of it's on you."

"We both know that's not how people work."

"I'm coming," Will said. "That's that."

"Suit yourself."

8

It was three days before Ezekiel was able to mount his horse and ride for any reasonable distance, and three more before he was able to travel at half of his previous speed. Ezekiel refused to let the family accompany them, despite Will's protests. They ended up staying at the campsite for an extra day. The boys and their mother left them as soon as she was able to effectively steer her horse.

On the eighth day, they arrived outside of Alexandria. The town was a sight to behold. Zigzagging protrusions of tall lumber, sharpened and angled outward, surrounded all-encompassing stone walls. Deep trenches ringed the land. Some were filled with murky brown water diverted from the Red River. Others were filled with smaller, spear-like branches. It wouldn't stop mortar fire, but it made charging successfully nearly impossible.

Mortars dotted the top of the stone wall at even intervals, and the black eyes of siege rifles stared out of small spaces cut in the wooden defenses. Two great blockhouses rose up at the sides of the fort's sealed gate. Ezekiel couldn't see them, but he knew there were soldiers inside, watching and waiting for any sign to open fire. The beads of their rifles itched on his skin.

A bridge linked to two chains crossed all the defenses and fortifications in a straight line that led to the gate. The shredded remains of the Confederate naval flag hung on the wooden portal—a testament to the enemy's defeat—right beneath a pristine Union flag.

"I guess we just walk right up," Will said.

"Yeah." Kate rolled her eyes. "Seems *so* welcoming."

"We can't approach without permission." Ezekiel brought his horse to a standstill just in front of the bridge. "They'd take us out before we made it across. We should wait until dark, sneak in, get what we need, and move on."

"Don't be ridiculous. They wouldn't shoot us," Will said. "They can clearly see that I'm one of them. I'll talk to them. Not everything needs to be a fight, you know?" Cupping his hands to his mouth, he called out, "I am Corporal William Taylor, Red River Division. My companions and I have traveled from the ruins of Natchitoches to rendezvous with the Union forces stationed here. May we enter?"

No response.

Will looked back at Ezekiel and Kate. "Maybe no one's stationed at the gate?"

He guided his horse past Ezekiel and onto the bridge. No sooner had its hoof contacted the first plank, a shot rang out and a Minie ball embedded itself into the wood. Will's horse reared back and threw him from the saddle. He had to roll into the trench alongside the bridge to avoid being crushed under the animal's hooves. The murky river water soaked him to the bone in an instant.

"They're in there alright," Kate said.

"I noticed." Will clambered out of the muddy trench and managed to calm his horse, though it rejected any attempts he made to climb back into the saddle.

Moments later the gate ground its way open with an awful, deafening sound. A squad of nine Union soldiers rushed out of the fort. Eight of them formed a ring of bayonets around Ezekiel and Kate, while the ninth herded Will into the circle with them before joining the surrounding soldiers.

"Does this seem familiar to anyone else?" Will asked.

"Stand down, men," a voice called. It was high and shrill, and made Will wince.

The soldiers lowered their rifles and fell into attention on the sides of the bridge. A blond man not much older than Will strode across the bridge, hands clasped behind his back. He wore the dark blue shoulder straps trimmed with gold—the sign of a high-ranking officer.

"You were up north," the young man looked Will up and down, "in Natchitoches?"

Will straightened himself and saluted. "Yes, sir."

"At ease, soldier," the young man smiled and waved his hand, then glanced at Ezekiel. "And you don't need to worry, we're all equals here."

"I'm sure," Ezekiel said.

"We're just passing through," Will said. "We'd hoped to get some supplies and then be on our way within the next few days."

"If not here, then where were you headed?" the young man asked.

Will hesitated. "New Orleans, to meet up with the navy."

The young man's eyes narrowed, the smile falling from his face. "You're deserters…"

Will's eyes widened. A hint of panic crept into his voice. "No, we were separated from our unit and are making our way back to them in New Orleans."

"Firstly, Corporal William Taylor, the navy is no longer stationed at New Orleans, since the capture of the city." He gestured at Kate. "Secondly, you expect me to believe this child served some purpose at a military installation?"

Will cursed. "She's my little—"

"Or are you Confederate spies?" the other soldier continued. "Saboteurs even? I've heard they've taken to using negroes as a means of avoiding suspicion in such cases of terrorism."

"I'd burn this whole state to the ground before I'd work with the likes of them," Ezekiel growled. "God knows there's enough cotton for it to catch."

The young man's face lit up. "Do you want to burn the people who enslaved you, boy?"

"I ain't your boy, *boy*," Ezekiel spat. "But if it burns, it burns. Don't much care who lights the match. Now, who the fuck are you?"

"Prentiss Banks, the man who believes he may have some use for you three. Bring them."

He snapped his fingers and the surrounding soldiers closed in, grabbing Ezekiel first and tying his hands behind his back. A burlap sack was slipped over his head and tightened by rope around his throat. He struggled, shouting, and lashing out so violently his wounds began to reopen. The sound of a gunshot froze him in place.

"Next one goes in your head if you don't cooperate." Prentiss's voice held no trace of the earlier conversation's forced warmth, just ice.

Rough hands grabbed Ezekiel and dragged him across the bridge and into the fort.

Their prison was an old barn, with dust and dry hay coating the floor and the interminable smell of animal excrement thick in the air. Red paint peeled off the walls, and misshapen slats let in trickles of light from outside. Soldiers talked in low voices outside the door. Ezekiel flexed his wrists now that his hands were no longer bound and reached down for his pistols to find they no longer hung at his waist.

"Figures," he said.

"They took the rifle, too," Kate said, brushing off her dress.

"I managed to pick this off one of the guys who brought us here." Will held up a bronze-barreled revolver. "Unfortunately, its owner didn't give us much to work with." With a flick of his wrist, the chamber fell open and revealed four empty chambers. Only the remaining two held bullets. Another flick sealed the chamber.

He tossed the gun to Ezekiel.

"How did you—?" Kate started to ask.

"Disarming people becomes very important when you don't want them to kill you, but don't want to kill them either. Plus,"—he held up his hands—"quick, steady hands."

"You'd make a hell of a gunslinger," Ezekiel said. "Or a thief."

"Nah, I'm already tired of being dragged into everyone else's nonsense."

"You're telling me." Ezekiel struggled to his feet and checked himself over. None of his wounds had reopened, but they all throbbed with an angry pain that made him woozy.

"This is kind of your fault though, Will," Kate said. "You wanted to talk to these guys."

Ezekiel said nothing, but eyed Will with the same irritation written on Kate's face.

"Fine. You're right." Will stood up and ran a hand through his shaggy hair in a futile attempt to slick it back. "From now on, it's your lead."

Ezekiel crept to the barn door, pressing his ear up against the cold, rotting wood. "I hear...four voices."

"That's two more than we have bullets for," Kate said, kicking at a pile of hay and filling the air with dust and dry pollen.

"Someone's coming," Ezekiel said, hurrying away from the door and tucking the revolver down the back of his pants. He untucked his shirt and smoothed it down to hide the weapon completely. Kate hopped up on a nearby bale of hay.

Will stood awkwardly in the center of the barn.

Prentiss entered the barn. The four guards closed the door behind him. He rolled a barrel in front of Ezekiel and perched on it with a look of too-practiced confidence.

"I do apologize for all of this." He gestured at the dusty surroundings. "But there are certain people here who would not approve of any of this."

"So, I just got to make a lot of noise, and someone will come get us?" Ezekiel deadpanned. He crossed his arms and leaned forward, towering over Prentiss with a scowl.

"Someone will come shoot you, yes," Prentiss responded, unfazed. "Now...let's talk business."

Ezekiel paced back and forth in front of the barrel. "Business?"

"I am not in charge of this fort."

"Shocking," Ezekiel mumbled. He cast a smug glance at Kate, who responded with a chuckle and kicked her feet into the side of the hay bail.

Prentiss's jaw tightened. "The general in charge is a weak-willed man. He doesn't have the strength to do what it takes to put these Confederate dogs in their place."

"At least he's not some kid who thinks he's the big man with all the answers," Kate snapped.

"I *am* a man," Prentiss slammed his hand down on the wooden barrel, making Kate roll her eyes in disgust. His lips peeled back in a furious sneer. "And I *will* be respected."

"You said the general can't do what now?" Ezekiel pulled Prentiss's attention back to him and the matter at hand. His hand had instinctively gone for the revolver when the young soldier had directed his fury at Kate, but he relaxed now as Prentiss pivoted to face him.

"He won't punish the traitors," Prentiss said, fixing the few strands of hair that had fallen out of place during his outburst. "Which makes the Union seem weak, something I won't stand for."

"Aren't the casualties of war punishment enough?" Will asked. He'd found a seat on a crate under Kate's perch and sat with his knees tucked to his chin.

Prentiss cackled like a hyena. "This war wants to bring everyone back into the fold as one happy union. The South *betrayed* us, the treasonous bastards, and last I checked, treason is punishable by death for all involved."

"So what," Ezekiel asked, "you plan to put the whole South to death?"

Kate's eyes went wide with horror. Her hands curled into fists at her sides.

"No, I am a merciful judge. But in the end, these dogs will come to understand just who is in charge, and exactly how much they need our support. They'll never dare try to split from us again. And if God won't bring a flood down on their heads, they'll learn through fire."

"Fire?" Ezekiel's brow furrowed.

"All those slaves picking cotton down here," Prentiss cooed. "So much soft, *flammable* cotton." He leaned in closer. "And so much of it right here in this fort."

"But the Union controls this fort." Will leaned forward a hint of fury building behind his eyes. "Your soldiers are stationed here."

Prentiss straightened. "Not for much longer. We're moving out in three days. That's why the general wasn't here to welcome you."

"And he put *you* in charge?" Kate raised a questioning eyebrow.

"And why wouldn't he?" Prentiss snapped.

"Seems a poor choice to leave a person whose methods you don't agree with in charge of the fort under your control," Ezekiel said, agreeing with Kate.

"He had his reasons." Prentiss tugged at the collar of his wool coat and stood. "The point is, I'm in charge, and I'm going to see to it that this, and every other bloody Confederate bastion, burns."

Ezekiel smirked. "You've got my attention."

"Ezekiel!" Will snapped, only to be kicked in the shoulder by Kate.

"Of course I do," Prentiss hissed. "Why wouldn't you want to strike back at your oppressors? Show them just how much hate you hold in your heart for what they did to you."

"What's the plan?" Ezekiel rested his palm on the now vacant barrel.

"We need someone to light the match."

"Why me?" Ezekiel bit back on pointing out that making someone else do his dirty work made Prentiss just as weak-willed as the general he so haughtily looked down on. A part of him railed against the idea —it was a waste of time, risky, and he loathed the idea of doing anything for the sleazy youth before him. The other part wanted nothing more than to stick it to the Confederates—this wasn't his war, not really, but they stood for everything wrong with this country. He pictured Pickett's plantation ablaze, and remembered feeling cheated that he wasn't the one to spark it to life.

Lighting the match would be satisfying, to say the least.

"All soldiers will be forced to depart once the general arrives,"

Prentiss said, his tone returning to one of false authority. "And we can't exactly burn the place down around ourselves, now can we?"

"You leave us behind to light the match." Ezekiel narrowed his eyes. "How do we know you won't turn around and shoot us when we try to get out ourselves?"

"Do I seem like that kind of man?" Prentiss asked, humility staining his voice like blood.

"Overwhelmingly so," Kate mumbled.

Prentiss ignored her. "Let me be quite clear. I am offering you the chance to participate in this willingly, but I am not *asking* you to do this." His eyes drifted across the three of them. "A negro with no freedom papers, a soldier fleeing from duty, and a runaway brat." He paused for effect, his eyes taking on a cruel glint. "The punishments one could come up with."

"No need for threats." Ezekiel crossed his arms over his chest. "I just want to be sure of where I fit in to everything. Aside from being the first spark."

Prentiss's face relaxed, some of the darkness in it fading away. "For now, just stay here and wait. Get comfortable if you can. Nothing matters until we depart. You'll be fed and treated well…if you're quiet and cooperative."

Ezekiel nodded, his face devoid of emotion.

Prentiss snapped his fingers and the four guards exited, taking their posts back at the door. "See you again soon."

The heavy wooden doors slid shut behind him with a dusty *thud*. The three of them were alone again in the dingy, hay-strewn barn. Ezekiel's placid face broke into a twist of irritation. "Uppity ass brat." He spat on the barn floor.

"What the hell was that?" Will stared at Ezekiel, incredulous.

"Obviously a lie to buy us some time," Kate snapped back.

"We're gonna do it," Ezekiel said.

"What?" both Will and Kate asked in unison.

Ezekiel shrugged, leaned back against a bale of hay, and said, "Gets us out of here with the least interference. And gives me more time to heal." His body still ached, and while normally he'd be inclined to gun his way free—this time he didn't like his odds.

"We're talking about burning down a whole town!" Will shouted.

One of the soldiers outside rapped angrily on the barn door. "Keep it down!"

Will lowered his voice and crawled closer to his companions. "How are you so calm about this? We're talking about destroying a city!"

"Sticks and stones," Ezekiel said. "It can be rebuilt."

"And the people?"

"You know better than me. Regular folk bolt at the first sight of the attacking army. Any soldiers will be taken as prisoners when they head out. Can't risk them joining back in the war effort."

Will deflated. "It just seems wrong."

Ezekiel closed his eyes. "There's a whole lotta wrong in this world. You either get used to it, or you get mad as hell."

"And we know which one you chose," Kate said.

"Damn right," he said slowly as he drifted off into a dreamless, restless sleep.

On the second day, the guards told them they could walk about, but that trying to leave the fort would earn them a fatal bullet. Soldiers stared at Ezekiel as they passed by. He glared back until eventually they averted their eyes. The soldiers' uniforms were in rough condition; tears, stains, and burn damage mottled the coats of those who had them. Some had even taken to wearing the color of their enemies, while still maintaining their caps and sewn-on blue patches so as to avoid confusion. Most had only stained white shirts and blue pants. Uniform was the last word Ezekiel would use to describe the soldiers' appearance. The only thing they all shared was the look of exhaustion that aged their faces well beyond their years.

"Notice anything?" Ezekiel asked as they walked up and down the streets, taking in the fortified town of Alexandria.

Will scanned their surroundings for a minute. "No civilians."

"Exactly."

"Feel better?" Kate asked.

"I don't know. It feels barbaric." Will wrung his hands. "Is this the kind of nation we're to be? The kind that scorches the earth in our wake, just to spite our enemies?"

"Yes." Prentiss stepped from an alley and regarded them. "Follow me."

Prentiss led them back the way they came, walking in what seemed to be an aimless pattern throughout the town. Ezekiel glanced around, as if he was in on the conspiracy that Prentiss had built around his actions. No one was paying them any mind, too concerned with their own situations to give a damn. Finally, Prentiss came to a stop in front of a barn not much different than the one they'd been kept in. He slid the heavy wooden doors along their tracks to reveal bags upon bags, each full to the point of overflowing with fluff. Cotton lay on the floor like fake snow blanketing the space in white.

"Your fuel." Prentiss's face lit with cold glee as he showed off the burlap-wrapped mounds.

Ezekiel made a concerned sound and clicked his tongue.

"What?" The young man's icy grin darkened, and his eyebrow twitched in irritation. Ezekiel had spoiled his excitement.

"It'll go up nice and easy, but most of these buildings are stone. Not sure it'll catch the way you want." Ezekiel shrugged. "Fire needs fuel, and rock ain't it."

"You think I didn't consider that," Prentiss snapped. "Come tomorrow, this will be placed near some key locations. Light it up, and *everything* will burn. Trust me."

Ezekiel scratched at the stubble starting to sprout on his jaw. "Guess that makes sense. And it ain't my plan, after all. I'm sure you have it all figured out."

Prentiss didn't seem to catch Ezekiel's sarcasm, instead looking pleased at what he took as a compliment. Prentiss cleared his throat and continued.

"You only need to light one. My soldiers will ensure the fire has all it needs to spread.

"And what about the people?" Ezekiel asked.

"The what?" Prentiss frowned.

"The ones that live here," Ezekiel continued, ignoring Will's attempts to catch his eye. "Or lived, I assume. They gone?"

Prentiss blinked in confusion, and then laughed. "Yes, yes, of course, the cowards fled when we first arrived. It was quite a sight. As I told you before, I am a merciful judge. Only their towns will burn. Though I must say, I find your concern for their well-being odd. Are these not the people who claimed to be your master?"

"At one point, your Union claimed the same thing." Ezekiel fixed Prentiss in a dark glare.

Prentiss's mouth snapped shut.

"And it ain't my concern." Ezekiel jerked a thumb back at Will. "It's his."

A man's gruff voice broke the silence around them. "There you are, Private Banks."

Prentiss's face froze in the expression of a child who'd been caught with their hand in the cookie jar. The man who approached them was well into his forties, with a full beard already greying at the roots. He regarded them with tired eyes and furrowed brow. His posture indicated a man who took himself seriously and commanded respect, but there wasn't a hint of arrogance. Ezekiel knew immediately the man was sizing them up and assessing their threat. No doubt he was the general.

"General Banks, you've returned early." Prentiss stumbled over his words. He closed the barn door with a too-loud thud. "Did something happen?"

"Who are these people?"

Without missing a beat, Kate said, "Refugees from Natchitoches. We escaped while it was burning. This boy let us in and gave us shelter." She toyed with the word 'boy', relishing in the twitch it brought to Prentiss's eye.

"Kindness. Very good." The general scratched his beard with a distant look in his eyes. "To answer your question, we were ambushed by a small group of Greybacks on the return, but otherwise the trip was uneventful. Is everything prepared for tomorrow's departure to Baton Rouge?"

"Yes, Dad."

General Banks raised a single, serious eyebrow. "We've discussed this."

Prentiss faltered and gave a salute. "Yes, sir. Everything is ready."

With a terse nod of acknowledgment, General Banks turned heel and set off to tend to whatever last-minute details needed to be taken care of. Ezekiel let out a low whistle.

"Going behind your daddy's back is mighty brave."

"Just do your damn job." Prentiss's face burned crimson as he stormed off.

9

The soldiers were all packed and lined up for the exit march from Alexandria. Prentiss rode at his father's side, casting a quick glance back at Ezekiel, who nodded in return. The general called the company to attention and pointed his saber forward. Hardly in sync, but trying their best, the exhausted soldiers began a slow, rhythmic march out of the town. When the last member of the troop disappeared out of the city fort, Ezekiel set to work.

Cotton had been strewn in a winding trail that coiled around almost every structure in the town.

"Lucky it ain't windy," Ezekiel said.

The three of them would each take a single focal building and ignite it. Ezekiel had the town hall, Kate the church, and Will would burn down the barn with the remaining cotton. After that, they would ride off to New Orleans with the fire fading into distant memory. Will finally seemed mostly on board with the plan, though it was impossible to tell if it was agreement or resignation. He held his matches in trembling hands.

"We could just leave," Will said, one last time. "They aren't coming back, and they can't stop us from just…disappearing."

"You're following my lead, right?" Ezekiel asked. Will's jitteriness had him ill at ease. The boy's nervousness was infectious. For a minute he weighed their chances of escape—slim to none, he figured, assuming the rest of the troops would turn on them whether they agreed with Prentiss or not.

Will said nothing but nodded glumly.

Ezekiel clapped a hand on his shoulder. "It'll go up quick, but fire won't spread anywhere near fast enough to cause us problems. We get it done, and then we're gone." He'd seen towns burned and rebuilt, over and over since the war began. Losing Alexandria might even make the Greybacks give up on their petty little rebellion.

"A good bonfire is always fun," Kate chimed in. "Gran used to make them on people's birthdays. Mom would get so angry, but she never stopped us." Her face fell a little, then perked up again. "Just try to have fun with it."

Will's jaw dropped. "Fun? We're about to burn down a town!"

"Mama always said to seek out new experiences."

Ezekiel shook his head. "Something is truly wrong with you, girl."

Kate shrugged. "Saved your ass."

"Matches?" Ezekiel ignored her and thumbed open his box. His companions held up theirs in response.

Town hall was the closest. Ezekiel leaned up against it as the other two wandered off to find their own targets. After a few minutes, Ezekiel struck the match and tossed it onto the trail of cotton. It went up in a spectacular display of flames, the fire almost instantly devouring the cotton trail as it raced along the makeshift path. The dry wood of the building caught a moment or so later, crackling as burning red tongues lapped at it. Ezekiel stared up at the growing inferno, cracked his neck, and turned to head back to the town center.

Something thudded inside the building.

Ezekiel froze. He craned his neck and listened.

Nothing. "Just the fire," he said.

Will's voice rose over the crackling flames, screaming his name.

The boy's voice cracked in panic, and Ezekiel's stomach lurched. He broke into a full sprint in the direction of the barn, sliding to a stop in front of the young man and the open barn door.

Will was fine.

Ezekiel's cheeks burned with frustration. "What the hell are you—?"

"Look." Will pointed into the barn.

Ezekiel squinted to see into the dark interior. Something moved under the fluffy mountain of cotton. More motion to the left, and then the right. A head emerged from the white coating, and a man, bound and gagged, stared at them with pleading eyes. Prentiss must have gagged them and bound them so they couldn't escape or call for help.

"People…" Sweat dragged a chilly finger down Ezekiel's spine as he remembered the noise from inside the town hall. Not splintered wood, or crackling flames, but people. People *he* just lit on fire. He turned to the red-orange glow from the town center.

"Stop Kate," Ezekiel barked.

"What about them?"

"They're fine for now. Go!"

Will hesitated a second longer, and then that focused glaze filmed his eyes once more. He nodded and sprinted around a nearby corner, heading to the church, and to Kate.

Ezekiel turned heel and ran back to the town hall, never taking his eyes off the growing red-orange blaze that now towered above most of the buildings in the town. The whole city center was aflame.

"This was supposed to be simple." He scanned the area for anything to help him douse the flames. "Burn the town, avoid a fight, no one gets hurt." He kicked at a burning plank of wood that had dislodged from a nearby building. "Fuck!"

He pulled his scarf up over his face, the all-too-familiar sting of smoke and heat swirling around him, blurring his vision and choking his lungs. His leather duster was torn, barely holding together after being savaged by Jonathan. Still, he pulled it tight around himself and carefully approached the door to the building.

The door was too big to kick open, and he could feel the heat building on the other side. His heart raced and sweat broke out all over his body, only to immediately evaporate in the intense heat. He stared in awe and terror at the towering inferno. A flaming tongue licked at his arm and jolted him back to focus.

"Okay." Coughs wracked his body in a painful fit, and the pain of the cauterized wounds on his skin sparked to life as if woken by the fire. "New plan."

He took enough steps back until he felt safe, yanked the bronze-barreled gun from his waistband, and fired a shot at each of the building's two front facing windows. Fire roared out of the open portals, blowing out the rest of the glass and clawing for the sky like a demonic genie escaping its lamp. The smoke and chaos muddled the screams of the people inside.

Using the remaining leather holding together the arm of his coat, he brushed away the jagged glass teeth of the shattered window. He took a deep breath and hoisted himself into the building. His skin cracked in the intense heat, his wounds popping open like blisters. He couldn't see anything through the glow of the crackling flames.

"Make more noise!" Ezekiel coughed violently as he sucked in more smoke, burning his throat. "I can't see you."

Muffled cries came in response, and he made his way towards them. The building's other windows blew out as well, spraying shards of glass outward from the building. Finally, Ezekiel saw them. Or at least the shape of them. There was a struggling mass of people and, as he got closer, he saw that they were all tied together, hand and foot, with a single line of thick cattle rope. The rope steamed, still damp even in the heat.

Ezekiel ungagged the first person, a gasping man with a handlebar mustache and frizzing grey hair. An ember caught his mustache and Ezekiel pinched it out. The man opened his mouth to speak but Ezekiel cut him off.

"Is it just you, the people in the barn, and the church?"

"As far as I know."

Ezekiel picked up a jagged piece of glass and cut through the man's bonds. "What's your name?"

"Dan."

"Help me save your friends, Dan." Ezekiel shoved the glass into the man's hands and picked up another piece for himself. "Be quick about it."

The two worked to free other people, and in turn those people helped to free even more people. Wood cracked and collapsed like gunshots in the superheated air, and Ezekiel did his best to ignore the sounds of the town hall coming down all around them.

An eternity in hell later, all the captives were free.

"Move!" Ezekiel shouted. He led the way to the window and leapt out first, tucking into a roll, smothering the flames lingering on his body with the dusty ground.

Will and Kate were waiting for him outside.

"Thirty people in the barn, seventy in the church." Will tried—and failed—to give the report without revealing his internal panic.

Ezekiel rose to his feet and counted each captive as they came through the windows. "Fifty in the town hall."

Will gave him a disapproving look.

"Save it," Ezekiel snapped. "I know I fucked up. Right now, we have other priorities."

"My God." Dan pressed a hand to his mouth. "How the hell can we stop this?"

Ezekiel's mind raced as the fires spread around them.

"Well?" Will's tone wasn't accusatory but held an urgency that did nothing to calm Ezekiel's nerves. A crowd had gathered around them now as the other townsfolk joined them at the center of the town.

"The nearest source of water?" Ezekiel searched the faces covered in ash and sweat.

"The river," said a familiar voice.

General Banks stood at the end of a nearby road while soldiers around him sloughed buckets of water to fight the encroaching fire. The general's tired eyes had grown sharp and glinted with a renewed vigor. Beside him, Prentiss fumed as hot as the surrounding flames. The general surveyed them a second longer and added, "My soldiers have buckets to share. Gather water and we'll douse the flames."

There was a tension in the air as the Union soldiers and the recently freed Southerners stood opposite each other in a heavy silence. The flames danced and grew and leapt from surface to surface.

"And why the hell would we trust you?" Dan spat. "When that boy of yours and his thugs are the reason we're in this situation."

"What are you talking about?" Prentiss sputtered and pointed at Ezekiel. "He set the fire; it was all his idea."

Ezekiel bristled, his face darkening with a rage that bubbled so close to the surface it threatened to consume him. He stormed at Prentiss. "You kidnapped us, locked us in a barn, and threatened to kill us, you pretentious piece of shit! I ought to—"

"Hey!" Will pushed his way between both crowds, even pushing Ezekiel back from Prentiss. "The town is *burning*. It will burn to the ground just like Natchitoches if we don't act!"

As if to mark his words, another house caught fire. Its windows burst from the heat; the rush of oxygen sent the flames pluming into the sky like demon's claws reaching to drag heaven down to the earth.

The townspeople and the Union soldiers sized each other up. Dan moved first, reaching down to grab one of the buckets sitting between the two groups.

Another man followed suit.

When the third man moved, the soldiers resumed their task— fetching buckets of water and fighting back the flames side by side with the townspeople. They worked as fast as they could, with silent, somewhat coordinated efficiency.

Ezekiel took up a bucket brought by the soldiers and hurled its contents at the nearest building. The fire that sought to expand its reach hissed away, rearing back like a serpent. Muffled noises came from within the building.

Ezekiel and Dan shared a horrified look.

"There are more people." Ezekiel snatched a bucket from the

nearest soldier and barked, "Work on getting them out of there. Check the other houses too."

The soldier raised an eyebrow and gave General Banks a questioning look.

The older man nodded slowly. "For now, listen to him as you would to me."

Another house burst into flames. The muffled screams that followed were cut short by the sound of collapsing wood. Ezekiel saw the fear etched onto the faces of the people around him. The house creaked as wooden beams weakened by the growing fire began to bend and snap.

A Union soldier returned from the river with a bucket of water. Ezekiel snatched it and dumped it at the ring of flames, moistening the ground and making a small opening in the ring of fire. He kicked open the door to the house and stared into the terrified faces of a small family.

"Stay calm." Ezekiel stepped forward, but the floor ignited right in front of his face and drove him away from the entrance.

The family did not stay calm.

Ezekiel didn't hesitate, he dove through the wall of flames and set about undoing the family's bonds. Just as he freed the father, a beam overhead snapped free and plummeted down on top of one of the daughters. She began to scream as the burning log pressed into her, searing through her dress and down to her skin. Ezekiel and her father grabbed the beam and heaved at it with all their combined strength. Even with the calluses built up on Ezekiel's hands from years of toil and hard living, the heat of the flaming wood scorched his hands until he wanted to scream. The beam lifted as his wounds reopened, only to sear shut again as the flames wreathed his body.

"Can you move?" Ezekiel grunted.

The daughter scurried from beneath the burning wood and grabbed her sister by the hand, pulling her towards the open door, now doused by one of the soldiers. Ezekiel motioned for the father to free the girl's mother, and finally, mercifully, dropped the beam. He looked down at the angry red of his hands and shook them out, doing his best to block the pain from his mind. He staggered from the building and slumped to his knees just outside the range of the flames.

Whistles blared around him as the Union soldiers hurried to and fro like worker ants, fighting the fire and eventually reducing the blaze to a few trapped conflagrations. As the fires began to dissipate, people rushed from the houses and into the streets, freed by the combined efforts of the soldiers and their own neighbors. Sweat stuck Ezekiel's clothes to his skin, and the fire burrowed deep, creating a sizzling nest in his lungs that burned every time he breathed. General Banks walked over and placed a bucket of water in front of him. Ezekiel dunked his hands in, relishing in the wet, cooling sensation that eased the angry burning in his hands. He closed his eyes and gasped at the pain.

"My soldiers can handle the rest."

"If you stand right there, the shade is perfect." Ezekiel gasped around each of the words.

The general stepped aside, allowing the sun's rays to resume their scorching assault on Ezekiel's cracked and blistered skin. "Did you start that fire?"

Ezekiel hung his head until his nose was inches away from the water in the bucket. "How many?"

"Sixteen dead, several more with burns ranging from incidental to,"—General Banks paused to look out over the smoking town—"well, we'll treat them as best we can."

"Never intended for anyone to get hurt."

"Explain."

"That boy of yours." Ezekiel looked up and held the general's interrogating gaze.

"Are you accusing my son of something?"

"He held us hostage. Said he wanted to burn the town to teach the South a lesson,"—Ezekiel chuckled, then coughed, and regretted both—"said you were too weak to do it. We thought the houses were empty." Ezekiel clenched his fists around handfuls of dirt. "Ask my companions and the townsfolk, hell, interrogate your own soldiers, they'll tell you straight…if you don't trust someone like me."

General Banks's ice blue eyes searched Ezekiel's face. "In justice, there is no room for prejudice."

"If only everyone thought like that." Ezekiel's wry smile cracked the skin of his lips, and he tasted blood. He licked it away and spat it at the ground.

"I've already spoken to several people." General Banks dusted his hands, then offered one of them to Ezekiel. "They confirmed your story."

Ezekiel clasped the man's hand and pulled himself to his feet. "Then why ask me?"

"I prefer to make my own judgments and not let the words of other people dictate how I approach a given situation, or in this case, a person."

"You wanted to see if I'd lie."

General Banks nodded. "In short, yes."

"Honestly, it was your son's plan, but I wanted to." He gestured with burned, exhausted hands. "I *wanted* to burn all this down. To dish out just a little bit of revenge for what these motherfuckers put me through on their plantations, but..."

"But?"

"It wasn't these folks who slapped me in chains."

General Banks regarded him. "So you risked your life to undo your mistake?"

"I couldn't live with myself if I didn't."

"Then you are a better man than most." General Bank maintained a stony expression as he gripped Ezekiel on the shoulder. "Regardless of the color of your skin."

Ezekiel scoffed and stepped out of the general's grip. "I don't aim to be. I just wanna get where I'm going, and I'll do what I got to do to get there with as little shit on my conscience as possible."

"I see." General Banks sniffed imperiously. "As it is, my son has wronged you. Lest I be accused of favoritism, and since you are the wrong party, I leave your punishment in his hands."

"You serious?"

General Banks's eyes flashed. "Do I look like a man who wastes time on jokes?"

Ezekiel didn't answer.

"The boy needs to learn that he is not as superior as he may think." General Banks turned and gestured for Ezekiel to follow him. "He's already tied and waiting, along with all of the conspirators I could root out."

A large crowd gathered in front of the church that Will had managed to prevent Kate from burning. Soldiers and civilians stood side-by-side. In the center of the circle, a heavy post had been driven into the ground. Prentiss's hands were tied at the wrist by a rope secured to the post. His coat and shirt were nowhere to be seen as he sat on his knees, his head hanging solemnly down to his chest. Five other soldiers shared his predicament. When Ezekiel and the general entered the circle to stand over him, he looked up.

"Father..." he started.

"I, General Jefferson Emmanuel Banks, do, in the best possible faith, extend a formal apology to the people of Alexandria for the misbehavior of my soldiers. Worse even, that one is my own flesh and blood." He glared down at Prentiss. "In bearing with the Union martial laws, he will be tried here and now, and punished for his actions."

"And what about the others?" Dan asked. The crowd of Alexandrians riled at his question, demanding an answer.

"For their treason they will be executed by firing squad," Banks said. "You understand, however, that I cannot bring myself to do this to my son." He swallowed hard and paused, inviting any disagreement. "And so, since I will already be accused of softness in his favor, I leave the choice and...execution...of his punishment to the man who was coerced into acting on his behalf." He gestured towards Ezekiel and stepped back. "I will not interfere." The ice in his voice broke on the last word with a strained creak.

Ezekiel glanced down at Prentiss, who quivered bare-chested and tied to a post, as he tried not to cry in front of everyone gathered. The scars on Ezekiel's back throbbed with agonizing memory. He opened his mouth, then closed it, biting hard on his tongue. His hands tightened into fists, and he stepped forward.

This was different. Wasn't it?

"Please," Prentiss said as Ezekiel got closer, "have mercy."

"Would you have?" Ezekiel tossed his head towards the crowd of Alexandrians. "If they had begged?"

"I-I-I…"

Ezekiel crouched down and leaned in as close as he could without his face touching the young man's. "I don't think you would have." He spoke in a menacing growl. "You were going to let them burn. *Alive.*"

Prentiss broke from Ezekiel's gaze and craned his neck to beg for his father's mercy. "I just wanted to make you proud. To show you I was strong."

General Banks turned his head in silence, mouth a grim line, arms crossed over his chest.

"Don't look at him." Ezekiel grabbed Prentiss by the jaw. "Look at me. Right now, I own you." The phrase sent a chill down Ezekiel's spine. His words faltered, and he searched the crowd, hoping to see Will or Kate.

He couldn't find them.

Ezekiel willed himself to keep talking. This needed to be done. "If you're gonna pray, I suggest you start,"—Ezekiel pointed to the sky—"but not to him, he ain't listening. It's just you, and me."

Ezekiel glanced down and saw that Prentiss had pissed himself.

"I don't want to die," Prentiss said.

"Shame." Ezekiel rose, brushing the dust from his knees. "No man should die in his own filth."

Prentiss began to scream and thrash against his bonds. Ezekiel locked eyes with the general and drew one of his revolvers. General Banks closed his eyes in resignation, hiding their pain from the world, but Ezekiel had seen it. He knew.

Two soldiers unhitched Prentiss from his post. He fought and cried and begged. Ezekiel knew just how strong a desperate man could be. He had been that man. The two Union soldiers forced Prentiss down to his knees as Ezekiel cocked his gun. He aimed for Prentiss's head and wondered what Will would say.

Sixteen dead. Don't you think enough people have died today?

The words rang as clear in his mind as if Will were whispering it in his ear. The next thought was his own, a conscience that hadn't spoken since the night he spared Collin Pickett—he'd told himself it died all those years ago.

Is this what Anna Marie would want? A man unwilling to show mercy...

Ezekiel bared his teeth and snarled, but he lowered the revolver's hammer and put it back into its holster. General Banks raised a single eyebrow. The whole crowd fell silent, waiting to see what he would do instead. He motioned to the two Union soldiers.

"Let him go."

Prentiss shook out his arms and rubbed his wrists.

"You asked for mercy." Ezekiel stripped out of his duster. "So here is my mercy: you get a choice. I can put you down like the disgrace of a man you are. That would be what you deserve. Or you can face your punishment like a man and fight to survive." Ezekiel raised his fists and bent his knees into a fighting stance.

Prentiss stared in horror. "I'm not going to fight you. You're twice my size."

"You'd prefer to tell the devil what you've done?" Ezekiel asked.

"It's not fair!"

"Neither is being bound in your home while it burns around you." Ezekiel cracked his neck. "Or being sold into slavery because of the color of your skin. Life isn't fair, you little shit. Now fight, or die."

"Fine." Prentiss's eyes flashed with hate, and he growled like a wounded cur, slapping his bare chest before raising his own fists. "Don't forget, *boy*, I'm a soldier. You're just a runaway slave!"

"Careful, kid, you're starting to sound like the Greybacks. Guess that means I should follow through and punish you." Ezekiel ground his teeth, biting back the anger that flared at Prentiss's comment. It was proof—or at least served to reinforce his belief—that even the

North wasn't some great land of the free. Not for people like him. Henrietta's words rang through his head.

So I can have white folk smile in my face and tell me I'm free all the while they're lookin' down their nose at me 'cause I'm black?

Prentiss wasn't fighting because he viewed slavery as an abomination, he just wanted to cause pain. He was no different than a man with a whip—raining down suffering simply because he had the power.

General Banks turned away, disappointment twisting his lips down at the corners.

Ezekiel shook his head. "You're breaking your daddy's heart."

Prentiss screamed and swung a haymaker aimed at Ezekiel's left temple. With little effort, Ezekiel brought up his arm and blocked the blow. The hit was pathetic, but the culmination of his injuries sent pain shooting through his entire body. He let Prentiss pull back and fire off a jab and a hook in quick succession, dodging them both with ease. As he did, Prentiss launched a third strike, lower, and he snatched one of Ezekiel's revolvers from its holster. He didn't even manage a shot before Ezekiel's fist smashed into the side of his jaw with a sickening crack. Prentiss went limp and the gun dropped to the ground. Ezekiel picked it up and slid it back into its holster.

"Never forget, I was the better man."

The two soldiers hoisted Prentiss's unconscious body and Ezekiel stopped them. "Don't set his jaw. It'll heal wrong and act as a reminder of the day he *didn't* die, even when he should have."

General Banks's hand pressed on his shoulder. "Thank you for showing mercy, even though it was truly undeserved."

Ezekiel tracked the tired lines that dug deep chasms on the man's face. He looked decades older now than he had before. "He won't eat normally ever again, and after you execute those other soldiers, the rest of your men will hold him responsible for the deaths of their brothers. I didn't grant him mercy; I just didn't kill him." Ezekiel pulled away from the general's touch. "So, you're welcome for that."

Banks stared at him a moment, then followed the soldiers who'd taken his son.

The crowd dispersed now that Ezekiel's judgment was passed. Some grumbled, unsatisfied with the outcome, while others seemed stunned at the brutality of Ezekiel's single strike. None openly complained. Will and Kate filtered through bodies until only the three of them remained.

"You did a good thing." Will placed his hands on Ezekiel's shoulders and gave a warm smile. "More bloodshed wasn't going to fix anything."

Ezekiel tensed at the touch and shifted away. "I knew you'd be pissed if I shot him."

"I think that might be the nicest thing you've said to me since we met."

"I think you should have killed him." Kate kicked at the ground. "He was an ass." She cocked her head to the side and thought for a moment. "But I guess if you killed every asshole, there'd be no people left."

Ezekiel staggered to a charred wall and slumped against it. "Probably not."

10

The troops came to a coordinated halt.

Ezekiel slowed his horse as Will rode back from the front to meet him.

"Here he comes." Kate rolled her eyes. "Just as pleased as punch."

Ezekiel choked out a single throaty chuckle.

Will had been adamant that they ride to Baton Rouge alongside the Union troops under General Banks. When questioned, he had simply said, "Strength in numbers." Ezekiel couldn't argue with that logic, even if Will had been annoyed when he referred to the other soldiers as 'ghoul fodder.' Still, the young soldier had taken Ezekiel's agreement as a victory and had high spirits since, despite what lay behind them.

"We're stopping to make camp." Will jerked on his horse's reins, bringing the beast to a sharp stop. "The general doesn't want his men exhausted, just in case."

"In case of what?" Ezekiel asked.

"Confederate ambush, or retaliation from the Alexandrians."

Ezekiel looked around.

To their east was marshland that stretched out toward the horizon, dotted with waterlogged trees, and overgrown with moss. The smell of mildew and grime hung thick in the air. Even with the sun shining, thick, velvety shadows swam throughout its nooks and crannies. To the west, an open field of high grass sprawled, terminating at the edge of a thick and tangled forest that bushed the horizon line. The distance would provide ample opportunity to see an enemy approach, but if the enemy was fast enough…

"You don't like it, do you?" Will asked.

Ezekiel stayed silent for a long moment, then dropped from his horse. His boots sank an inch and a half into the muddy ground. "Your general gonna give us a tent?"

The red sun sank down below the overgrown horizon. Ezekiel whittled away at a wooden stake, sharpening the end until it reached a deadly point.

Kate came over and sat beside him. "Gimme one."

"Only one knife."

Kate slid a knife out from the belt around her dress. "Didn't ask for your knife."

Ezekiel tossed her a post.

"Where'd you get these?"

"Stole 'em," he said. "From Alexandria." He glanced over to see her reaction.

"Sure." She didn't look up from her post. "Not like they needed them to rebuild or anything. Where did you actually get them from?"

"Been in my saddlebag since before I came across you or the boy." Ezekiel dropped the one he'd been working on to the ground and picked up a new one. "Ain't had time to sharpen them until now."

"These actually work?"

"On the ones like Jonathan? I don't know. But on the ghouls that like to come out at night? You ain't seen a fire 'til you stake one of them through the heart."

"I think I've had my fill of fire." She glanced out at the darkening sky. "Think we'll see any tonight?"

"Group this size? It's possible some might try and pick off a few of us while we sleep. Like any hunter."

"You nervous?" She cut a deep gash into her post, wincing as she pulled the knife free.

"What about?"

"Running into another vampire."

Ezekiel paused his whittling. "No." He peeled off one last strip of wood before setting the stake aside and starting on a third post. "It caught me off guard the first time, but now I know."

"You'd have died on the side of that road if it weren't for me."

"You're whittlin' it wrong." He pulled the post from her hands and demonstrated how to peel strips to get a nice point, instead of digging chunks out like the knife was a shovel and the stick was a mound of dirt. "And keep each side even if you want it to be real sharp." He tossed it back to her.

"Are we the first people you've kept around since…?"

"Yes."

"Explains a lot." Kate smirked. "You got no manners."

Ezekiel laughed. "You're not much better yourself."

"Gran always said manners are for when you want something." She stopped whittling and placed her hands on her hips. "Otherwise, it's best to talk real."

"Smart woman."

"But then Mama always said that you won't go nowhere in life without your manners," she continued. "Never knew which one to listen to."

Ezekiel tossed another finished stake onto the ground. "Both."

Kate narrowed her eyes and stared at him. She shook her head. "Not helpful."

"You'll get it—"

"If you say 'when you're older'…"

"—eventually," Ezekiel finished. "I was going to say 'eventually'. Age's got nothing to do with understanding. It's about experience."

"Oh." Kate blinked. "Thanks."

"What for?"

"Not treatin' me like a kid." She held up an almost perfectly whittled stake. "Gran never did, but Mama was different."

"I wouldn't know how to treat a kid if I tried." Ezekiel took the stake and added it to his growing pile. He handed her another post. "Never liked kids. Maybe I only like you 'cause you don't seem like a kid."

"I am a kid," Kate murmured. "But I hate being treated like one."

Ezekiel deadpanned. "Don't make me change my mind about you."

"How many of these do we need?"

"Enough."

"That's not a real answer."

"No, it's a polite answer," Ezekiel said. "The real answer is 'enough to kill every last bloodsucking motherfucker in this godforsaken country.'"

Kate cackled so hard she snorted. "That's a much better answer."

Night fell like a silent curtain, suffocating the light in its creeping shadow. Kate had fallen asleep shortly after insisting she wasn't tired. Ezekiel opted to keep watch rather than leave her in the tent alone. A shadow drew closer, and Ezekiel reached for one of the revolvers at his belt.

"Not everything needs to be shot on sight." Will entered with an exasperated sigh. His shirt and pants hung from a lanky form so much smaller than he appeared in his heavy wool coat. He scratched at a few angry hairs on his neck, then focused.

"We need to talk."

Ezekiel raised an eyebrow.

"General says there's movement in the forest to the west." He rubbed his face. "I tried to stop him, but he sent some troops in to check it out."

"What kind of movement?"

"Wolves, he thinks. Maybe a bear?"

Ezekiel sighed deeply and reached for one of his freshly whittled stakes. "Better hope it is, or those soldiers ain't coming back."

Screams ripped through the night.

Kate bolted upright, and Ezekiel rushed out of his tent to see the source of the sound.

A lone soldier emerged from the tangled woods. He clutched the bloody stump of a shoulder that used to be his left arm as he half-ran, half-limped toward the rest of the company. Will started to move, but Ezekiel grabbed him by the shoulder.

The soldier made it a few yards from the forest before a shadow descended on him, ripping out his throat and dragging him back into the winding dark. The trees came alive with gleeful howls and fleshy tearing sounds that rattled the canopy like wind from a storm. And then it fell silent.

"Not wolves. A ghoul nest." Ezekiel clutched the stake in one hand and a revolver in the other. "Tell your general not to send any more men into the forest. Unless he wants them to be the second course."

"He's going to have questions."

"He's allowed to," Ezekiel said. "But it would be better if he just listened."

"Six of his men just died!"

"And if that's a nest, many more will die before the night is through. There's nothing to be done but wait for the sun to save us and then haul ass to Baton Rouge."

"We could move camp now," Will argued. "Push to whatever the nearest town is."

"Oh, the ghouls would love that, give them a *real* hunt."

"Then we can kill them. That's what you do, right? You're a vampire hunter for Christ's sake!"

Ezekiel looked at him like he was crazy. "You wanna go over there and fight those things…in the dark…in an unfamiliar forest…without knowing how many there are? Be my guest. I'll wait for whatever comes to try and take me here, where I can at least see my black-ass hand in front of my face."

"Then at least tell the general what we're up against!" Will crossed the tent and grabbed Ezekiel by the collar. "Stop being a stubborn ass and do something useful."

Ezekiel looked Will up and down, then turned to Kate. "You see this?"

"Looks like that stick in his ass turned into a spine."

"Still, it's about time." Ezekiel pressed his palms into his knees, massaging them before rising and cracking his back. "Alright, kid, take me to your leader."

General Banks's face was whiter than fresh-picked cotton when Ezekiel entered his tent. Prentiss was laid out on a cot in the back of the fabric structure; his jaw was wrapped, but still hanging at an odd angle. Ezekiel tipped his hat at the general, before sitting in one of the two chairs positioned around the war table. Prentiss mumbled something unintelligible under his breath but fell quiet when Ezekiel gave him a second glance.

"General Banks." Will stood beside Ezekiel and flashed a salute. "My companion has some important information about what just happened."

Banks placed himself in the chair on the opposite side of the war table and nodded.

"I heard you lost some men." Ezekiel resisted the urge to kick his feet up on the table. "Actually, I think everyone heard that."

"Those screams…" General Bank's face flushed red with anger. "Is that funny to you?"

"Not in the slightest."

The general cleared his throat and regained his composure. "Wolf attacks are not unknown to us. It's unfortunate I sent my men into their territory and doubled the normal guard, but it's nothing to warrant any other response on our part. Predators are predators. If we leave them alone, they'll likely move on."

Ezekiel shook his head. "I assume by the color of your face when we entered, that you saw that last soldier get taken. That look like a wolf to you?"

"Six of my men are dead." General Banks struggled to maintain his calm demeanor. "I've no time for you to dance around the subject. What the devil was it?"

Ezekiel folded his hands and leaned on the war table. "I just need to make sure you're ready to hear what I have to tell you, otherwise tonight is just going to become more of a hassle."

"Out with it then."

Ezekiel rubbed the stubble on his chin that threatened to sprout into a full beard if he didn't shave soon. "Vampires."

General Banks's face went blank and expressionless. "Vampires?"

"More specifically a ghoul, a person corrupted by a vampire's venom." Ezekiel pointed a finger on the war table map indicating the forest. "And that seems to be their nest."

The blank expression on the general's face darkened, and anger flickered behind his blue-grey eyes. His voice dropped to a cold, venomous hiss. "Get out. I'll not have you mock my men's death. I thought you a better man than this, Mr. Blackthorne."

Ezekiel kneaded his forehead. "Wanna back me up, Will?"

"All due respect, sir, he's not lying. We've come across a few between Natchitoches and here, and Ezekiel, well, he hunts them."

Banks stared back and forth between the two men; his face twisted in disbelief. "You're both absolutely mad."

Ezekiel stayed calm and shut his eyes. "No," he worked the words out slowly, trying to maintain an air of patience, "we're not." His eyes snapped open. "But general, six of your men are dead. How many are you willing to let die to your disbelief?"

"What?"

"Sixty? Six hundred? How many death notifications do you think you can write before your hand cramps up permanently? So answer me, do you want to stay ignorant, or do you want to save as many of your men as you can?"

"If I believed you," General Banks ground his jaw in frustration, "what would you tell me to do?"

Ezekiel blew out a long low breath, puffing out his cheeks as he did. "You're gonna hate this, but our best bet is to burn the forest."

"Let me get this straight." General Banks narrowed his eyes. "You want to start *another* fire?"

Ezekiel held up his hands. "I know, I know, but fire and sunlight are the only things that can kill them en masse. Unless you want to wander in there and try to stake them one by one…"

The general ran a hand through his greying hair, then dabbed at his forehead with the sleeve of his coat. "How?"

"The forest is surrounded by marshland on the back," Ezekiel rolled his neck, "which will act as a natural barrier to keep the flames in check on that side."

"And if the fire spreads towards us?"

"Rather be burned alive than become one of those things," Ezekiel said. "But you can dig a ditch as a firebreak to keep it from getting too close. Have some buckets of water on hand, too. As far as your soldiers: groups of four men at different points along the forest's edge. Three to watch, one to light the fire. Once it gets big enough it'll start to push them back, trapping them between the fire and the slow-moving water of the marshlands. Any survivors will be burned at sunrise when there is no dark canopy to protect them."

General Banks frowned down at the map.

Ezekiel raised an eyebrow. "Well?"

When the general looked back up, the wrinkles in his skin and the dark circles beneath his eyes seemed to have tripled in intensity. "I'll inform the men." He rose slowly, gave Ezekiel a slight nod, and headed to the tent's entrance.

"Oh—" Ezekiel snapped his fingers. "How much silver do you have? And how many crosses?"

General Banks's shoulders slumped as he held open the tent flap. "Go speak to Holloway, the chaplain. He'd be the best place for those questions." He disappeared outside the tent, leaving Ezekiel alone with Will and the moaning Prentiss.

"How do you do that?" Will asked.

Ezekiel regarded Will out of the corner of his eye. "Do what?"

"Command situations despite…well, you know…" Will fidgeted, then gestured at Ezekiel's face. "I mean, sure this is the Union army, but even then…it's just impressive."

"In the ten years I've spent searching for Anna Marie, I've been threatened, harassed, beaten, imprisoned, enslaved again, and left for dead. You wanna know what I learned?"

"What?"

"There are two kinds of people: those who give and those who don't. I don't give." Ezekiel jerked a thumb at the mouth of the tent. "Man's old, tired, just wants to be done with the war. Sure as hell doesn't want to deal with vampires. He gives."

Will scratched at his head. "Do I give…or not?"

Ezekiel shrugged. "That's up to you. Now, where's this chaplain?"

"No silver," Ezekiel grumbled, guns drawn, about ten yards in front of the soldiers assigned to prevent the spread of the fire towards their encampment. "Bet that preacher was lying through his teeth."

"You said that this would work just as well." Will aimed his standard issue at the forest and stared down its iron.

"It complicates things."

Will hesitated and cast a nervous glance at Ezekiel. "It *will* work, right?"

"It better." Kate aimed the rifle she'd used against Jonathan in the forest, loaded with the last of Ezekiel's silver shells. "Or we're all gonna die."

"That's the spirit," Ezekiel said dryly.

They stood alongside several Union soldiers that General Banks had given them to oversee, a defensive line against whatever might try to escape the forest during the burning. The wall was loose, and only covered the main section of the camp, but it would have to do. Several yards in front of the line, a row of crosses, like a makeshift graveyard, separated them from the forest. It could repel a few ghouls, but a frenzy of the sons of bitches would be unlikely to even notice as they swarmed over them. Ezekiel scanned the sky, hoping morning would soon be on its way.

The general joined them on the line, stepping in between Ezekiel and Kate. He glanced down at her, and looked as though he were about to speak, but instead shook his head and focused his attention on the forest instead.

"Remember," Ezekiel turned both ways and shouted down the line, "without silver, destroying the head is the only way these bullets will put them down."

The skepticism of the soldiers was clear in their faces, the jokes they cracked, and the lackadaisical ways in which they held their weapons. Most of them hadn't even responded to the summons until the general began threatening corporal punishment. Ezekiel ground his teeth at their nonchalance but knew there was no way to make them believe…until they saw.

Fires burned at the base of the forest's outermost trees, casting a dim, flickering light in the otherwise inky blackness of the night. The men who lit them sprinted back towards the defensive line, their shadowy silhouettes all that could be seen. Maybe they didn't believe in vampires, but they knew that *something* killed their companions.

"And now we just stay like this 'til dawn," Ezekiel muttered.

The first shriek—a howl unlike that of any animal—rose into the air as the trees began to catch, and the fire spread throughout the canopy. Ezekiel pulled back on the hammers of both revolvers. A shadow broke from the forest, screaming through a gap in the spreading flames and racing towards their line. Ezekiel tracked its path and opened fire. His first shot was echoed by the volley of the other soldiers. He was hoping their aim would be better, and that they wouldn't all shoot at once. The creature writhed and shuddered under the impact of the volley, most of which missed. A last single shot burst its head like a melon. Its shriek died in a wet squelch as it collapsed to the ground. After a moment it burst into flames like a sack of gunpowder touched with a match.

It hadn't gotten far.

In the firelight, the ghoul's form became visible, and the line of soldiers began a collective murmur of growing panic.

General Banks cut through it with a bark of: "Reload!"

The soldiers hurried to prepare their rifles for a second volley.

Everyone waited to see what came next.

The silence was deafening. Sweat shone on the soldiers' foreheads despite the night's chill, and it wasn't just from the growing fire. Rifles shook in unsteady, fearful hands. The ghoul's inhuman figure twitched as it lay burning in the grass, a sign of what lurked just out of sight.

Now the soldiers believed.

Now they were *scared*.

Animals began to flee the burning woods now: red wolves, rabbits, squirrels, even a lone black bear and her cubs hurried away from the spreading flames. Ezekiel steeled himself as they went. Things lurked in those woods that could be given no quarter. It was better for the fleeing animals to find another place, a place not corrupted by evil.

The cacophonous sound of shrieking legions erupted over the roar of the inferno. Smoke billowed into the night sky, blotting out the stars. And then came the ghouls. Not one, or two, but twenty, all at once, even as the forest continued to scream.

About ten feet away from the makeshift graveyard, the creatures stopped, confused. Ezekiel smirked as the ground at their feet began to hiss and bubble, and the shrieks of rage turned to howls of pain and fear. Holloway hadn't been able to provide silver, but he was an ordained minister. He'd been loath to bless the murky, man-made creek—calling it blasphemy and witchcraft—but had eventually acquiesced when the general stepped in. Now a nearly invisible line of holy water acted as the first deterrent between them and the ravenous ghouls.

"Gun 'em down!" Ezekiel shouted.

The night crackled with a chorus of gunshots punctuated by inhuman shrieks as the soldiers opened fire, and bullets ripped through the wave of ghouls. There were more approaching. Ezekiel reloaded and rejoined the assault, firing his silver bullets until every last visible ghoul lay sizzling on the grass in a muddle of their own foul blood.

Nothing stirred save the dancing flames.

The soldiers began to cheer, and Ezekiel started to join them, but the sound caught in his throat as the temperature plummeted. Within seconds, it grew cold enough that he could see his breath steaming out in front of him. Darkness smothered the forest fire until the golden blaze vanished completely. In the forest, more ghouls began to howl once again, not in fear or rage, but in something akin to the soldiers' cheers. It was a horrible, creaking wail that made Ezekiel's head spin. A centipede of horror skittered down his spine.

"Palaiologos," he said under his breath.

"What?" Will approached, still keeping an eye on the now inky black forest.

"He's here. Palaiologos." Ezekiel sprinted from the line and into the encampment. "Show yourself, you bastard!"

Will called after him, but the words died in the wind rushing past Ezekiel's head.

The scream came from the general's tent.

Prentiss.

Ezekiel made it to the tent first, but General Banks wasn't far behind. Ezekiel held up a steadying hand, reloaded, nodded at the general, and ripped open the entrance flap.

Prentiss sat in his cot, mouth a wide rictus scream. His eyes were glazed over, and he stared past them as they entered. Hunched over the back of his left shoulder, shark teeth buried deep into the fleshy side of the young soldier's throat, stood Palaiologos. The vampire moaned in pleasure and ripped away from Prentiss's neck, stretching the skin, muscle, and tendons until they snapped. He straightened his back, chewed, then spat the lump of flesh from his mouth.

"Oh my." He offered a grin that dripped blood down to the grassy tent floor. "I fear you've caught me at a rather embarrassing moment. Chewing with my mouth open."

Ezekiel didn't hesitate. His first shot pierced right between the vampire's eyes. The canvas material of the tent soaked up the spray of black blood that burst from the back of the Palaiologos's head.

The wound began to hiss and sizzle.

Palaiologos looked upward, as if he was trying to see the opening in his head. Blood vessels popped in the whites of his eyes as they rolled back down to look at Ezekiel. "Does poor etiquette warrant execution these days?" He reached up with one clawed hand and dug into the bullet hole. Small chunks of skull and brain matter dropped to the grass at his feet until finally he hooked his finger deep and plucked the bullet from his head.

Beside Ezekiel, General Banks gagged.

"Silver. I wondered why it itched more than usual." The spent bullet sizzled in Palaiologos's fingers, but he licked it clean of his blood and smirked. "Can't leave these things in or they'll be stuck once I heal. It's a real headache."

Ezekiel's blood ran cold.

"I admit," he continued, "that this is quite a shocking scene, and yet…your reaction was calm and—" he held up the silver bullet "—you were prepared. Do I…know you?"

Will burst into the tent followed by Kate, who immediately pointed her rifle at Palaiologos and fired. A bloody hole opened in Palaiologos's side, but he didn't seem to notice as he continued to stare at Ezekiel. Ezekiel put a hand on the barrel of Kate's rifle and pushed it down, so it was aiming at the grass.

"He didn't even flinch," she said.

Will held up a crucifix and thrust it toward Palaiologos.

"What did you hope to accomplish with that?" The vampire's eyes flicked toward the symbol and away again. "It's far too small to hang me from."

"I thought—"

"I believe in your 'Christianity' no more than you believe in ghosts, or goblins,"—Palaiologos flashed a shark-mouthed grin—"or vampires!" He fell into a fit of cold laughter. "*Belief* in a symbol is what gives it power, not the symbol itself. So put it away, you're just embarrassing yourself."

General Banks found his voice. "What have you done to my son?"

Palaiologos looked down at Prentiss's bloody wound. "As I said, you caught me in the middle of something." He unhooked his jaw and sprayed bile-colored liquid into the ragged gap in Prentiss's throat.

Prentiss seized, then collapsed. The general rushed to his side, and Palaiologos stepped out of his way, a serene, serpentine smile plastered on his face.

"You'll forgive me." Palaiologos bowed. "It came to my attention that one of my sons, Jonathan, recently passed. So I decided to make a new one. I happened to see your marvelous display of courage against those ghouls and well...but about Jonathan—" he leveled his gaze on Ezekiel "—you wouldn't happen to know anything about that, would you?"

"Bastard." Ezekiel ground his teeth. "Do you know who I am?"

"I've been around so long I do tend to forget faces." Palaiologos cocked his head to the side. He blinked in realization. "Oh wait," he grinned, "did I happen to borrow your wife?"

Ezekiel willed himself not to react, but his gun trembled in his hands.

"Of course, yes, I do remember you. Is this what you've made of yourself? I'm not sure whether to be proud or horrified." Palaiologos clapped his hands together the way an excited child might. Beside him, Prentiss's skin had taken on a rotten grey color, and his teeth began to fall out, a scattering of white amidst the green- and red-stained grass.

Ezekiel considered shooting Palaiologos again, if only for the small amount of satisfaction it might bring, but he thought better of it. If he threw his life away here, he'd never get Anna Marie back.

General Banks shook Prentiss. "Son, can you hear me?"

"Oh, that reminds me," Palaiologos spun on his heel to address Prentiss, "son, how are you feeling? Are you ready to go?"

Pronounced canine fangs protruded from beneath Prentiss's lips, and he shuddered as clammy sweat oozed like slime down his skin. The sweet smell of rot radiated off of him in waves, filling the tent.

His response was mechanical, completely devoid of emotions. "Yes, of course, Father."

"What is this foolishness?" Banks drew himself up to his full height and stared down at Palaiologos. "Prentiss is my son, and he will not be going anywhere with you."

"General…" Ezekiel warned.

Palaiologos pouted and shoved the general aside. "Well, that can't be right. He just called me 'Father'." He cupped a hand on Prentiss' cheek and turned the young soldier to face him. Palaiologos's eyes flashed red. Prentiss's flashed in return.

"I am your devoted son."

"See?" Palaiologos shrugged. "He's made up his mind, I'm afraid."

General Banks's mouth hung open. Ezekiel hated to think that Anna Marie was under the same spell, mechanically doing whatever thing the perverse creature in front of him desired. He shook the thought from his mind.

"Ten years." Ezekiel stepped forward.

"Hmm?" Palaiologos looked away from his new son.

"I've tracked you for ten years with nothing to show for it, why here? Why now?"

Palaiologos blinked and let go of Prentiss's face. "You've been hunting me this whole time?" He turned as if truly regarding Ezekiel for the first time. "I admit, I'm flattered, but sorry to say I haven't given you…any thought at all. At least not until you were here, shooting me in the head."

Ezekiel's temper burst from his throat with an animalistic roar. He dropped his gun and charged the vampire, swinging his fist in a wide arc. Palaiologos closed the distance between them first, catching Ezekiel by the throat. He squeezed, not hard enough to kill, but enough to make Ezekiel's head swim as he gasped for air through his constricted windpipe.

"I let you live once," Palaiologos growled. "Do not make me regret that choice."

"Fuck. You." Ezekiel choked out the words, spittle flying from his mouth.

"I'd heard that more ghouls had been dying than usual. I figured it was just the war heating up. Them getting caught in fires, or accidentally killed by soldiers with the odd silver ornament." Palaiologos laughed to himself. "I never would have figured it'd be *you*. All this for one woman? Truly?" His grip around Ezekiel's throat loosened, enough to let in air, but not enough to fully release him.

Ezekiel struggled. "Anything for that woman."

"How noble." Palaiologos spoke thoughtfully as he looked Ezekiel up and down. "And romantic." He worked his ice-cold fingers into an iron grip around Ezekiel's left forearm. "Let's test that resolve."

Ezekiel groaned as the bones cracked, and their jagged edges began to grind together. Sharp nails drew blood from his ebony flesh and shredded his skin to ribbons. He wouldn't scream for this bastard.

Kate raised her rifle and racked the lever.

Palaiologos shifted Ezekiel so that his body acted as a shield from any additional fire. "I would rather not be shot again. And I believe he wouldn't enjoy it much either." He scowled down at the shredded side of his burgundy smoking jacket and the grey shirt beneath. "I'm sure you've already more than ruined this outfit."

With one quick motion, Palaiologos tore Ezekiel's arm from the socket attaching it to his shoulder. A wet sucking sound filled the tent, followed by a loud pop. At first, Ezekiel felt nothing. He stared dumbly at the place his arm had once been. Palaiologos held up the detached limb and waved it in front of his face. It sprayed blood over the cotton duck fabric of the tent, and Ezekiel became aware of a slick warmth running down his left side.

The pain registered, and he finally screamed.

Palaiologos cackled, a hollow, far away sound, and dropped Ezekiel into a pool of his own warm blood. "See you again soon. I'll tell your wife you said 'hello.'" He dissolved into a cloud of smoke, sweeping Prentiss up into his darkness and vanishing into thin air.

Ezekiel stared up at the tent ceiling from the bottom of a long, black well. Will peered down into the depths, looking at him from above, haloed by a shining golden light. The light went out, and Ezekiel was left in darkness.

11

Pain throbbed in the darkness.

Ezekiel's left side burned as he tried to move his arm, to position it in a way that didn't hurt. Nothing moved, and his shoulder screamed in pain at the effort. Sensation flooded back to his body, everywhere wracked with agony except his left arm. Where there should have been pain, there was only the awful static of absence. Memory came flooding back all at once, a chaotic picture show of events. The fire, the ghouls, the dark, Palaiologos...and his arm. Ezekiel's eyes shot open, and his vision swam like too much paint swirling in a murky bowl of water. He frowned, willing his eyes to focus on a singular thing: the beige tarp of the tent overhead.

The fire in his left shoulder increased in intensity as he stepped further into consciousness. He rolled his head left and looked at the bloody rags wrapped around the shoulder where his left arm had been. Though there was nothing there, he was horribly aware of the tingling absence, the knowledge that *something* should be there, attached to the white wrapped lump. He screwed his eyes shut and strangled the first groans of a sob. When he opened them again, it was with a desperate hope that it had been a dream, and his arm would still be there, connected as it always had been, as it always *should* be.

It wasn't.

He wanted to scream, to hurl the cot beneath him, to shoot something, someone, *himself*. Between the pain and the exhaustion, and the lingering, dry, dizziness that pinned him down, there was nothing he could do but stare up, aware of his current nightmare.

"You're awake." Will's voice came from the foot of the cot.

Ezekiel struggled to sit up.

"Don't," Will said. "You lost a lot of blood and—"

A lance of pain shot through Ezekiel's side as he tried to use his left arm to prop himself up and collapsed instead, with nothing there to support him. He gasped and gulped down shaky breaths as light-headedness turned his stomach.

"You might accidentally do that," Will finished with a sigh. He helped Ezekiel readjust himself into a comfortable position, propping him up against the head of the cot. "I want you to know I begged the company surgeons to re-attach your arm, even though it might never have worked the same, but the damage was… Jesus, man, he tore it off like a branch from a tree. I did what I could with the muscles and everything on the shoulder…you're lucky I was able to burn away most of the infected tissue. Your body managed the rest, thank God."

Ezekiel opened his mouth, but only managed to cough on the dry, sticky interior.

"Oh, sorry." Will brought a canteen over. Ezekiel snatched it with his right hand and drank. He gulped down the water greedily, but too quickly, choking on it and coughing violently. As soon as the coughing stopped, he drank more, until the canteen was empty. He gasped for breath and dropped the container.

"How long was I out?"

Will grimaced. "Little over a week."

Ezekiel took a deep breath. "I can still feel my arm. It…itches."

"Phantom limb." Will glanced at the bloody bandages. "It will happen from time to time. Pain, an itch, or just awareness. Once the wound is fully healed, you'll be able to massage the…massage your shoulder to help with it." He tried his best to give a reassuring smile. "It's nothing serious, lots of amputees get it."

"Sawbones," Ezekiel muttered. "Sure you know all about amputees."

"Ezekiel…" Will's words trailed off. "I'm sorry."

Ezekiel glared. "Don't be. I'm not about to bitch and moan about this. I…"—the fire went out of him—"I've been through worse."

Will said nothing.

"Do you want something or are you just here to feel bad for me?" Ezekiel pounded his good fist on the cot. "It's an arm, I'm not dead. Feel bad for me then!"

"Like it or not," Will kept his voice soft, soothing, "I do feel bad for you. The loss of a limb is…horrifying and life-altering. But I also know that you're a tough son of a bitch, and this isn't likely to put you off of your quest for long." Will shrugged. "It's who you are. With that in mind, I had the smith start on something for you. A present for your no-pity party. It'll be done in a few days. Until then, you need to rest, and I need to change your bandages."

Ezekiel narrowed his eyes. "You scheming?"

"If I am, it's your fault."

Ezekiel coughed out a throaty chuckle. He laid down on his right side to give Will easier access to the bandages. "What'd you do with my arm?"

"I think Kate has it. Or at least, she still has the hand." Will stared down at the ground and awkwardly cleared his throat. "She said we should keep it, for the Voodoo Queen. I guess it reminded her of something Henrietta did when a slave lost his finger."

"You're letting her keep my severed arm?"

"I'm not the one who lost it in the first place," Kate said as she entered the tent, one hand on her hip, the other holding a small wooden box. "And technically, it's just the hand—chopped it off to transport it easier. Heard they're using the rest for soup." She grinned wickedly.

Ezekiel stared at the box, ignoring her joke. Thoughts whirled through his head, but the moment he reached for any one of them, they slipped through his fingers. At last, he forced a single word from his dry throat. "Okay."

She jabbed Will with her elbow. "You were supposed to come get me when he woke up."

"I needed to make sure he was okay first," Will said.

"Of course, he is," Kate said.

"Yeah," Will said, "of course."

Kate held up the box. "Your hand, covered in salted dirt to help with the smell," she said.

"For the Voodoo Queen?" Ezekiel asked.

"Yep."

"Why?"

"Did you know Henrietta practiced voodoo?" Kate asked.

Ezekiel remembered the diorama of statues, and the old woman's admission of enchanting Kate's mother and grandmother. "No," he lied. "I didn't."

"Thought so," Kate said. "Well, she told me a little about it when she nannied me. It's,"—she frowned in thought for a minute—"sympathetic," she said finally.

"It feels bad for people?" Will asked.

"No," Kate and Ezekiel said in unison.

"It acts on relationships between things," Ezekiel said. "Dolls represent people, and you use a bit of them on the doll to strengthen the connection. Like hair."

"Or a hand," Kate said. "If hair is enough, imagine what a hand could do! Besides, it's not like you're using it anymore."

Will winced at the comment, but Ezekiel didn't seem to mind.

"Smart girl," he said.

"Finally, someone notices!" she replied.

Ezekiel turned to Will. "Where are my guns?"

"Kate still has the rifle."

"Tattle-tale," she grumbled.

"That's fine, she can keep it," Ezekiel gestured at his bloody, bandaged shoulder. "Needs two working hands. The pistols?"

Will pointed past Ezekiel to a barrel that acted as a table at the head of the cot.

"One's yours," Ezekiel said, picking up the gun belt and holding it out to Will.

"I don't—"

"That bastard tore my arm off *after* I shot him in the head," Ezekiel said. "I won't ask you to kill any people—"

"He's got me for that," Kate interjected.

"Just vampires," Ezekiel finished. "You have my word."

"I might ask you to shoot some people," Kate said. "If they piss me off."

"No," Ezekiel said, "she won't. All I expect is that you don't let yourself get killed over some moral complex against killing. Your life's on the line, you defend it, you hear?"

Will hesitated for a moment then sighed. He walked to the head of the cot and pulled the pistol out of the left-hand side of the gun belt, sliding it, without looking, into his own empty holster beneath his uniform coat. "Okay," he said. "Okay."

Ezekiel laid back down, exhausted from all the interaction.

"You need rest," Will said. "To heal."

"Yeah, I feel like shit," Ezekiel said. "You gonna change these?"

***

Ezekiel pushed open the door to the little shack on the Pickett Plantation with his left hand. His surroundings seemed to bleed like watercolor. Anna Marie sat in her chair, rocking back and forth in front of the dying embers of a fire. She looked up as he entered.

"Anna Marie," Ezekiel said breathlessly.

"Welcome back," she said, rising to pull him into a tight embrace. "They kept you out there all day."

"Pickett was supervising," Ezekiel said. "Whip in hand."

"He get you?"

"Kept my head down. Old Caesar though…" He trailed off. "The others are takin' care of him now. I needed to come see you."

"And I got something I need to tell you." Her smile faltered and turned sad after a second. She tried to revive it but couldn't.

"What is it?"

"You're gonna be a father," she said. "I haven't bled for three months now."

Ezekiel's mouth hung open. "I—You—" He knelt down by her chair and took her hand in his. "A father?" he asked.

Anna Marie nodded. "Yes, my love."

Tears welled in Ezekiel's eyes, and he fought to keep them from falling. "A father," he repeated. "What will we name them? I—"

He saw the poorly concealed sadness on Anna Marie's face.

"What is it?" he asked. "Is something wrong?"

"You will be a father," she said. "A wonderful one. But our child will be born into this." She gestured at their surroundings. "Born a slave. And Pickett…" Her face contorted and tears streamed down her face. "The things he'll do to our child." She shuddered from the force of her sobs. "He'll take them away from us."

Ezekiel's stomach dropped. He'd been so caught in the moment he hadn't thought that far. His child, born in hell with no say in the matter. He tightened his jaw and closed his eyes.

"We have to leave," he said finally. "Escape. Take our child somewhere where they can live free."

Anna Marie's eyes went wide. "We'd never make it off the property," she said. "You remember what happened to Simon."

"They shot out both his legs right from under him," Ezekiel said. "Tied him to a horse and dragged him back, whippin' him the whole time he was bleedin' out. Of course I remember," he said. "They made me ride the damn horse."

"I couldn't watch them do that to you," she said.

Ezekiel stood. "We won't get caught," he said. "We'll go soon. Start packing us some stuff to take." He placed his hand on her stomach. "I won't let our child suffer as we have."

Ezekiel woke in a cold sweat. He couldn't hold back the tears this time. They ran down his cheeks, mixing with the beads that glazed his skin in response to his body's rising temperature. Will had predicted the fever but hadn't warned Ezekiel of the dreams—the memories that would haunt him in his weakened state. A cool rag pressed against his forehead and pushed him, gently, back down onto the cot. Will's outline sat by his bed in the dark. If the boy saw Ezekiel crying, he had the decency and wherewithal not to comment. Ezekiel closed his eyes, and pictured his wife and child, now almost ten years without their real father. Son or daughter, he could hardly imagine a man like him as any decent kind of father.

"Please," he mumbled, "stay alive. I'm coming…"

"She knows," Will's voice whispered back as Ezekiel slipped again into the darkness.

"Both of them?"

12

The light of the sun burned against the backs of Ezekiel's eyelids, rousing him. He glanced around, feeling the soreness become sharper as his body continued to wake.

Kate remained in the chair at his side. Her head rose, and she looked at him with sleepy eyes as he stirred.

He swung his legs over the side of the cot and fumbled for his gun belt. He went to put it on but couldn't. "Two-handed job."

"Just this once," Kate stood. "Better not take it off after this."

She helped him get the gun belt fastened around his waist and let him use her shoulder as a support to work his way to his feet. He stood, wobbled for a moment, then straightened.

"Whole world spinning?" Kate asked.

"Thought it was just me," Ezekiel stumbled past her and pushed open the tent flap. He stepped out into the bright morning light, shielding his eyes. The encampment wasn't exactly where it had been. The trees were a distant memory on the horizon, and far less menacing in the light of day.

"It's only been a day since the last time you woke up." Kate emerged behind him. "Banks kept us moving, but slowly. Lots of people got hurt."

"I figured."

Kate blew out a sharp breath. "Since you're up, the general wanted to talk to you if you survived. Think you can make it to his tent?"

"The hell's he want with me?"

"Your vampire stole his son," Kate said flatly. "Well, the thing that his son became."

"Turned into a ghoul?"

"Didn't look like it. Seemed like he got the full blessing."

Ezekiel's nostrils flared. "He's building his family, one stolen soul at a time."

Kate's voice grew small. "Will told me about your wife. If Palaiologos turned Prentiss, do you think—"

"No," Ezekiel barked. "He didn't. She isn't."

Kate's mouth was a thin, grim line. "Will also wanted to see you when you got up."

Will was talking to another soldier when they approached.

"Oh good, you're awake," he said, shooting a glance at Kate, "and walking."

Kate shrugged. "You know him."

"I rested enough, I think," Ezekiel said. "More than a week."

Will sighed and kneaded his forehead. "Well, it's actually good you're here. You need to try it on."

Ezekiel raised an eyebrow.

"Your no-pity party gift," he said. "Got to make sure it fits." He turned to the other soldier and whispered something while fidgeting with an object Ezekiel couldn't see. Then looked back at Ezekiel. "Remember how Holloway told us there was no silver?"

"I remember wanting to punch him in the face for it," Ezekiel said.

"Well, I didn't do that, but I did have him spend most of the last week going through every crate and container, and lo and behold."

"Silver."

"Mostly some fancy dinnerware, and a misplaced coin or ring here or there." Will said, beaming with pride, hands hidden behind his back. "Not a lot, mind you, but enough."

"Enough?"

"For this." He pulled his hands out to reveal a contraption made of leather straps, wood, and a few small pieces of iron, with two silver hooks protruding from the top.

"What is it?" Ezekiel asked.

"A new arm for you," Will said. "Here let me show you." He pulled Ezekiel's wrapped stump towards him and began unwinding the cloth bandages until only a thin layer of material was left. He positioned the stump at the hollow bottom of the contraption. "There may be some discomfort with this part." He shoved the contraption against Ezekiel's shoulder, then, reaching around, fastened a few clips beneath his remaining arm.

"Fuck, that hurt," Ezekiel said, trying to pull away.

Will held his arm tight. "Let me finish," he commanded in a voice unlike he'd ever used before. He pulled two leather straps out of his coat pocket and tied them both around the base of the hook contraption's sleeve, tightening them before asking. "How does it feel? Too tight?"

"It'll slip off the second I go to give you the middle finger," Ezekiel said.

Will tugged the straps tighter and gave a questioning look.

"Feels about right, I guess," Ezekiel said. He alternated bending and extending the false elbow and rotating the strange device that now replaced his hand. Certain motions caused the pain to flare up until it was almost unbearable, but in general it was little more than a persistent, phantom throb that ran the length of his missing arm. He held both hands, flesh and false, out in front of himself, palms inward. The silver gleamed in the sun.

"It's not going to replace your real hand, not really," Will said. "But I figured something would be better than nothing. It can loosely hold reins, maybe balance a rifle, and—"

"Leave some nasty claw marks on a bloodsucker's face," Ezekiel said. He fixed Will with his most serious stare and held it in silence for several moments. "Thank you," he said, finally. He extended his hand. Will gripped it tight and shook. Ezekiel pulled him in and clapped him on the back, before releasing his hand and pulling away.

"If I told you that you needed more rest before setting out, would you listen?" Will asked.

"This time, yes," Ezekiel said. "Besides, apparently the general would like to yell at me."

"I don't think yelling is where he is mentally or emotionally at this moment," Will said. "He won't let anyone in his tent unless they bring him,"—he gestured like he was drinking from a bottle—"so good luck."

"Knock knock," Ezekiel said, stepping into the general's tent. He held up a half-full bottle of bourbon. He placed it gently on the table as he sat down in the chair across from the general. Careful not to tip the bottle, he pulled his arm back, sliding the bottle's neck from between his hooks. "I heard you were thirsty. Hope you don't mind that I plucked this from the supply crates."

Banks's eyes were sunken and red-rimmed. He stared at the cot in the back of the tent, still stained with Prentiss's blood, now a dry, caked brown.

"You still come with jokes," he said, his voice marred by whiskey and a parched tongue. "My son is whisked away in the night by a demon straight from hell, and you still come with jokes."

"I wasn't joking," Ezekiel said. "Have a glass."

"I think I've had enough." The general snatched the bottle and downed a large swig.

"I can tell."

The general's tired eyes turned from the absent cot and locked on to Ezekiel. He glanced down at the bottle and, with a rasping sigh, lifted it and poured Ezekiel a drink as well. The bottle stayed in his hand as he spoke.

"What do you want?"

"I didn't come here to talk to a drunk man," Ezekiel said. "I came to talk to a general."

Banks narrowed his eyes. "I am still a general."

Ezekiel raised an eyebrow and took a sip of his whiskey. He relished the burn as it trickled down his throat. His breath came out hot, and the tension left his body as he swallowed more of the drink.

"Is there any way to bring my son back? To turn him back from that pale specter he became?"

"You're not going to like my answer to that," Ezekiel continued.

"Answer me, damn it." Banks slammed his fist on the table.

"No. Once they change there's nothing to be done but—" He stopped himself from saying 'putting the bastards out of their misery.' He cleared his throat. "Your son is gone."

Banks nodded. "Then that's that," he said, downing another gulp of whiskey before wiping his eyes. "Thank you for your honesty. You may go." He went to drink again, but Ezekiel took the bottle and emptied the rest into his own glass.

"That's it?" Ezekiel said.

"I've grieved my son this whole week," Banks said, "all day and all night, for seven days, holding on hope that maybe he could be returned to me...to his mother. At night, sometimes I swear I still see him..." He gave a grim smile that barely reached his face before beginning to quiver. "Your words killed that glimmer. There's nothing more to be done."

"And you're fine letting Palaiologos get away just like that."

The general's eyes hardened, losing their unfocused luster. "There is a war on," he said. "One that must be won, for all the men and sons who still live." His voice broke. "I must do my duty," he said quietly.

Ezekiel hung his head. "I am sorry," he said. "I...know how this feels."

Banks rose in fury and hurled his glass across the table, narrowly missing Ezekiel's head. "You know what it's like to lose the son you loved from the very moment he was born?"

Ezekiel remained calm. "That same vampire," he said, "took my wife and unborn child from me ten years ago. I've been hunting him for the same amount of time." He laughed a dry, hollow laugh. "Hunting and hoping they're still alive and not…"

"Not vampires," Banks said, trembling as he returned to his seat. "I didn't know."

"I'm not much for sharing," Ezekiel said. "But my two most recent ass-whoopin's have shown me that I don't stand a chance against this thing alone."

"I can't help you," Banks said.

"I know," Ezekiel said. "War, duty, all that bullshit. That's your cross to bear. I just wanted you to know that I will not stop hunting him down until he's dead."

"And my son?"

"What do you think?"

Banks closed his eyes tight. "Are you certain beyond a shadow of a doubt that there is no cure? No blessing or great panacea that can restore him?"

"Ten years, and not even a hint of such a thing," Ezekiel said.

"Then send him to God," Banks said. "Let him be at peace."

"At your word, General," Ezekiel said. "And good luck."

"May I never see you again." Banks turned back to the blood-stained cot. "Or the misfortune you bring."

"Reckoned you'd feel that way," Ezekiel said.

13

———

Where's Will?" Kate asked.

"Talking to the general," Ezekiel said, tightening the straps on his prosthetic the way Will had shown him. "Needed to get leave from the war to join us."

"Always by the book, that one," she said.

"It'll grow on you."

"So will a rash if you let it," she replied.

Ezekiel's eyebrows rose. "That how you really feel?"

"Of course not," she said with a devious smirk. "But if I tell him otherwise, I'm pretty sure it will go straight to that head of his."

"Well, I'll try not to let it," Will said, entering the tent.

Kate frowned. "You sneaking around listening to us talk?"

Will frowned. "I'm traveling with you two, you know?"

"Oh right. Sometimes I forget," Kate said.

"Sentences like that make it very hard to believe what you just said," Will replied. He walked over and checked Ezekiel's prosthetic in silence. "Feel alright?" he asked after looking it over.

Ezekiel nodded.

"You're an idiot if you can't figure out when I'm just pulling your leg," Kate said, rolling her eyes. "Obviously we like you, otherwise one of us would have shot you by now." She grinned.

"You both ready?" Ezekiel asked.

"I was honorably discharged from service," Will said, holding up a scrap of parchment bearing the general's signature in blotchy black ink. "I can go wherever, whenever."

"And I'm thirteen, and you're my guardians," Kate said, crossing her arms. "I'll go when you do. Unless I don't want to."

"Alright then," Ezekiel said, sauntering off in the direction of the tethered horses. "It's about a two-day ride to New Orleans the way we're going."

"Are you sure it's a good idea to avoid Baton Rouge altogether?" Will asked. "We don't know what's out in the southern swamps. General Banks is taking his troops down to New Iberia and—"

"Yeah, but we do know what's in the city," Ezekiel said. "And I'm getting tired of obstacles that I can't just shoot my way through. That, and trudging along with these folks."

"Maybe we'll come across an alligator," Kate said, opening and closing her mouth while exposing her teeth, like she was gnawing on something. "Or an alligator *vampire*."

"Vampire venom kills anything that ain't human or vampire," Ezekiel said. "Least, everything I've come across. Hell, I've seen the shit melt rocks…"

"But maybe—"

"Look, I've seen all kinds of critters get torn apart by vampires that couldn't find a person to eat. They die and melt down to the bones. Smells like an open grave the whole damn time, too."

Will gagged.

"Hell with that." Kate wrinkled her nose.

They rode for several hours before they came to the transition. Green fields gave way to brown mud flecked with barely thriving blades of green grass too sporadic and covered to be noticeable. Finally, they reached the swamp. They stopped at the edge of brown water over-grown with thin reeds that blew in the wind. Bald cypress trees rose up from the murky water, covered in moss and thick verdant vines. Ezekiel held up a hand for his companions to follow and guided his horse slowly to the edge of what appeared to be solid ground.

His grey stallion stalled. He urged the horse forward, but it wouldn't budge. Ezekiel dropped the reins and slid out of his saddle. Brown water splashed around him as he sank, calf deep into the water. He looked back at the horse.

"That ain't nothing for you," he said.

The horse gave a panicked whinny. In the silence after, a low grumble mixed with a throaty hiss, and the sound of moving water came from behind him. He made eye contact with Kate who already reached for her rifle. Ezekiel shook his head and held up a hooked hand.

"That's not a hunting sound," he said. "It's a warning."

"Guess you got your gator," Will said.

"I mean, they're really common around here," Kate said calmly. "I was just trying to scare you."

"I should have known."

Moving as slow as he could, Ezekiel turned to face the sound of the noise. A single grey reptile glared at him with film-covered eyes. Its head protruded from the water, mouth ajar, but the rest of its body was hidden. By the size of the head alone, Ezekiel figured the whole thing had to be about eight feet long. His eyes darted around until he saw it. Half buried in the mud a few feet to his left, a clutch of white-brown eggs.

"It's a mom," he said.

"What do we do?" Will asked.

"We'll go around. I'm not shooting her," he said. "The young would die without her."

"She won't follow?"

"Maybe for a bit, but she won't want to leave the eggs unattended for too long." He pulled himself back into his saddle and used the reins to turn the horse to the right, taking care to stay on the muddy bank and not slip into the water. He'd seen what an angry or hungry gator could do to a panicked horse.

The gator's head tracked them as they moved, watching for a while before disappearing under the water, only to appear again after they had traveled a few feet. She tracked them for an hour until finally, Ezekiel saw no sign of her in the murky depths. He kept an eye out for any other hungry reptiles and, seeing none, guided his horse into the water and set off on a makeshift path into the swamp.

Progress was fine at first, but the thick muck and sudden drops into deep muddy holes under the water slowed their progress drastically as they entered the swamp. Night had fallen and the buzz of insects mingled with the occasionally hiss of a basking gator hidden by night and swampy water. Ezekiel had considered stopping for the night but was determined to make up as much of the time he'd lost recovering as possible. They pressed on with him in the lead, knee deep in the green-brown waters of the southern swamps. He led his horse by the reins with his good hand and told Kate to keep an eye for "anything might need shooting". She rode, eye down the length of the rifle in her hands even despite the lack of visibility.

"The horses can't take much more of this," Will said as his horse struggled to lift its leg and continue their forward progress.

"I'm with him on this," Kate said, lowering her rifle. "We need to find a place to stop."

Ezekiel ground his teeth. He turned back to his companions to tell them to keep moving but stopped when he saw the weary state of both the horses and their riders. He was about to speak when movement caught his eye. What had appeared as brown earth, rippled, and a thin black snout peaked above the surface.

"Will," he shouted, just as the alligator sprang from the water. It toppled the young soldier's horse and sent Kate's horse galloping away in fear. The mother gator had been a murky green color and a thick snout. This was a black gator, twice the length, with golden eyes and a rough, rocky hide. It hissed and snapped, a living bear trap out for blood. The reptile caught Will's boot in its thin but powerful jaws and began to drag him towards the patch of swamp water, now visible from the motion. Ezekiel went for his gun, but the silver hooks and his hand simply clanked against the wooden butt, making him fumble the motion.

"Damn it," he spat, switching to his right hand and jerking the gun out of the leather holster. His first shot went wide, striking the water and disappearing into the swamp.

Will screamed, kicking at the gator with his free foot. It growled in response and continued its furious fight back into the water. Ezekiel took a deep breath and rested the barrel of the revolver across the wooden part of his prosthetic arm and looked down at the sight. It had been a long time since he'd had to actually check his aim. He pulled the trigger and gunpowder sprayed as the hammer struck. The crack made the reptile jump and release Will as the bullet struck one of its hind legs.

"Damn it," Ezekiel spat, adjusting his aim.

Will scrambled backwards as the reptile rounded on Ezekiel. The bullet hardly fazed it as it rushed him, quicker than he expected, and brought him down to the ground. Ezekiel tried to clamp his hands over its mouth to keep it closed, but the prosthetic slipped, ripping the scaled flesh of the gator's snout, and making it even angrier. It clamped its jaws on the wood of the prosthetic and pulled. It seemed to grin at him the same way Palaiologos did, all teeth and unfeeling coldness. He roared and jammed the gun barrel into the creature's mouth alongside the false hand and fired five shots, one after the other until the gator stopped moving. He yanked his clawed hand free from its mouth, bringing blood and fleshy chunks with it, and shoved the creature off of him. His breaths were deep, laborious struggles as he walked over to Will and offered him his good hand.

"Thanks," Will said.

"You almost died," Ezekiel growled. "I gave you my damn gun. Why didn't you shoot it? Your pacifist bullshit makes it hard as Hell for me to—" He stopped mid-sentence.

"To what?" Will asked.

"I can't shoot as well with my right," Ezekiel said, jaw tight and rigid. "Relying on me to save your ass will get you killed."

Will pulled out the revolver hanging at his belt and rubbed a hand over its polished surface. "Sorry, it just...doesn't come naturally to me. Never did. But you're right."

"Everyone okay?" Kate said, riding up, her horse back under control.

"Yeah," Will slid the gun back into its holster, "it's handled."

Ezekiel relaxed and looked down at his silver appendage with a grim scowl. "Alright," he said. "Let's find something solid and get some rest."

Their something solid ended up being a half-submerged rock with a single cypress tree growing up above it, exposing its roots like a living, makeshift shelter. They tethered the horses up in the muck that came up to the animals' ankles and climbed up onto the moss-covered stone.

"I'll take the first watch," Ezekiel said. "Rest up, we're not stopping until New Orleans tomorrow."

He stared into the dark, watching the horses as they slowly drifted off to sleep standing up, releasing the occasional twitchy snort as they did. The swamp was calm; there wasn't even enough wind to disturb the surface of the water. Beyond that the world faded into an impenetrable blackness. He kept expecting another gator, or perhaps the same one, back for revenge to emerge and finish what it had started. Movement made him jump, and instinctively move for the gun on his left. He cursed quietly as Will slid up and sat next to him.

"You should be sleeping," Ezekiel said without looking.

"I have to ask you a question," Will said.

"That's rarely true."

"I want to ask, then."

"Then ask."

"Both of them?" Will asked.

Ezekiel regarded the boy out of the corner of his eye. "Both of who?"

"When you were feverish...you talked to your wife, I guess. Told her that you were coming for her. I told you that she knew, and you asked me about 'both of them?'"

"Oh," Ezekiel said.

A heavy silence blanketed them, interrupted only by the occasional soft sounds of Kate's sleeping breaths. Will stared at Ezekiel, patient, but intent. Ezekiel sighed.

"It was a fool's dream," he said. "Nonsense from a sick mind."

"That's a lie," Will said.

"No," Ezekiel said. "It's not. My wife was pregnant when she was taken from me. I know she's still alive, Palaiologos said as much, but he took Prentiss to be his child. Why would he do that if—" Ezekiel stopped before his voice cracked. "If I still had a child in this world."

Will thought for a moment. "What if it's a girl?"

"What do you mean?"

"With Prentiss he said that now he had a son," Will said, "not that he now had a child. A son specifically. Maybe your kid was a girl."

Ezekiel sat quietly. "Yeah, maybe," he said. "It's just...hard...not to despair."

"What would you name her?"

"What?"

"If it was a girl. What would you have named her?"

"I,"—Ezekiel paused—"I never thought of it. He probably already gave her a name..."

"Maybe think of one, and one for a boy, too, just in case. Their true parents should name them, right? Not their kidnapper."

"But if they're dead..."

Will clapped him on the shoulder.

"You've been doing this for ten years with no proof your wife was even still alive until today," Will said, standing up and moving back to his sleeping position. "You may be familiar with despair, but you're no stranger to hope either. Give it some thought."

Ezekiel let a half-smile cross his face in the dark. "No stranger to hope," he repeated.

"Get up," Ezekiel said, shaking his two companions. Red-gold light filtered into their shelter through the gaps in the tree's roots. "Sun's coming up."

"Did you watch the whole night?" Will asked groggily. He stretched with a wide yawn.

"Too restless to sleep," he said. "Kate—"

"I'm up, stop talking." She sat up and glared at both men, before running her hands violently through her hair in an unsuccessful attempt at untangling it.

The horses also grunted in disapproval at being woken so early. They hooved the submerged ground and snorted as their riders untethered them. Will and Kate spent several minutes soothing the creatures before they were able to mount them. Ezekiel patted his horse's side as he waited.

As soon as they did, Ezekiel urged his horse in the direction of the rising sun. Minutes faded into hours and eventually the swamp gave way to drier land. Ezekiel's clothes clung to him and chafed in all the most uncomfortable places. He pulled at the material, trying to unstick it, with limited success. Relenting to his discomfort, he made his way to his horse and checked its hooves. The large animal stayed calm as he used his knife to scrape them free of gunk and mud before wiping them down with a relatively clean and dry rag. Will did the same with his horse—borrowing the knife—and then, despite her protestations, finished with Kate's.

They found the road, a dirt path long since turned to packed and trampled mud. The road led them past carts and wagons all departing the city of New Orleans on the way to other places, for some, less Union occupied, for others just farther away from the war. Men, women, and children alike gave them strange looks as they passed. Ezekiel looked down at his clothes and saw that he looked as grimy as he felt.

"Gonna need at least four washtubs," he said. "And that'll just be for my damn clothes."

"Got good news for you then," Will said, and pointed ahead of them.

On the horizon, the shapes of homes, a church, and many other buildings were easily identifiable. All that stood between them and it, were a field of mushy grass and the few above-ground mausoleums that made up the city cemetery.

Ezekiel's boots squelched as he walked through the above-ground graves, glancing at the names carved into the bone white marble. He dragged his hand along the smooth white surfaces and a chill ran down his spine. The wind whispered through the final resting place of these people and beckoned him. He shook his head and touched the cool metal of his hooks gently against his forehead.

"The spirits are restless," a voice thick with a Cajun accent said. The owner of the voice, an emaciated, dark-skinned man appeared from around the corner of a nearby tomb. He regarded them with eyes concealed by cataracts so thick, he appeared to have no pupils. "You make them restless, because you are expected, but you are late."

"Who's expecting us?" Ezekiel asked. He already knew the answer.

"This way. This way," the man said. "The Voodoo Queen awaits."

14

The man led them to an unassuming house some distance away from the rest of the homes near them. It was squat, only one story high, but wide. He gestured towards the door.

"After you," Ezekiel said.

"I am not allowed inside," the man replied.

Ezekiel looked the man up and down and nodded.

The house had no porch. It sat directly on the ground beneath it. Two wooden posts disappeared into the ground out front supporting the wrap-around awning that extended from the roof. Ezekiel strode up to the door, an old, peeling thing, and tried the knob. It was unlocked.

"She in there?" he asked.

"When she needs to be," the man said.

"Kate, my hand."

"Left side saddlebag," she said.

Ezekiel backed away from the door and circled around Kate's horse, rummaging in the leather bag until he was able to grab the wooden box. The smell made him gag.

"Did you expect a more floral scent?" Kate asked. "Nothing but wet heat between then and now. That thing's rancid."

Ezekiel held the revolting thing as far away from his face as he could while walking back up to the house. When the warm wet liquid trapped in the box started leaking into his hand, he almost dropped it in disgust, but managed to switch it over to be cradled in the nook of his hooks. He wiped the fluid on his mud-caked pants and turned the doorknob, pushing inward as he did. The moment he stepped across the threshold, the door slammed shut behind him and locked. Will pounded on the other side, shouting, and jiggling the knob to no avail.

"I was told I was expected," Ezekiel said to the dark, empty house.

"You are," said a woman's voice. "You've *been* expected."

"And yet no one's here to greet me," Ezekiel said dryly.

The woman's voice laughed, a sound like wind chime. Sconces on the walls began to blaze with a purple light, casting the interior of the space with dim, dancing shadows. The whole house was just one room. Lush red carpet covered the floor, and each sconce was intricately formed out of a metal that looked suspiciously like real gold. The final sconce blazed to life, revealing a black woman in nothing but a red chemise, lounging on a chaise longue. A black ribbon wound up the length of her forearm. One end was tied around her wrist, and the other in the crease of her elbow.

"Oh, look," she said in a voice laced with false surprise, "someone here to greet you."

"Are you the Voodoo Queen?" Ezekiel asked.

"Is that what people are calling me now?" she asked, sitting up. Her chemise hung loose from her body, revealing her chest slightly with the movement. She fixed it and with a snap of her fingers the black ribbon unwound itself from her arm and snaked around her torso, tying the garment tight against her body. "I suppose it's what they called my mother."

"Well?" Ezekiel asked.

"You're ruder than expected," she said. "Yes, I am now the one people are calling the Voodoo Queen, as my mother was before me. I am Heloise, the Eucharist, some say." Her eyes wandered the room until they landed on Ezekiel. "And you are here for my help." Her gaze continued down to the box resting on his metal appendage. "What is that? I can smell it from over here."

"It's a hand," Ezekiel said. "…my hand."

Heloise's eyes flicked between Ezekiel's prosthetic and the box that held his hand. "You cut off your hand to bring it to me as an… offering?"

"I didn't cut off my own damn hand," Ezekiel snapped. "I'm here because of what did."

"Give it here, then."

Ezekiel handed her the box. "Why don't you know what I'm here for?"

"I'm a witch, not a mind reader." She looked at him like he was stupid. "I know what I know. I knew you were coming, and that you needed help. With this I'll be able to see why." She held up her hand when Ezekiel started to speak. "I don't need you to tell me," she said. "You'll get it wrong, all emotions and desires, muddying the truth."

Ezekiel closed his mouth.

Heloise grimaced as she opened the box and attempted to wave away the smell of Ezekiel's putrid severed hand. "You couldn't have gotten here sooner?" she said.

"Losing my hand took a bit of the wind out of my sails," Ezekiel said.

"Yeah, well receiving your hand is taking a lot out of my stomach," she snapped.

Ezekiel shrugged.

Heloise reached into the box, pulling the severed limb out by the middle finger, dangling it in Ezekiel's general direction, before tossing the box aside.

"This won't do." With a flick of her wrist, she tossed the hand into a nearby brazier that Ezekiel hadn't seen when he entered. Heloise produced a match from inside her robe and lit it. She tossed it in, and the brazier roared to life with a crackling purple flame. "Give it a minute."

To Ezekiel's surprise, the smell of burning flesh did not immediately fill the room. Instead, just the smell of smoke and heat teased his nose. His phantom limb throbbed, and a tingle of pain, as if it were still attached as it burned, made him wince. He clutched at the prosthetic and moved to get a closer look, but Heloise held up a hand, stopping him.

"All due respect," she said, "you'll mess something up, so just be a dear and stay over there." She gave him a sweet smile.

The fire belched a green burst of smoke.

"Oh, it's done." She reached her hand into the flames, causing Ezekiel to gasp. Her musical chime laughter filled the room again at his reaction. When her hand came out of the flames it was completely unharmed, and holding his dry, desiccated hand. The appendage was not blackened and charred like he expected, more mummified than burnt.

"Now then..." She clasped his severed hand as if she were strolling with a lover and plunged her hand back into the fire with it. "Let's take a walk."

Ezekiel groaned as an invisible rope tightened around his intestines and tried to pull him down into the floor. His head spun, and his mouth went dry.

"You may want to sit down for this," Heloise said. "Or your body will find its own way to the ground."

Ezekiel attempted to steady himself as he sat down on the soft carpet. His body went limp, and he sprawled out on the floor. He blinked once, and found himself standing by Heloise's side, her fingers laced through the fingers of his left hand.

"How?" he asked.

"We're in your head," she said. "Now hush."

She stepped forward, pulling him with her, and they stepped out into the ruins of an abandoned plantation. Pickett's plantation.

"What are we doing here?" Ezekiel hissed.

"You were born here," she said. "And in creation, there is truth."

Ezekiel saw himself amidst the ruins of the main house. He was on his knees in front of the corpse that had once been Silva. The bloody cross was still in his hands. He was praying. This was back when he'd still prayed.

Heloise walked around the vision of Ezekiel's past, running her hands along the ethereal images that shimmered at her touch until she came to Silva's bestial corpse.

"I see," she said.

With a snap of her fingers, they were back in her room. Ezekiel felt as though someone had captured a gust of wind and shoved it deep inside his body. He bolted off the floor gasping for breath. He looked down at his left hand and saw the cold silver hooks, gleaming up at him. He gripped the base of the prosthetic, feeling where his arm stopped, and the contraption began. Heloise eyed him coldly.

"Vampires," she said.

"You know about them?" Ezekiel asked, still sucking down air and clutching at his chest.

"My mother warned me about bloodsucking demons as well. They're a dark kind of magic." She threw Ezekiel's hand back into the fire and it burned away into ash. "I can't help you."

"Excuse me?"

"I'm sorry," she said, "I'll see you out."

"The hell you will," Ezekiel slammed his hooked hand into the wall, gouging out a chunk as he withdrew it. "I came all the way down here, almost died, and lost my goddamn hand all because I was told you could help me." He crossed the room and stared right into Heloise's face. "I'll be damned if I leave this place empty handed."

"You can't threaten me," she said. "I'm not afraid of you."

Ezekiel held her gaze.

"You're afraid," Heloise said thoughtfully.

"I'm not." Ezekiel's throat tightened. "My wife—"

"Might be dead," Heloise said.

"She's not!" Ezekiel snapped and slammed his fist into the wall of the room. "He's keeping her alive in some kind of demented family." He trembled. "Please," he said. "I can't... I can't beat him alone. I'll die. They'll die." He gestured to the door, with Will and Kate waiting outside of it. His voice rose again as anger took hold. "I need help."

Heloise sighed. "Come with me."

"My companions?"

Another irritated sigh. "Bartholomew! Let the other two in," she said, before turning and walking towards the back wall of the room. Ezekiel followed as Kate and Will caught up behind him.

"What'd she say?" Will asked.

"No."

"Then why are we following her?"

"Because we hope she'll say yes," Ezekiel said, with a grim smile.

Heloise placed the palm of her hand against the back wall of the dimly lit room. In response to her touch, the room shook and lit up, and a door faded into existence beneath the palm of her hand. She looked back at the surprised faces staring at her.

"A woman should be versed in many kinds of magic, in a world such as this," she said. "Voodoo is just the beginning." The door swung open letting out a blinding light. Ezekiel shielded his eyes.

Heloise stepped through, with a final 'follow me' gesture, and disappeared into the glow.

"I am not going first," Kate said.

Ezekiel said nothing and stepped toward the luminous portal.

He found himself standing on a landing at the bottom of a pair of white-stained stairs, the foyer of a massive plantation style home. Several more emaciated figures like Bartholomew shuffled around doing various tasks, from sweeping and dusting to carrying silver trays of food from room to room.

"Where are we?" he asked. His hand instinctively went to his gun. This was a slaver's house.

"My house," Heloise said. "What? You thought I lived in that tiny room?" She laughed. "I take clients there, so they don't know how to get to me except in the way I want them to."

Kate and Will tumbled into the foyer, and each looked as surprised as Ezekiel. Will went to the window and looked out at the open expanse of dry grass that seemed to stretch on forever outside of the house.

"We're not still in New Orleans, are we?" he asked.

"Spirits, no! You should never live where you work, especially in my business," Heloise said.

"You have slaves," Ezekiel said.

Heloise looked around as if noticing for the first time. "Hardly," she said. "They're all dead." She snapped her fingers and one of the emaciated figures immediately came to her side with a cup of tea. "Thank you, Bartholomew."

"But Bartholomew—" Will started.

"I call them all Bartholomew," she said with a wave of her hand. "Keeps it simple."

"You keep them from heaven?" Will asked.

Heloise looked truly offended. "Of course not, their souls have long since gone to the other side. These men and women offered their bodies to me after death. A repayment for some deed I, or my mother, did for them," she said. "Not slavery, willing servitude."

Ezekiel counted twelve emaciated bodies milling around the house. With each one, his anger grew. "Could you free them?" he asked.

"I could," she said. "A little salt under the tongue, and the body will crumble to dust."

"Then why keep them?"

"This way my husband doesn't need *real* slaves to work for him," she said.

"Your husband?"

"He's a good man," she said, "but he's a white man, and for a white man to make a profit down here, good or otherwise, he needs cheap labor."

"And that makes slavery okay?" Ezekiel didn't bother to temper the disgust in his voice.

"No," Heloise said, "thus, zombies." She sighed. "Slavery is an abomination. It offends every sensibility of decent folk. But it's ingrained down here, and if you want to succeed, hell, if you want to survive down here, it's necessary. This is my lesser of two evils." Heloise paused, waiting for a reply. "Now then, do you want my help, or should we continue discussing my morality?"

Ezekiel stared at the floor, his hat hiding his face in shadows.

"That's what I thought," she said. "This way."

She led them out the front door of the house and down the porch steps, following a path until they came to the fields where more zombies went through the automatic motions of farming. Heloise stopped by a green shoot growing out of the ground and bent to pick it up, revealing a full bulb of garlic. She plucked up another and a third, all while mumbling something to herself.

"This should be enough," she said, finally, holding up the three bulbs of garlic.

"Garlic?" Kate said. "Are we gonna cook for the vampires?" Her eyes lit up. "Are we going to *cook the vampires?*"

Heloise wrinkled her nose at the thought and said, "No, little girl, we aren't doing any of that." She paused and wrinkled her forehead, before crouching down in front of Kate. "Would you like to learn some magic, little girl?"

"Call me little girl again, and I'll make your teeth disappear," Kate said. "Like magic."

"Feisty," Heloise said. "I like it. Well then *young lady*, magic? Yes, or no?"

Kate grinned wildly. "Naturally!"

"And us?" Will asked.

"Entertain yourselves," Heloise said. "I don't teach men. There are enough of you with too much power as it is." She held out her hand to Kate who took it and followed behind as Heloise led her towards a smaller structure off to the side of the house.

"She could have just told us to stay inside," Will said.

"But that wouldn't have inconvenienced us," Ezekiel said. "At least, not as much."

"We're not just gonna hang around out here, are we?"

"No," Ezekiel said. He began walking back towards the main house. "Help me find some salt."

Will jogged to catch up with Ezekiel. "We're gonna destroy her zombies?"

"We're gonna free her slaves," Ezekiel said.

"But you heard her," Will said. "She does this, so her husband doesn't need to use real slaves. And they gave up their bodies to her."

"Do you really believe that?"

"The lady can walk through walls," Will said. "I'm not sure she needs to lie. Plus, I'm sure she'd just make more."

"Then let her when we're gone," Ezekiel said, pushing up the large plantation doors. "I won't stand by and do nothing while—"

"Oh, hello there," a voice with a distinctly British accent said. "Who might you be?"

Ezekiel turned and saw a middle-aged white man, dressed in a riding suit that was perfectly prim save for the mud and grime caked on the boots.

"Oh, fuck me," Ezekiel said under his breath.

"We came to see your wife," Will said in a hurried voice. His eyes went wide at the realization that two strange men coming to see another man's wife might elicit an unwanted response. "I mean, we came for her special services. I mean—"

Ezekiel sighed and kneaded his forehead. "You know your wife is a witch, right?"

"Of course, everyone around here does," the man said.

"We came for that," Will said.

"I figured."

"Right."

The man extended a hand to Ezekiel. "Albert Harris," he said, beaming at the both of them. "It's always a pleasure to see the clientele that magnificent woman brings in." He stared off in the direction of the smaller house where Heloise worked her magic. "So what are you here for?" He glanced between the two of them. "Wait, let me guess,"— he pointed to Will — "something for stamina? No offense of course, it's just common amongst boys your age."

Will's face went red.

Albert turned to Ezekiel. "And you—"

"Vampires," Ezekiel said, with a wry smile.

Albert's face went blank for a second. He then broke out in a fit of laughter. Ezekiel forced himself to join in.

"That's a good one," Albert said. "You almost had me going with that serious face of yours. Vampires." He scoffed. "Magic is one thing, but monsters?"

"Exactly," Ezekiel said, giving Will a knowing look.

"No, but seriously," Albert said. "What could a strong-looking man such as yourself need?"

Ezekiel placed a hand on his stomach. "Digestive problems," he said.

"Ah," Albert said thoughtfully, "the richness of Southern cuisine can take its toll on people unaccustomed to it."

"You said it," Ezekiel quipped.

"Well, please, come in." Albert beckoned. "I know how she gets with men in her shed." He chuckled. "I'll make us some tea." He put a hand to his mouth conspiratorially. "The British kind, not the sweet kind."

He led them into a wide sitting room with more lounging chairs like the ones from Heloise's strange room, as well as a long couch and several armchairs. On the back wall was a large hearth with a rack mounted over the fire. A silver cart held an assortment of items including a tea kettle. Albert busied himself preparing the tea and filling the kettle with water.

"You don't have the servants do all this for you?" Ezekiel asked.

"I don't like to waste them on menial tasks," he said. "It feels… beneath the honor they deserve for what they gave up." He hung the kettle on the rack and sank into an armchair, grinning. "And besides, they're American, they'd ruin it."

Ezekiel forced a chuckle. Will caught his eye and gave him a look.

"Please, sit." Albert gestured at the various seating arrangements. "Be comfortable."

Ezekiel found an armchair opposite the man and sat.

Will found himself on the couch, which caused him to lean back and yawn. "We've been riding and sleeping on cots for so long," he said. "I forgot what this felt like."

Albert nodded enthusiastically.

They sat in silence, reveling in the relaxation, until the kettle started to whistle. Albert sprung up and went about the work of placing loose tea into a separate pot. He poured the water into the pot and waited before filling each cup on the car with the steeped tea. "I'm afraid I've misplaced my sieve, but I can assure you the tea will still be delicious."

He wheeled the cart over to Will first, who took his cup and saucer before moving towards Ezekiel.

"How many are there?" Ezekiel set his tea on the arm of the chair. "The servants."

"Thirty-two," Albert said, returning to his seat beside the hearth. He poured his own tea and leaned back in the chair. "No, wait, thirty-one. Isaiah was released just yesterday. Apologies."

"Isaiah?" Will frowned up at the man. "But your wife calls them all—"

"Bartholomew, yes." Albert sipped his tea. "Bartholomew was the first person to offer up his body at the time of his passing. Now, the people who do it often refer to it as 'becoming Bartholomew', so my wife tries to honor that in how she refers to them. I keep a list to honor the individual, and she honors the collective."

"Why didn't she just tell us that?" Will tried to take a drink but hissed when it touched his tongue. He blew on it a few times and tried again.

Albert shrugged. "Heloise is an impatient woman. She perceives the world quicker than most and doesn't like to waste time explaining things."

"What did you mean by 'released'?" Seeing both of the other men drinking, Ezekiel risked a taste of his own tea, and was shocked to find it good, though a bit floral for his taste.

"Each person offers their body for a certain amount of time, from a few months to forever." Albert set his tea on an arm table to his left. "Isaiah's four years were up."

"So it's not slavery?" Will asked, eyeing Ezekiel.

"Gods, no," Albert said, his face turning red with indignation. "I can't—I won't support that abomination that plagues this country. The fact that it continues here nearly three decades after its abolition in England…" He shook his head.

"What if your wife decides she doesn't want to let one of her servants go?" Ezekiel spoke up before either Will or Albert could continue.

Albert gave him a hard stare. "She can't. From what I do understand, the person sets the length of their indenture when the spell is cast. So the spell only remains in effect for that long. Afterwards, their body returns to dust."

They sat in silence again.

"It's all very clean, neat, and orderly," he said, "and no one gets hurt or exploited."

"Okay," Ezekiel said.

"And they aren't all black, either," Albert said, nodding his head at Ezekiel.

"What?" Ezekiel said. His voice was louder than he meant.

Albert shook his head. "All kinds of people offer themselves up. Rachel, dear," he called.

A white woman, who would have appeared young if not for the cataracts in her eyes and the emaciated state of her body, entered the room.

"Obviously just showing you one is not a huge statement," he said, "but I assure you there are others like Rachel here, as well as a few other races floating around this dusty old house."

"Thank you, dear, that was all."

Rachel nodded and exited the room.

"Have I passed?" Albert asked, casting a humorous glance at Ezekiel.

"Excuse me?"

"Well, you were planning on 'destroying my zombies' before you came in," he said nonchalantly. "What do you think now?"

Ezekiel stewed in his chair. "If everything you say is true," he said, "then…yes."

"Wonderful," he said. "I appreciate your concern. It can be quite shocking and gruesome at first, but I think it's rather humane."

Ezekiel nodded. "Better than the alternative."

The flames in the fireplace roared to life and crackled like a thousand tiny fireworks. A billowing puff of smoke burst out of the brick opening, and from it emerged Kate, followed by Heloise.

"Please tell me you did that?" Will said to Heloise. "And not her?"

"Nope, that was all your girl," Heloise said with a wink in Kate's direction.

"You're done?" Ezekiel said.

"We've been working for days," Heloise said. "You just didn't notice."

Ezekiel scoffed. "What did you come up with?"

"Something useful, I'm sure," Albert offered.

"Naturally, my dear," she said, sauntering over to give her husband a kiss. When she pulled away, she added, "Guaranteed to kill your vampire, no matter how powerful they may be."

"Oh," Albert said. "You were serious about that?" He looked up at his wife. "Vampires are real, and you didn't tell me?"

"Not now, dear heart," Heloise said. "Show them, Kate."

Kate held up a bottle about three inches tall, filled with a liquid that swirled silver, black, red, and yellow at various intervals. She shook it up and down and the swirls became more rapid and violent inside the glass container.

"And that is?" Ezekiel gestured with his hand.

"A concoction," Heloise said, "of silver flecks, garlic oil, dead man's blood, liquid sunlight, and a supplicant soul."

"A what?" Will asked.

"A soul taken from purgatory," she said.

Will's face went snow white.

"Don't worry, it'll go right back once its job is done," Heloise added. "You have my word."

"Give it here," Ezekiel said, holding out his hand.

Kate placed the bottle in his grip.

"Careful," Heloise said. "I can't make that again if you break it. Spirits aren't often happy when you snatch one of their own. There would be consequences for trying it again."

"How does it work?" Ezekiel asked.

"Make him drink it."

Ezekiel nodded.

"That won't be borderline impossible," Will said. "Here, drink this strange liquid, promise it won't kill you."

"That is not my problem," Heloise said. "You wanted to kill a full-grown vampire; I gave you a way. The rest is on you." She paused. "If you die, at least make sure to break the bottle and let that soul go free."

"I will," Ezekiel said.

"Wonderful." She draped herself over her husband's chair. "Now if you don't mind." With a wave of her hand, Ezekiel found himself back in the single room building from before. The sconces and brazier were no longer lit, and a cold shadow hung inside the room.

"I don't like that," Will said. "I really don't like any of that."

"Not my favorite either," Ezekiel said.

"I think it's great," Kate said.

"Learn anything interesting?" Will asked.

"Or useful?" Ezekiel added.

Kate held a finger up to her lips and grinned deviously. "That's a secret," she said. "Not for you two snoops to know."

"Sounds like a no," Ezekiel said.

"That's what I was thinking," Will replied.

Kate's face dropped. "What? No! I definitely learned some stuff," she said. "I just can't tell you."

"Sounds like an excuse to me," Will said. "What do you think?"

"A damn shame of an excuse," Ezekiel said, scratching at his chin.

"Fuck both of you," Kate said, storming out of the house.

Will cracked up and Ezekiel couldn't help it either. The two of them spent a few moments relishing in the laughter.

"You know, I think that's the first time I've heard you actually laugh," Will said.

"I haven't had a lot of reasons."

The two stood in silence for a minute before Will spoke up again. "I'm gonna head outside."

"Gimme a minute," Ezekiel said. "Gonna see if there's anything else useful in here."

Will nodded and left the room. Ezekiel heard him try to talk to Kate, only for her to hurl a stream of foul words at him. He paced the room, not actually expecting to find anything, but relishing in the first moment of calm he could remember having in a long while. As he walked, he glanced down into the brazier in which Heloise had burned his hand. In the ashes sat a simple doll made of dark brown burlap. Crosses were drawn in ink all over its upper half. Two black buttons stared up at him from the large head. It was him. He glanced around the room, half-expecting to find Heloise lounging once more on her chair, with her open robe, chiding him. The room was still empty and cold.

"Magic mumbo jumbo," he muttered in frustration, turning his back on the doll. A shudder ran down his spine as he did. He wheeled around to see the doll, sitting just as he left it. "Fine."

He stormed across the room and scooped up the doll, sending a shower of ashes falling to the floor like tainted snow. Inside the rough cloth that made up the doll's skin, he kneaded the familiar joints of his own severed hand. The rancid smell still lingered slightly behind the overpowering combinations of perfumes on the burlap. It only furthered his disgust. "Now what?"

The room was silent and cold, but without the chill from moments earlier.

The emaciated man waited outside in the dark of night, his cataract-filmed eyes staring at the door as they emerged. Kate had already mounted her horse and sat waiting for them. Her face tightened in a pout that served to remind Ezekiel how young she was. He looked to Will at his right and saw his youth as well. A deep sigh rose from his chest. Ezekiel stopped as he drew close to the man. He held up the doll.

"Anything to say about this?" Ezekiel asked.

"If the mistress has left it to you, then there is certainly a reason."

"That's about what I figured," Ezekiel said. He placed the doll in the pocket of his jacket, next to the vial of vampire-killing potion. His horse trotted over, and Ezekiel pulled himself into the saddle. As he prepared to leave, he paused and rode back towards the zombie servant.

"Is your name actually Bartholomew?" he asked, looking down from his horse.

"It is," the man said.

"You were the first person to pledge yourself to her?"

"I was."

"For how long?"

"Until the end of her days."

Ezekiel grunted a non-committal response and turned his horse around. Bartholomew's hand shot out and caught the edge of Ezekiel's coat. Ezekiel glanced back down at the man.

"I know what you seek," he said. His voice changed until it was not his own, but that of Heloise. His eyes filled with purple fire, and he spoke. "Search in Nouvelle-Ibérie. The spirits whisper of strange things there. Dark things."

Ezekiel grimaced. "Ain't that our luck."

15

Ezekiel laid back on the small bed in the corner of his room at the abandoned inn. It was nowhere near as comfortable as the chair at Heloise and Albert's plantation, but it would do for getting a few winks of sleep before setting back out. They decided to travel by the main roads and pass through Baton Rouge, which was under the control of the Union army, before making their way to Lafayette and finally down to New Iberia. Ezekiel wasn't keen on the idea, given that General Banks had wished to never see him again, but Will had pointed out that they might need Union support to get access to Nouvelle-Ibérie.

His damaged shoulder throbbed. Ezekiel looked over at the prosthetic on the table by his bed. He looked at the scarred patch of flesh that had once been his left arm and imagined moving the fingers one by one. The sensation grew duller over time. Frustrated, Ezekiel reached over to the table and grabbed the small bottle. He turned it around in the dark, watching as it shimmered with its own low light.

"Soon," he said.

Morning came before Ezekiel realized he'd fallen asleep. Will banged on his door as he passed for good measure. Ezekiel had slept in his clothes that now clung to his sweat-soaked body. He fought against the tangled sheets as he rose. After a few minutes he was free and met the others outside the inn. Will handed him the reins to his horse. Ezekiel nodded a silent thank you as he mounted. Kate leaned forward on her horse, head on her hands, but straightened up and followed as Ezekiel set off.

Baton Rouge was only just under a day's ride from New Orleans, and they arrived just as the sun began to slip below the lip of the horizon, back into hiding for the night. Sullen faces peered out of darkened windows as they rode into town. There was nobody in the streets, and the only sound was the rush of the Mississippi.

"Something's not right," Ezekiel said.

"Where are all the soldiers?" Will asked.

"Inside?" Kate offered.

Will shook his head. "We're not supposed to occupy civilian buildings, just set out our camps within the city boundaries," he said. "There should be tents and artillery and—"

He gagged violently on the coppery smell as it washed over them. Ezekiel pulled his mask up over his mouth and nose, and Kate shoved her face into the crook of her arm.

"What the hell is that?" she asked.

"A hell of a lot of blood," Ezekiel said. He pulled down his mask and sniffed at the air. "And bodies."

"But where?" Will asked. "And why?"

"The river," Ezekiel said. He spurred his horse towards the river and had to jerk on the reins to keep the creature from sliding into the muddy trench dug just below the sightline of the riverbank. He stared down into the ditch soaked, not with water, but with blood, and grimaced. "I found your soldiers. But I can't tell how many there were."

Will rode up beside him and went wide-eyed. He dropped from his horse and to his hands and knees, vomiting onto the ground. Kate pulled up the rear.

"What the hell got to him?" she asked.

Ezekiel held up a hand to stop her. "Not this," he said. "You stay there."

The ditch was full to the brim with the torn and dismembered remnants of Union soldiers. Blue uniforms had turned a deep purple as blood ran from torn eye sockets and severed limbs. The faces Ezekiel could make out were all twisted, frozen in a final look of abject terror. Where body parts hadn't been ripped and pulled, angry claw marks dripped congealing blood. Not quite fresh, but not dry yet. Ezekiel looked around them as the red light of the setting sun began to fade.

"We need to get across the river," he said.

"What do you mean?" With trembling hands, Will climbed back into his horse's saddle. He couldn't take his eyes off the shredded bodies on the ground.

"Whatever did this is still here," Ezekiel said. "This isn't a mass grave, it's a feeding trough for ghouls."

Will turned to Ezekiel and froze, staring past the man. "You're right," he said.

Ezekiel looked over his shoulder and saw the source of the boy's fear. He spun his horse around to face the threat. Hundreds of ghouls were trickling out of the city buildings and filling the streets, all congregating and moving toward the ditch. Toward them.

Ezekiel reached for both his guns. His good hand found the one on his right hip, but his hook only scraped the skin of his left side as he drew empty with the prosthetic.

"Damn it," he hissed. He balanced his single revolver on the prosthetic instead.

Bestial sounds rose and fell from the gathering crowd of creatures. Ezekiel tried to count but kept losing track. He figured the whole city must have been turned. They couldn't fight their way out of this one.

"Too many," he said. "Get to the water." He drove his horse towards the madding crowd, then wheeled it around, charging towards the bloody ditch. A lash of the reins made the horse leap over the gory feed trough, and charge toward the river. Will and Kate followed his lead, Kate's eyes scrunched tight as her horse cleared the gap.

The ghouls shrieked, an unholy cry that grew louder and more painful to hear as each demonic voice joined the raging choir. Ezekiel risked a glance and saw that most of the creatures, predators that they were, focused on the easier meal. They descended on the lukewarm remains of the soldiers. A smaller portion, still hundreds deep, was more interested in live prey, rushing after them with rabid looks plastered on their faces. Less than fifty yards ahead, the grass gave way to the mucky riverbank.

"Are vampires afraid of rivers?" Kate's shout was panicked despite her dry sarcasm.

"I've heard that they can't cross rivers," Ezekiel called back. "Never tried it before though—never got chased by this many."

Will's scream interrupted their conversation. Both brought their horses to a skidding stop and turned to see Will's horse go down as a ghoul latched fangs first into its ankle. The horse's fall flung Will to the ground where he landed and rolled a few more feet. He rose winded and began to sprint, trying to keep ahead of the much faster creatures pursuing him.

"Damn it," Kate hissed, spurring her horse forward toward their fallen companion.

"Kate," Ezekiel called.

"Just shoot something," she shouted back.

Ezekiel took stock of the situation, searching out the ghouls that presented the most threat. Many had stopped to feast on Will's fallen horse, but several still pursued the boy himself. One in particular had its clawed hand outstretched, reaching for the nape of Will's neck.

Ezekiel leveled his gun, careful not to shoot too close to Will, and fired. The creature gurgled as the bullet tore through its throat, leaving a hissing hole. It fell to the ground, clutching and tearing at its own neck, trying to get the bullet out. Seconds later, it burst into flames and ceased moving before crumbling to dust. Ezekiel tracked the rest. Kate's rifle cracked twice in quick succession and two more ghouls went up in flames. He smirked. The girl was a dead shot.

Kate's horse slid up next to Will who jumped and grabbed onto the saddle, scrambling his way up the side until he was seated behind Kate. She didn't wait for him to settle, jerked the horse around and spurred it hard. The horse shrieked, kicked up dirt and mud, and bolted just as the first ghoul reached out to slash at its rump.

Ezekiel managed to use his prosthetic to cock and fire his revolver three times in a row, taking out the nearest three ghouls. The third shot only struck the last creature's arm. It screamed and gripped the wounded appendage, digging in with hooked claws until black blood poured from the wound. With a furious scream, the creature gave a mighty pull and ripped the arm off at the shoulder, discarding the limb just as it burst into flames. The creature heaved and hissed before locking its eyes on Ezekiel.

"Come and get it," Ezekiel said, aiming down his revolver's sight.

As soon as the creature began to move, he fired, tearing a hole right through its left eye socket. It didn't even have time to scream before it fell over dead and began to ignite.

Kate was finally back by his side, with Will gripping her by the waist so as not to fall off. She flashed Ezekiel a grin and said, "We're never letting him live *this* down, are we?"

"Let's make sure we live before we get to that," Ezekiel said.

They raced to the water hoping to find a boat to carry them across. Most of the vessels were smashed to splinters along the shore. Ezekiel began to lose hope as his eyes only found wreck after wreck.

"There," Will said, pointing up the river.

A long pier extended from the back of a house, spanning about half of the river. Ezekiel kicked his horse and turned, guiding the beast toward the stretch. The horse's hooves thundered down the length of wooden planks. Ezekiel put his head down and drove the horse forward, pulling up on the reins at the last minute. The horse leapt into the air and splashed down into the greenish-brown water.

Ezekiel's senses were consumed by the frantic movements of the horse and the splash and burble of the sluggish river sluicing past his ears. He clung to the reins as tightly as he could. Finally, he broke the surface. Beneath him the horse began to calm as it oriented itself and began its trotting swim. It shook its mane with a huff, spraying him with water.

Kate's horse crashed into the river a few moments later. She had a less difficult time bringing the steed under control and soon made her way alongside Ezekiel. Will's soaking hair clung to the front of his face, and he shivered, almost slipping from the saddle in the process.

Ghouls surged towards the pier, shrieking and moaning. The rest of the town must have finished their meals because bloody mouths dotted the crowd. At least one creature still held a partially-gnawed arm or jaw in its mouth as it sprinted towards them. It careened into the river, and Ezekiel watched in morbid fascination as the slow-moving water wicked away its flesh like a flame melting candle wax. Moments later nothing remained but floating bones.

"We're too heavy for the horses to make the whole swim." Ezekiel fumbled free of his stirrups and drifted away from his mount. He didn't know how deep the river was, but the bottom was well out of reach. "Turn them loose and we'll make our own way."

"What if they get eaten?" Kate slid off her horse even as she asked. She gave the animals a final, tender pat before releasing her hold on the reins.

Will was the last one in the water. He floundered for a moment, then caught his rhythm, treading water with his head just barely above the surface. "Like mine."

Ezekiel shook his head and pointed. The ghouls had gathered along the riverbank and clustered on the part of the pier still on land, but none of them ventured beyond that boundary of water that lapped at the ground. "They can't get them in the water. Plus, horses are smart. They'll bolt once they make it across. See?"

Both horses shied deeper into the river, eyes bulging at the sight of the amassed crowd of ravenous monsters. After a moment they began to swim in earnest, leaving their riders behind as they tread across the sluggish water to reach the other shore. The second their hooves hit solid ground they bolted off into the distance.

"They're safer than us, now." Ezekiel nodded at Kate and began to swim.

They crossed the river in silence, each of them focusing on trying not to get swept away by the river's current.

Ezekiel's lungs burned as he sloshed out of the water, half-swimming, half-walking one splash at a time until he made it to the bank, sprawling out on the mud as he did. Will and Kate flopped down on either side of him, and for a minute the only sounds were the river and their labored breathing, slowing with each passing second.

Ezekiel forced himself to sit up and looked across the river. Amidst the gathered ghouls, two humanoid faces stood out. The first he recognized immediately. It was Prentiss. His skin was grey and stretched too thin over his skull. He grinned with shark-like teeth, a grin so wide it cracked and tore at the dry skin at the corners of his mouth. Black blood dribbled down his chin.

The second face stared back at him with nothing but contempt, and it took Ezekiel a minute to process what he saw.

"Collin?" he whispered under his breath. It struck him what Palaiologos had said before, that his other brother had survived. Ezekiel had killed Silva but left Collin alive. Palaiologos must have found him and turned him. His heart sank. If the rest of Palaiologos's bastardization of a family were turned, the hope of his Anna Marie still being human grew slimmer.

He dug his hand into the soft soil of the riverbank, clawing up a handful of dirt and hurling it into the water with a shout. "Fuck you, goddamn bloodsuckers." He fell to his knees and pressed his forehead against the cold earth. "Fuck you."

Will placed a gentle hand on his back. "Come on," he said, "let's get a move on before they find a way that they *can* cross the river."

Ezekiel gave himself an extra moment before sucking in a deep breath. "Right," he said, rising to his feet. He gave one last hateful glance to the assembled monsters on the other shore before turning his back on them.

"We'll have General Banks send a group over to burn that place to the ground," Will said. "They'll just hide in their houses during the day and come back out at night to cause harm if we don't."

Ezekiel wiped at his eyes. "Ain't that a little violent for you?"

Will shook his head. "Those aren't people, not anymore. Like you said, death is the best hope they have."

Ezekiel nodded. "That it is." He looked out in the distance, his vision shortened by the darkness. "We've got another day of walking ahead of us."

"Through another swamp," Kate groaned.

"You should know better," Will said. "It's Louisiana, it's all a swamp, sometimes it's just dressed up nice and pretty for us."

"And sometimes it's a pain in my ass," Kate said. "Just like you."

"Start walking," Ezekiel said. "Or I'm leaving you both."

16

<hr>

It started to rain. Heavy water droplets pounded down in a relentless torrent as they trekked through knee high mud. There was nothing solid in sight. Even the trees seemed to sink down deeper into the soggy, squelching earth. Ezekiel pulled his leg up and out of the mire as he took his next tedious step. He turned to see Kate, almost waist deep in the muck.

"Will," he said, motioning back to her with his thumb.

Will glanced back and trudged back towards Kate. She gave him a "what do you want" look. Without saying anything, Will squatted down and motioned for her to get on his back.

"Are you kidding?" she asked, visibly annoyed.

"He said you're moving too slow. Hop on," Will said.

She scoffed, and Will shrugged.

"Fine," she said, unsticking herself from the mud and clamoring up his back. "But I hate this."

"And you're heavy," he said.

She kicked him in the ribs with her heels. "Watch what you say, pony boy."

Ezekiel figured they'd walked all night and then some. He could see the sun, fighting unsuccessfully to poke its warming light through the thick grey clouds. His legs and feet screamed for rest, but there was nowhere in sight. He looked down and saw that they had come across another, smaller river, brown with mud and debris. A small, open-decked steamboat drifted towards them. Ezekiel waved his hands, hoping to get the attention of the captain or a deckhand. The boat didn't stop, and no acknowledgement came; no smoke plumed from the singular stack affixed to the vessel. Ezekiel pulled out his revolver and fired twice into the air. Still nothing. The boat listed right and began to turn sideways as it journeyed down the river.

"There doesn't look to be anyone on board," Will said.

Ezekiel mustered his strength and dove into the murky water. Leaves and branches caught in its flow clung to him as he struggled his way towards the ship. His palms slapped against the wooden hull, and he struggled to keep from being pulled under in the vessel's wake. He dug his nails into the wet wood and ground his teeth, clinging as tightly as he could. A rope ladder unfurled down towards him. Ezekiel grabbed the rungs and pulled himself up.

Will called out to him, but Ezekiel couldn't make out the words over the roar of the freezing rain. He climbed up the side of the ship and flung himself gasping onto the deck of the ship. Rolling over onto his back, he rubbed the stinging water out of his eyes. He could finally make out what Will was shouting. One word: 'Greybacks.'

Ezekiel's eyes snapped open, and he looked into the scowling faces of five Confederate soldiers. Three glared daggers down at him, one frowned in confusion, and the last one smiled cruelly, a white-fanged scar across a pallid face. It was a smile that reminded Ezekiel of Josiah Pickett. They'd been hiding, waiting for him to get on the ship.

"Collin." Ezekiel lay sprawled in the center of the deck—rough unpainted wood scraping his skin—staring up at the cloudy sky. Heavy raindrops pattered around him. "You got here quickly."

One of the soldiers brought the butt of his rifle down hard into Ezekiel's stomach. "Don't you talk to the general like that," he slurred.

"General?" Ezekiel said, coughing as he tried to laugh through the pain. "Didn't realize they let you pick your own titles now."

The rifle came down again, but Ezekiel was prepared. He pulled his knees to his chest and rolled to his side. The hard wood struck a glancing blow against his ribs that elicited a pained hiss from the back of his throat.

"For some reason, rushin' water sort of loses its effect if it's all rushin'," Collin said, gesturing lazily at the rain. "And you already know we're faster than you," he added.

"Uh-huh, and where's your new nephew?"

"Back where you left him. Rallying the troops," Collin said. "Well… I say rallying, but enslaving is probably more accurate." He grinned as realization dawned across Ezekiel's face. "That's right," he said. "Four million black, expendable resources, to aid our war. Game over, Union."

"And hello vampire Confederacy," Ezekiel grumbled. Tattered flags posted along the sides of the boat whipped in the stirring wind. "Where everything human is nothing but a slave."

"You've got it. And you're just in time," Collin said.

"For what? A speech?"

Collin laughed. "I'm not like my brothers. Either of them."

Ezekiel was hoisted to his feet and a sharp burning pain stabbed into the right side of his neck. One of the soldiers had lodged its fangs into his throat, right through his slave brand. The venom raced through his veins like thorny vines dragged through a pipe.

It was like being ripped apart from the inside. He screamed and lashed upwards with his hooked hand, slashing across the soldier vampire, melting the surrounding flesh as he dug savage gashes in its face. The soldier jerked away, and Ezekiel wheeled around, tackling the soldier, and embedding his silver claws into his throat and tearing. With his right hand, he drew his revolver and fired his last loaded shot in the direction of one of the other soldiers before slumping to his knees. A satisfying shriek quickly died in the open air, followed by the crackling of unnatural flames.

His bullet had gotten intimate with one of the other soldier vampires.

Ezekiel struggled for breath as he knelt atop the gurgling corpse. His chest heaved, and hot sweat made him shiver in the cold rain. His vision blurred and focused in strange pulses. He felt himself wobble.

There wasn't much space on the deck of the ship. It was wide enough for Ezekiel to have room to dodge and maneuver, and about twice as long; empty save for the damaged stump that had once held the wheel.

"See, he weren't top brass," Collin said. "So you ain't gonna become like us. You're just gonna die. And I promise, it will be slow, and hurt the entire damn time. Course, you deserve it."

Ezekiel composed himself and willed his body to stop shaking. His hot breath turned to steam in the downpour. "I liked you better when you were just a slave-owning piece of shit," he said, forcing himself to his feet. He glared at Collin over his shoulder. "I don't suppose you'll just stand there and let me gut you, huh?"

Collin flashed his shark-like teeth in a wicked smile. "Always fightin' like the dog you are, Ezekiel. Thomas said to kill you slow, but I remember what you did to my daddy, and what you did to Silva." Black bat wings erupted from his back, ripping the remaining two soldiers apart, their steaming intestines spilling out onto the deck of the boat as they stared at their general in shock. The halves of their bodies thudded onto the wood planks.

"I see." Ezekiel chuckled grimly as he turned. "You want to experience it firsthand." He tossed his revolver aside and raised his fist and his claw up for the fight. "Let's go, boy."

17

The lazy drift of the boat as it pitched and yawed down the sluggish river brought an unsteady nausea to the fight. Collin was faster than Ezekiel on a good day, and as the vampire venom burned its way through his veins, Ezekiel received a painful reminder that today was not a good day. Managing to stand upright was a challenge; avoiding the vampire's furious assault bordered on impossible. He just barely avoided five ragged claws raking through his face, and the action left him sprawled on the deck of the ship. Ezekiel returned the favor, slashing at the vampire's leg with his hook and tearing into the grey flesh. Collin hissed and stumbled backwards, his eyes bloody and teeth bared. Ezekiel took the opportunity to right himself and shed his coat and shirt, revealing his burns. Collin hissed at the sign of the cross in multitude across Ezekiel's torso.

Both men stumbled as the boat ran aground on the opposite bank of the river.

"I'm so glad you ain't your brother," Ezekiel said, charging Collin. He tackled the young vampire, wrapping him up in a bear hug in the process. "You believe in the cross."

Collin's skin sizzled in Ezekiel's grasp. The rotting, burning smell was amplified by the rain, choking Ezekiel with each laborious breath. He pulled back and slammed his fist into Collin's face, imprinting the four symbols as swollen burns across his eyes. Collin screamed, his wings struggling to expand in Ezekiel's grip. He bit down on Ezekiel's chest, only to rear back in agony as the holy burns did their work. Collin's eyes cracked open beneath the burned flesh; he pulled his head back and slammed it forward into Ezekiel's nose, cracking it and making the hunter release him and pinwheel backwards with a string of expletives.

Collin hissed as the skin around mouth steamed in the downpour. His face changed from that of a pale human to a darker, more bestial visage. Gone was the form of a man, and in its place snarled an ebony demon with flaming eyes, just like the one from the forest.

The demon flared its wings in an intimidation display, letting loose a raptor-like cry before flapping precariously into the air. The crack of a rifle rang out above the downpour. Something whizzed through the air and tore through the demon's wing, leaving a wide and ragged hole in its place.

The creature shrieked as it lost its orientation and plummeted back down to the wooden deck. Ezekiel stared over the side of the boat and saw, through pouring rain, Will trudging down the riverbank with Kate, smoking rifle pointed at the boat, perched on his shoulders. He could just make out the wicked grin on her face.

Smiling hurt, but it didn't stop a proud smirk from showing on Ezekiel's face. It didn't last long. Pain hitched in his chest, doubling him over and making him wretch violently. His whole body ached. He coughed and looked down at his hand; blood and teeth rested in his palm and were washed away in the torrent. He could feel his new teeth, razor sharp, pushing their way forward and out his gums. A scream clawed its way from his throat.

Ezekiel leapt at Collin, ripping into the obsidian flesh of his other wing with silver claws and raining down blows with a branded fist. Collin fought back, grappling Ezekiel, and ripping his prosthetic off of his wounded arm, tearing open the scabby stump in the process. The contraption skidded to the side of the boat.

Ezekiel bit down on his tongue until it bled, just to keep from screaming. He cradled the wounded arm with his other hand. Collin's one good wing lashed at him, tearing a fresh gash along his chest, and knocking him away.

Kate's rifle cracked again, like thunder, the bullet ripping through Collin's arm and embedding itself in the ship's deck, sending splinters scattering into the air. Collin shrieked as his arm hissed and cracked from the silver wound.

Rainwater pooled, red with blood at Ezekiel's feet. He let go of his arm, letting the aggravated stump hang at his side. He stared at the sky, panting, trying to catch his breath. A bloody grin streaked across his face as he looked back down at Collin.

"You look like you're in as much pain as me," he said.

"I'm gonna drain the blood from your skull," Collin shouted. "I'll pluck out your fucking eyes and eat them like olives."

"I've noticed you sons of bitches threaten a lot more when you know you're about to die. Whether you know it or not." He stomped on a loose deck plank, snapping it in half longways. A single unsteady hand reached down and snatched up the broken half, pointing the sharp end at Collin. He raised his arm and pointed the wood at the sky. "Sun's coming out."

The rain began to slow, until finally it came to a sudden stop. Collin's eyes went the size of saucers, and he sank to his knees, screaming in agony. Ezekiel lowered his makeshift stake and swayed over to the vampire.

"How do you want to go?" He stood, his shadow blocking out the sun. Collin looked up. "No pain?"

The vampire didn't respond.

"Pain." Ezekiel stepped to the side, letting the faint golden light of the sun that filtered down from the clouds land in searing rays across Collin's skin. "I can give you either. Just depends on if you cooperate."

Ezekiel's whole body throbbed. He looked at his arms to see that his veins were dark and pulsing beneath his skin. It was everything he could do not to throw up and pass out. He rocked side to side, ultimately blocking the sun again. He glared down at Collin's charred body. "Choose."

Collin choked out a laugh. "If I'll die either way, why should I help you?"

"You ever seen one of your own go up in the sun?" Ezekiel forced a chuckle. "Guess not, else you wouldn't be here right now. It ain't pretty. Lasts a while, too."

Collin's eyes narrowed.

"You can be skeptical all you like, but vampire or not, you're still a young man, and I'd be willing to bet…death and pain…they terrify you." He dropped his voice to a whisper. "And they should." He stepped back out of the sun's path. Collin shrieked, shrinking away, trying to find some cover from the light.

He hissed and screamed. "Fine, just make it stop!" Third degree burns and worse covered Collin all over as he huddled and shook from the pain. Ezekiel choked back the vomit that rose in protestation of the smell.

"Where is he?"

"Who?"

"Don't be cute. Palaiologos, where is he?"

Collin's lips pressed into a thin line surrounded by angry red burns. Ezekiel made like he was going to move.

"The island!" Collin shouted. "The one south…in the bay."

"See," Ezekiel said, "easy."

Collin resumed his human form, bruised, burned, black with blood, and breathing like a snake through cracked ribs and ruptured lungs. "Take me below deck?"

"Excuse me?"

"I answered your question," Collin said, "you promised me no more pain. I need to get out of the sun."

Ezekiel's head spun. "I said I could give you pain or no pain. I didn't promise I wouldn't kill you."

Collin's eyes widened. "You're not a son killer," he said, coughing up inky fluid. A hint of panic was creeping into his garbled voice. "Remember? You said that once."

Pain burned cold in Ezekiel's veins, clouding his vision, and filling his ears with a high-pitched ring. He stared coldly down at the smoldering vampire in front of him.

"Your father was a monster," Ezekiel said, stepping to the side and letting the sunshine down on Collin in full, finally igniting him. "Your brother was turned into one by the man who's pretending to be your brother."

"He is my brother!" Collin shrieked, lunging at Ezekiel in a last-ditch attack. Ezekiel brought the stake up at the last second. Something cracked and then popped. A geyser of black blood erupted from Collin's mouth, spraying over Ezekiel's shoulder, and splattering the side of his face. Collin's burnt body twitched violently, bones snapping as he looked down at the stake now embedded in his chest. He slumped, his weight sagging down onto Ezekiel.

"You'll be one happy family in hell." Ezekiel shrugged the vampire off, stumbling backwards until he sprawled out on the deck, and lost consciousness.

18

This was the second time Ezekiel had woken up on a military cot, but the first time he found himself bound to one. The ropes weren't tight, but they weren't exactly comfortable either. They chafed at his skin as he struggled against them. Sunlight filtered in from the small gap in the tent flaps.

"It wasn't our idea," Kate said, entering the tent. Her clothes were waterlogged, and her hair hung in slick clumps around her face. "But General Banks saw the bite marks on your neck."

Memory flooded back over Ezekiel and made him shudder. The burning sensation in his veins was gone, leaving only a heavy nausea in the pit of his stomach.

"Do you know how long you have?" Kate hesitated.

"Go on," Ezekiel said. His voice sounded hollow even to his own ears

"It's just… Prentiss went pretty fast…" For the first time, he saw concern etched on her young face. "It's already been almost six hours, and you've been spitting teeth like God willed it."

Ezekiel looked down at his chest. His skin was still the same dark brown, complete with darker burns all over. Fear flickered through him. His own branding would—at best—condemn him to even greater suffering once the transformation was complete. He licked his teeth and hissed in pain as he cut his tongue on the serrated fangs that now filled his mouth. The blood tasted orgasmic. He shuddered with pleasure, before relaxing. There was no more pain coming from his tongue. He stuck it out and pinched it. His hand came away wet, but without blood.

"I'm fine," he said finally. "Let me out of these."

Kate hesitated.

"Kate—" He saw the look in her eyes. "Dammit, girl," he said with a sigh. "I'm not gonna hurt you."

"And how do we know that?" General Banks asked, entering behind Kate, and placing a comforting hand on her shoulder. The man's eyes flashed with madness. Red rings and dark bags beneath bird-like eyes told of a severe lack of sleep.

"General Banks," Ezekiel said. "I'd say it's good to see you—"

"Then we'd both have to lie," the general said.

"Where's Will?"

"My son," Banks started. "Every night,"—his voice faltered—"every night when it rains, he comes, and he taunts me as he picks off my men. He doesn't kill them. I hear their screams as he carries them off to God knows where. Do you know how many nights it's rained?"

Ezekiel thought of the pit of soldiers in Baton Rouge.

He knew where those men ended up.

"I'll wager quite a few nights," Ezekiel said. He flexed against the ropes, watching his muscles strain against the bonds. "I've mentioned that being tied up brings back bad memories, right?"

"I recall no such statement on your part."

"I'd like to talk to Will," Ezekiel said.

Banks shook his head. "The corporal has been redrafted and is currently leading a detachment of soldiers to Baton Rouge after informing me of what you encountered there."

Ezekiel cursed Will and his unfailing honesty. "How much silver did you send them with?"

"My soldiers took nothing but their standard issue armaments and materials to burn the city to the ground."

Ezekiel fumed. "In the rain? You've said yourself it's been raining forever, how are they going to start a fire? They will all die. Call them back."

Banks gave him a cold stare. "My son was there, and you didn't do what you promised. So now we must do things my way," he said.

"Look, General, we have a way to kill Palaiologos. The Voodoo Queen—"

"Yes, yes, your magic bottle," the general said, holding up the small vial. "I'll hold on to it for now." He glared down at Ezekiel. "In case we need it for more pressing matters."

"I know where he is," Ezekiel shouted.

"Be that as it may," Banks said. "You're not going anywhere."

Ezekiel roared with frustration and strained harder against the ropes. They gave slightly, but not enough to free himself. "Call them back and let me the hell out of these before I make myself a damn problem."

"You already are," he said. "Watch him, Kate, and don't trust him." He tucked the vial in his coat and left.

The second he was out of earshot, Kate's normal demeanor returned, her voice a low whisper. "So he's gone full nuts."

Ezekiel's brow furrowed in confusion.

"What? You think I'd give up on you that easily? Banks is insane and his army still thinks they have to follow orders. Personally, I would like to make it past thirteen."

A weight lifted from Ezekiel's chest. "That-a-girl," he said with a smirk.

"Are you sure you're alright?" she asked.

"I got a mouth like a shark, and blood tastes an unholy type of good, but I don't have an urge to hurt nobody but the bastards that did all this," he said. He left out the fact that he felt like he'd been dragged underneath a train.

"Sounds like the same old asshole to me," Kate said. She produced a bayonet from beneath her dress. "Let's get you out of these." She sawed at the ropes until all of them had been cut. Ezekiel sat up, slipping at first when he went to balance on his prosthetic. He looked at Kate in confusion.

"Couldn't find it," she said. "Must have ended up in the water."

Ezekiel remembered the false arm skidding to rest near the edge of the boat. "Must have," he said. "That complicates things a lot."

"Why didn't it grow back?" she asked.

"What do you mean?"

"Vampires heal from anything unless the wound is from silver or something, right? Shouldn't your arm be back?"

"Guess it doesn't work after the fact," Ezekiel said, staring down at the gnarled stump. "Shame."

"What's the plan?" she asked. "Aside from killing the vampire before you turn." She caught the look he gave her. "Sorry."

"Were you able to stop Will?"

She shook her head solemnly.

"Then we have to go after him," Ezekiel said.

"No," Kate said.

"What?" His head was still swimming.

She rolled her eyes. "You need to get that vial back from the general and get to Palaiologos. You said you know where he is?"

"Yeah, he's on an island south of here."

"Then focus on that. We don't know how long he'll stick around there." She paused seeing the concern on his face. "I'll go after Will."

"Alone?"

"I'm not a little kid," she said. "And close as you are, you're not our father. You have a mission. See it through." She gave him a defiant smile. "Don't make me think you've gone soft, now."

"Never," Ezekiel said, his voice crackling out of a hoarse throat.

"That's what I thought."

"Where is Banks's tent?" Ezekiel asked.

"Center of the camp this time," she said. "Guess he got paranoid after—"

"Wouldn't you?"

"No," Kate said, "I'd have hunted the fucker down and killed him by now."

Ezekiel nodded. "Anything else useful I should know?"

"The soldiers are tired, and don't want to be here," she said with a shrug. "Might work to your advantage."

Ezekiel grimaced. "Not worth it," he said. "Can't trust 'em."

"Good luck," Kate said, rushing up and giving him a quick hug before pulling away. "Tell no one."

"About what?" Ezekiel asked, imitating Kate's sly grin.

"Exactly, now get a move on." She disappeared outside the tent, and he listened as her footsteps squelched away on the muddy ground.

"My turn," Ezekiel said.

In his paranoia over losing so many soldiers, General Banks had put all his resources into the nightly guard. Men who clearly hadn't slept properly in days barely kept their footing as Ezekiel crept through the shadows on his way towards the center of the camp. He was glad to be dealing with Banks as he was, broken and verging on madness. The man he'd met in Alexandria would have never made it so easy for him to move about. *His* guard would have been alert, well-rested, and ready to fight. As Ezekiel moved past guards and the lantern light spilling from open tents, he made a point to check any unloaded barrels and crates, hoping to find his prosthetic stored away, but to no avail.

"One-handed it is," he grumbled to himself.

The sentence triggered a phantom sensation in the place where his hand had been. The cramping pain started in the tips of his missing fingers, traveling up his arm and clawing at the back of his mind. His breath hitched in his chest as he tried not to vocalize the discomfort. He closed his eyes and pictured his left hand, gently clenching and unclenching, trying to trick his mind into relaxing a limb that wasn't there. While doing this, he clenched and unclenched his right hand as well. Slowly, the pain subsided. He looked down at his arms and saw the black, bulging veins, a stark reminder of what was to come. His tongue explored his teeth, carefully this time to avoid laceration.

"Don't think about it," he said.

His adrenaline was wearing off, making way for the whole-body pain that burned and twitched its way through every muscle in his body. He saw Banks's tent ahead and willed himself forward. Banks's shadow paced back and forth inside the tent, illuminated by a single, low-burning lantern. Ezekiel steeled himself, tiptoeing around to the open flap of the tent. He peered inside.

Banks ambled back and forth, face blank and zombie-like. He clutched a daguerreotype in his hand, muttering to himself. Ezekiel couldn't see it, but he knew it was a photo of Prentiss. Ezekiel scanned the rest of the space, and his breath hitched in his throat.

Sitting on a cot, in much the same way as Ezekiel last truly saw him, was Prentiss. His skin was a sickly shade of grey mottled with shadows in the flickering lantern light. Eyes that had been blue now pulsed an alternating grey and red, and he whispered through a wolf-like smile, never taking his eyes off his father. Ezekiel remembered how Palaiologos's eyes had flashed at Prentiss shortly after he turned; how Prentiss had gone from afraid to subservient. And how Pickett had been made to think Palaiologos was his son Thomas. Prentiss was doing the same thing to his father.

Banks looked up and seemed to notice Prentiss for the first time. His eyes went wide.

"My son," he said, dropping the photo and holding out his arms.

Prentiss hissed. His eyes flashed violently red, and Banks recoiled, rocking back and forth before returning to his stupor. He picked up the photo.

"They're here," Prentiss hissed. "The ones who turned your son. The vampires."

"My son. My poor son." Banks's voice was flat.

"They're hiding, disguised as your soldiers," he said. "All of them. You've been betrayed."

"Betrayed," Banks repeated. He began to grow irate. "Betrayed!"

"That's right. You've killed several over the past nights, but there are still more, and they grow in numbers. Tonight you must end it. The camp is lost. Burn it."

"Burn," Banks said. "Fire to purify."

"It's what your son would want."

Banks's arms dropped to his sides, limp.

Ezekiel had heard enough. He stepped into the tent. "What is it with you and fire, kid?"

Prentiss hissed. "It's him," he said. "He's been bit. He turned your men. Kill him, kill him first!"

Banks rounded on Ezekiel.

"Really?" Ezekiel asked. "You're gonna make an old man fight me?"

Banks drew his pistol, but Ezekiel was already there. He slammed his shoulder into Banks's chest, toppling him over and knocking him unconscious. A swift kick sent the pistol sliding out from under the tent. Banks groaned.

"Stay down," Ezekiel said. "And you—" He turned to Prentiss, only to catch the flashing red of his eyes.

"Just sleep. And dream," Prentiss hissed.

The world began to melt away around him until there was nothing but blackness. The darkness laughed, and then fell silent. Ezekiel fell, deeper and deeper, plummeting through sleep as his senses grew fuzzy. Everything stopped with a jolt.

19

Ezekiel woke in a bed in a house he didn't recognize. It wasn't the shack he'd been a slave in, nor was it Heloise's strange room of magic and trickery. His gut told him the house was his, but the memory of how and when he acquired it flitted just out of reach. He rolled over and saw a second pillow, with a fresh indent, and blankets moved by someone who just recently left the bed. A door closed on his other side, and soft footsteps tiptoed into the room.

"You're awake." The voice was soft and kind. And familiar.

Ezekiel's heart raced at the sound. He shifted around in bed and saw his wife staring down at him with a soft, vacant smile. "Anna Marie," he said. His voice was hushed, and reverent. "How—?" He winced as sharp pain popped behind his eyes.

Anna Marie placed a concerned hand on his head and sat beside him on the bed. "Were you hurt that bad? Don't you remember?" she asked. "You don't have a fever or nothing, do you?"

"Remember...?" Ezekiel's head throbbed when he tried to think. "Remember what?"

"How you rescued me, from that monster." She smiled softly at him. "You stormed his castle with your rifle and your crosses, and you sent that devil back to hell."

Ezekiel frowned. "Palaio—"

She pressed a finger to his lips. "Don't say his name," she said. "It's an ill omen. Besides, he's gone, we should move on with our lives." She pulled her finger away, but Ezekiel caught her hand in his. Both his hands. He blinked, looking down at the five fingers on his left hand.

"But I—" He looked back up at Anna Marie, who held him in a serene gaze. He shook his head and stroked the top of her hand with his rough fingers, feeling the softness of her hands. He squeezed, feeling her warmth.

"I did it," he said. "After ten years. I missed you."

"You did, my love."

He pressed her hand against his cheek and closed his eyes. Pain stabbed in his head sending red sparks dancing in the dark behind his eyelids. He snapped back to attention and looked around the room, frowning.

"What's wrong?" Anna Marie asked.

"Where are Will and Kate?" he asked, sitting up in the bed.

She ignored his question. "Oh, by the way, your son is outside waiting for you to take him horse riding like you promised," she said.

"Son…" Ezekiel's mouth went dry. Will and Kate were forgotten in light of the shocking news. "We have a son?"

"You really did hit your head if you don't remember little Elijah out there," she said. "You rescued him when you rescued me. My pregnancy?"

Anxiety gnawed at Ezekiel's chest. "Where are we?"

Anna Marie pulled her hand away and frowned at him. "Don't you recognize it?" she asked, gesturing to the room around her. "It's the old Pickett house."

"That house burned down," Ezekiel said. "To the ground."

Anna Marie shrugged. "I guess someone rebuilt it."

Ezekiel scowled.

"Oh, don't give me that face," Anna Marie said, rising and crossing her arms over her chest. "It's a nice place."

"Why the hell are we back here?" Ezekiel snapped.

"Because we own it now." She said it dismissively, as if it were the most normal and obvious thing in the world. "We live here."

Ezekiel narrowed his eyes and scowled harder. His head rang as he tried to focus his thoughts and remember how all this could have happened. "So what, I kill Palaio—"

"Don't say his name," Anna Marie snapped, her face twisting in rage and then softening immediately. "I'm sorry," she said. "I just... I can't stand hearing it after everything I went through. I still can't believe I'm not crazy."

"Right, I'm sorry." Ezekiel relaxed his scowl. "I'm just so confused. Where are Kate and Will?"

"I don't know," she said. "I suppose he went back to fighting, and she went home."

"Will doesn't fight," Ezekiel said.

"He's a soldier, in a war. Are you gonna argue with everything I say, or are you gonna go out there and show that boy how to get his ass on a horse?" Anna Marie placed her hands on her hips, giving the appearance of a strict older mother. It didn't look right on her.

"I'll go," Ezekiel said.

She nodded. "Good."

The hallways of the Pickett house were exactly as Ezekiel remembered them, down to the finest detail. The exactitude of the renovated craftsmanship weighed uneasily on his stomach, and as he stepped outside from the two main doors and saw the plantation in its full glory, that weighty feeling grew heavier and denser: an angry knot in the pit of his gut.

People toiled in the fields. He shielded his eyes from the sun with his hand to get a better look but was interrupted by a tugging on his pants. He looked down into the face of a small black child, staring up at him with big eyes and a bright smile. It was like looking into a mirror of the past. Except the eyes.

"Daddy," the child said in a questioning voice. "What you looking for?"

Ezekiel looked down at the boy, words catching in his throat. He finally managed to croak out, "You're...my son?"

The boy laughed, a sound like a windchime. "Don't be silly, of course I am."

"Right," Ezekiel said with an awkward smile. "Of course you are." He tried to remember how he'd ended up here. Nothing came. No fight with Palaiologos, no emotional introduction to his son, just darkness, a laugh, and a splitting headache.

"What's wrong?"

"Nothing, I guess I got more wiped than I thought fighting Palai—"

The boy screamed, a shrill piercing sound. "Don't say his name. Don't say his name."

Ezekiel knelt down beside the boy. "Okay, okay. I won't say it," he said in a calming tone. He placed his hands on the boy's shoulders.

Immediately the boy stopped screaming and gave a bright smile. "Good. Can we ride horses now?"

Ezekiel opened his mouth to speak, but something caught his attention, motion at the edge of his peripheral vision. A white man was walking towards them, and Ezekiel instinctively placed himself between his son and the man. Confusion washed over Ezekiel as he saw that the man was dressed in rags and bore the marks of several whip lashes all over his body.

"I am so sorry to bother you, Master," the white man said, stumbling over his words. "But one of the other slaves has passed out in the field."

"What did you just say?" Ezekiel asked.

A look of panic crossed the man's face. "We tried to wake him up so we wouldn't have to—"

Ezekiel's son stepped from behind his father, shouting at the man. "What are you doing here?" he asked. "Why aren't you working? You want a whooping?"

"Hush, boy," Ezekiel snapped.

The boy's mouth snapped shut, but he continued to glare at the white man.

Ezekiel continued talking to the man. "What did you just call me?" he asked.

"M-master? I—is that not what you wanted to be called?" the man asked. "I'm so sorry, I—"

"I'm the master?" Ezekiel furrowed his brow.

"Yes," the man said. "Of course. You own" — he gestured around — "all of this…all of us."

Ezekiel scowled. "Show me."

The man nodded his head hurriedly. "This way."

"What's your name?" Ezekiel followed him.

The man paused mid-step and gave Ezekiel a confused look. "You don't give us names, Master."

"But Daddy, you said—"

"Not now," Ezekiel said. "Go inside." The boy took in a deep breath and looked as though he was about to scream, but Ezekiel bent over and got in his face. "And if you start that screamin' again, I'll give you a reason to scream. Go."

Fear and anger flickered in equal measure across the boy's face. He turned on his heel and ran back inside the house shouting for his mother.

"Continue." Ezekiel gestured toward the man.

They passed several more of Ezekiel's slaves as they walked to the field, all of them white men and women. Disgust at the sight knotted in Ezekiel's stomach. His head throbbed as he tried to remember anything before waking up in bed. He knew Will and Kate had traveled with him, but…

A group gathered in the center of the field, huddled over an unseen figure. They all straightened and backed away as Ezekiel approached, led by the unnamed man. Murmurs of fear started but stopped just as quickly. All the assembled people were white, men and women, dressed and scarred in the same fashion as the first man.

"This is him," the man pointed at the unconscious man on the ground. "He was working and then he just collapsed. We tried to wake him up, but he wouldn't budge, and so—"

Ezekiel held up a silencing hand and looked down. Ice gripped at his heart.

"Will." The word came out louder than he meant.

The gathered slaves gasped at the use of a name to refer to one of their own. He dropped to the ground and shook Will by his shoulders. The young man's eyes fluttered open a tiny bit, then went wide. He wrenched himself from Ezekiel's grasp and scuttled away in fear, breathing heavily, eyes darting around the gathered crowd.

"I passed out again." He wiped his forehead, smearing dirt across his brow in the process. His eyes were sunken and tired, and his body was corded with misshapen muscle that bent his back like a much older man's.

"Are you okay?"

Will's eyes locked onto him, and hatred flashed in them as his face darkened. He dusted himself off and rose to his feet. "Oh...you. Still pretending like you care about me?"

Ezekiel furrowed his brow. "What are you talking about?"

"I traveled with you, helped you kill vampires, helped you kill *the* vampire, and the second you get your family back, you turn around and do this." He gestured at the plantation. Many of the other slaves were shushing him, trying to pull him away or hold him back, but he pointed an accusatory finger at Ezekiel. "You're no better than the men who put you in chains."

Ezekiel clenched his head in his hands. "I didn't want this," he shouted. "I just woke up to it. I don't,"—his head pounded behind his eyes like an angry drum beat—"I can't even remember how I got here. What happened after we beat Palaio—"

"Don't," Will shouted back. "I don't want to hear your excuses. Just...punish me and let me get back to work," he spat onto the ground beside him, "Master."

Ezekiel hauled back and slammed his fist into the side of Will's face. "You're not listening! I don't know what's going on." He towered over Will but extended his hand to the young soldier. "Something is wrong. Now stop acting a fool and talk to me."

Will wiped the blood from his mouth. "Go fuck yourself, Ezekiel Blackthorne. You're just another monster."

Before Ezekiel could respond, Anna Marie called him from the house. He gave Will a hard look. A pang of guilt needled its way into his chest. He rolled his shoulders and tried not to show the pain that gripped his heart. "This isn't over."

"Lucky me." Will nursed his already swelling jaw.

His wife called his name the entire time he walked back to the front of the house. He stopped outside the large front doors and stared up at the plantation home. Images of it burning flickered through his mind. He scratched at the paint on the two white columns that flanked the door. No signs of charring beneath the white paint could be found.

"How the hell is that possible?" he muttered. "If I beat Palaio—" He stopped himself; the name didn't frighten him, but he couldn't bring himself to say it. "After what they went through it makes sense they wouldn't want to hear it. Best get into that habit now."

He pushed open the door and found the whole interior of the house was blanketed in darkness. No candles burned, and a chill draft blew through the front hall. His head began to throb worse than before, the incessant pulsing threatening to make him sick.

He massaged his temples. "Anna Marie?" His voice echoed throughout the house, calling back a hollow answer to his question.

Anna Marie didn't answer him.

Ezekiel stepped deeper into the darkness of the house. The light from outside vanished, and he turned to find that the door had disappeared completely. When he turned back around, he found himself standing in an empty black space, where the vague outlines of human shapes danced like blurred ghosts at the edges of his vision.

"Anna Marie, where are you?"

"Daddy." His son's voice echoed in the black. "Why couldn't you play nice? I just wanted to learn how to ride a horse."

"You couldn't settle down and accept things as they were," Anna Marie's voice chimed in. "We could have been happy here. Together. Until you drew your final breath."

"I don't understand." Ezekiel dropped to his knees. "I saved you! I hunted that bastard all across this damn country. But this is wrong. I just wanted you back. I would never—"

"We gave you your perfect world. One where we are free from slavery, avenged, your family back together like you always wanted."

Both Elijah and Anna Marie stepped into view from the darkness. Their voices joined together as one. "But you wouldn't accept it."

"How could I?" Ezekiel looked up at them. "We wanted to be free, not to take away everyone else's freedom. Anna Marie would never—" Something itched at the back of his mind. "Anna Marie would never want this."

"How can we be free while others are free to hate us?" Anna Marie stared down at him with unblinking eyes full of scorn. "After everything we went through as slaves, did you really think those two whiteys were what? Your friends?"

"They're...like my kids." The carpet pulsed before his eyes as he spoke. "Every day they find new ways to piss me off, but—"

"I'm your son." Elijah's shriek cut him off. "Me! Me! Me!"

"I don't even know you," Ezekiel shouted. "You're a ten-year-old boy I've never met!"

Elijah winced at the words and his lower lip began to tremble.

"We *deserve* our time on top." Anna Marie placed her arm around the boy. "You know we do."

"Damn it, we can't become this." Ezekiel pounded his fist against the floor. "If this is what we do, the cycle just repeats until everyone is dead or dying."

"Maybe they should be." Their two voices melded back into one booming voice, making Ezekiel's skull feel like it was cracking from the inside, preparing to burst. The pain burst behind his eyes, showering his vision with dancing lights. Blood leaked, warm and sticky, from his nose. His memories flooded back all at once. The encampment. Banks. Prentiss. *Prentiss.*

"You bastard." Ezekiel's rage lit inside him like a wildfire. "This is one of your sick illusions, isn't it? You trap your daddy in one of these too?"

"This is your fantasy," the two replied, their voices taking on a sneering tone. "A perfect world inside your head to cradle you until you die. Returning the favor for your mercy."

"My perfect world wouldn't have slaves *at all*," Ezekiel barked. "But thanks for telling me where I am. I can work inside my own head." He adjusted the positioning of his hands, as if he were holding his revolvers. With a little focus, he felt cool weight appear in his hands. Two silver-barreled revolvers glinted in the darkness.

The illusory figures vanished into the darkness, and everything went silent, as though a thick blanket had fallen and doused all the sounds in the world. Ezekiel spun around, searching for signs of movement. He stepped forward and the first shriek filled the air. His son appeared out of the darkness on all fours, his head twisted around at an odd angle. He looked at Ezekiel with sad eyes that leaked bloody tears as he spoke.

"I don't want to kill you, Daddy." His sadness seemed genuine.

"You're not my son." Ezekiel set his jaw and repeated the sentence over and over in his mind until he truly believed it. "I don't have a son."

Elijah screamed. His face contorted in rage as he leapt at Ezekiel, razor-sharp fangs erupting from his mouth as he did. Ezekiel closed his eyes and squeezed the trigger. Even the gunshot was muffled in the strange dark space. He heard Elijah's breath hitch as the silver bullet of Ezekiel's mindscape tore through his chest.

Ezekiel opened his eyes and saw the boy trembling on the ground. There was no blood, but the bullet hole was clear. Elijah rolled over to face him, clutching at his chest.

"Why?" the boy asked. "It hurts."

"I'm sorry. You're not real." Ezekiel knelt down and placed a hand on the boy. This was his mind, and he would rip as much control back from Prentiss as he could. "There's no pain."

Elijah stopped trembling and blinked, a bright spot appearing in the darkness around him. "You're right." He began to fade away. "Get him, Dad."

Ezekiel fought back the tears, tightening his grip on his revolvers.

He squatted down and pressed the butts of the guns to his forehead, his body shaking as he tried not to cry. "Damn it! Damn it, damn it, damn it!"

"You could still stay." Anna Marie's voice dragged him back to focus.

Ezekiel could hear her, moving around in the shadows, creeping closer to him as it spoke.

"Stay with me until the end."

He took a deep breath. "It's not her…it's just her face. It's not her…"

"I could be." Bones popped in the darkness. "If you believed."

"I can't." Ezekiel stood and wiped his eyes. "My wife needs me."

"I am your—"

"No." Ezekiel fired at the source of the voice quicker than the illusion could react. The gunshot cut off the rest of her statement. Anna Marie's breath rasped through a ragged hole in her throat as she stumbled into view. "You're not."

"But… I thought you loved me…" Her face twisted in rage, lips peeling back to reveal blood-stained teeth. "I thought you loved me!"

Ezekiel fired again, and again, and again. He didn't stop firing until the illusion of his wife stopped moving. She lay on the ground, full of empty holes that seemed to leak darkness.

"You're a monster," the illusion croaked. "You killed your son. You killed me."

"I know you're not real," he knelt beside her, "but…I'm doing this all for you, Anna Marie. Ten years I've been searching, and God—God I wish that you were real right now. But not like this. Never like this."

"Shut up."

"I promise I will get Palaiologos."

"No," she screamed. "Don't say it."

Ezekiel nodded and gave a bitter chuckle. "So that's it, huh? That's why you hate me saying his name. Because when I do, it becomes real for me again. And how else do you break an illusion but with reality?" Ezekiel's tears had stopped flowing. "You're not worried that his name will bring him back, you're worried I'll remember he's still out there."

"You don't know anything!"

"Cause yeah, I've been trying to rescue you, but honestly, I don't even know if you're still alive...or human. But I know Palaiologos—"

The illusion shrieked and clawed pathetically at the air.

"—I know he's still around." Any sadness left inside him burned away and was replaced with an icy rage. "And I hate him." He placed a gentle hand on Anna Marie's shoulder. "I'll get him, and if you're still alive, I *will* rescue you and spend the rest of my life with you. But even if you're not, I'm going to put that bastard Palaiologos in the ground for good."

"Stop saying his name!"

"I promise." He squeezed the illusion's shoulder. Like with Elijah, a pool of light began to appear around the fallen illusion, spreading until all of the darkness was washed away.

"Please don't leave me," Anna Marie begged. "I'm scared."

"I'd never leave you." Ezekiel steeled himself against her pleas, so he wouldn't slip back into the illusion. "The hope that you were alive is what kept me sane all these years. You give me my strength. I could never abandon you."

The light became blinding, and Ezekiel had to shield his eyes for fear they would burn out of his skull. He was falling again, despite the growing white space that surrounded him. He flailed, searching for something to grab onto, but found nothing. His stomach dropped as weightlessness took hold of him, and then, with a sudden jolt, he stopped.

Ezekiel bolted up from the floor as all his senses returned at once, overwhelming him. Color. Sound. Breath. Pain. His muscles tightened until his body became one giant cramp. Slowly the tension began to fade, and he became aware of his surroundings once more. The tent was exactly as he left it. Banks unconscious on the ground, and Prentiss sitting on the cot, only now a look of disbelief was etched onto the vampire's face. Ezekiel looked down at his missing arm. He stared at the ground and clenched his one good fist until his whole arm shook.

"Prentiss." Ezekiel's voice clouded over like a thunderstorm. His fury mounted as the illusory dream began to fade from his mind. Only Anna Marie's face remained. "You *really* shouldn't have done that."

20

That's impossible." Prentiss scrambled on his cot until his back pressed against the fabric of the tent. "You can't do that. *No one* can do that!"

"Almost no one." Ezekiel lunged for the vampire and caught him in the crook of his good arm. The crosses imprinted there burned Prentiss's throat as the two tumbled to the ground. "You're lucky I've only got one hand to whoop your ass with." He planted his knee in Prentiss's chest, making sure he had a clear view of the remaining crucifixes that covered Ezekiel's own. Prentiss writhed beneath him as Ezekiel brought his fist down into his nose with a crunch.

Prentiss hurled Ezekiel to the side. He landed on the ground with a groan as his whole body spasmed. Rage and adrenaline had fueled him so well he'd forgotten that his body was slowly breaking down from the inside. Anna Marie's pleading voice echoed in his mind, and a new burst of fury got him to his feet.

Prentiss leapt onto him as soon as he stood, sharp nails digging into the sides of Ezekiel's head. His legs were positioned on the parts of Ezekiel that were covered, and he avoided looking at the crosses, though he still trembled slightly in their presence.

"You escaped." Prentiss held Ezekiel's head steady even as he struggled to look away. "That's impressive. This time I'll bury you so deep in your own mind you'll gladly rip out your own throat when I tell you to." His eyes flashed red.

"Get the hell off me." The colors of the world around Ezekiel started to melt again, sliding off of their surfaces like wax in the presence of a fire. He felt the first tug of the falling sensation and the fuzzy feeling of sleep, beckoning him down…down…down…

Ezekiel's good arm flailed as he slipped in and out of the darkness of unconsciousness. He reached out for the only light he saw: the lantern. He grasped the handle and swung it at Prentiss's head. The glass broke on impact, sending burning oil running down the vampire. His dry skin went up in flames like he was made of kindling.

Prentiss shrieked.

Ezekiel shoved, pushing Prentiss so hard that he tripped over the cot and toppled into the side of the tent. The cot, the side of the tent, and his whole desiccated body went up in flames. He flailed, slapping at himself, trying to douse the flames, but they continued to burn. With a final scream he lunged at Ezekiel, flaming claws outstretched, before bursting in a shower of ash that coated the tent's interior.

Neither he nor Banks would survive if Ezekiel waited for the flames to do their work. With great difficulty, he hoisted the general up and supported his dead weight on his back and shoulders. Light-headedness crashed over him in waves.

He burst from the tent, letting oxygen in, and magnifying the flames. The whole thing burned like a great bonfire at the center of the Union camp. Ezekiel rolled on the ground, smothering his own flames before patting the few flames that burned on the general's uniform.

Ezekiel spat ash from his mouth and wiped it from his face. He dropped to his knees, shoulders rising and falling with labored breaths. The flame spread, crackling behind him. Ezekiel stared at the dancing flames, watching the images of his wife and son fade away into the bright light of the inferno. In moments they were gone, and the memories began to dissipate as well, like a terrible nightmare…or the best of dreams.

"You shouldn't have used my family." Ezekiel let his head drop into his hands, and let out a strangled, broken cry.

The soldiers outside had smelled the smoke or heard the screams. Either way, they couldn't get in because the fire had spread to the tent's entrance. They began the process of dousing the flames with water.

General Banks stirred and opened his eyes. "You…" The coldness in his voice was gone, replaced with confusion. "What are you doing here?"

"I'm really not in the mood." Ezekiel panted, glaring at the general. "I fixed your vampire problem, so don't give me any shit." He pointed at the burning tent, surrounded by soldiers with buckets of water. "You're welcome."

Recollection dawned in the general's eyes. "Prentiss." His eyes widened in horror. "He was here. He made me…oh God."

"Yeah." Ezekiel coughed. "You're gonna need to take that one up with God and your men, I imagine." He paused, looking for some words of comfort or consolation. "Start with the men, then go to God, that way you're guaranteed to end with forgiveness." It wasn't what Ezekiel had hoped would come from his mouth, but he couldn't think of anything kinder to say. "Your son's gone," he finished. "At rest, I suppose."

General Banks's eyes filled, but he blinked away the tears. He rose to his feet and extended a stiff hand to help Ezekiel up. Ezekiel relented and let the man pull him to his feet. His body ached something fierce and wanted nothing more to lay down and await his fate. Pain and exhaustion threatened to end him quicker than the poison racing through his veins.

"He got in your head, too." The general was staring at Ezekiel.

"We're not swapping stories." Ezekiel's voice was low and hollow. "I don't have time for you to give a speech. You want to thank me, give me the vial you took from me, and let me go kill that bastard Palaiologos."

Pain ripped through Ezekiel's chest, as though his heart had burst. He doubled over, clutching at his chest through his clothing, his whole body shaking. His sweat, at one point dried up from the lapping flames, began to bead and run profusely all over his body. He exhaled shakily.

"You're dying…"

"Just give me the vial," Ezekiel growled through gritted teeth.

General Banks said nothing but reached into his coat pocket and produced the vial. Ezekiel all but snatched it from the man's hand. He looked around and saw four horses tied up just a few feet away.

"And a horse."

"Take one. It doesn't matter which."

"Thanks." Ezekiel turned and began to walk towards the tied-up horses.

"Ezekiel Blackthorne," General Banks called.

Ezekiel glanced over his shoulder.

The general hesitated a moment, then said, "Take care."

Ezekiel flashed a wry grin that quickly became a grimace. "Don't you worry about me, General." With difficulty, he pulled himself onto a grey horse with black speckles and situated himself in its saddle. The horse was nervous, blustering a bit at first, but Ezekiel stroked the side of its neck and whispered to it in a calming tone, relishing in the warmth radiating from its body. "I won't be a problem."

Reins gripped tight in his one fist, Ezekiel spurred the horse forward and rode out of the camp.

21

Ezekiel was glad for the light sprinkling of rain as he made his journey towards the bay. His horse charged forward, kicking up mud and reeds along the way. He discarded his jacket, letting the bracing cold keep his mind off the pain that wracked his body and screamed with each jostling bump of the horse's gallop. He was in sight of the shore if it could be called that. Marshy wet grass gave way suddenly to still black waters slicking equally dark stones with floating weeds protruding above small, ripple-like waves.

Ezekiel brought the horse to a stop.

Out in the middle of the ebony mirror of the Vermillion Bay—perfectly still save for a faint rippling caused by the breeze—sat the island, overgrown with thick black trees. From the midst of the tangled forest rose the grey-green spire of a crumbling castle. Ezekiel dismounted and sat cross-legged on the marshy ground. His breathing had evened out, and the anger left over from Prentiss's trap was starting to dissipate. He looked left and looked right. There wasn't a boat visible on the shore.

"Of course. Why would they need a boat? They can fly." He placed his face in his hands and breathed slowly, trying both to ease his pain and to come up with a plan. His revolver was useless; Palaiologos shrugged off silver like it was rock salt. Since the Christian faith meant nothing to him, Ezekiel knew his crucifixes would be just as unhelpful.

He sighed.

Death was bearing down on him like a charging war horse, and he had to stop and figure out how to get an ancient vampire to drink something specially designed to kill him, and hope it worked.

"Not a lot of room for fuckin' up," he grumbled. "Not a lot at all." He pulled out the vial, getting lost in the swirling contents. His hand instinctively went to his neck, feeling for the bite marks. He dabbed at the blistered skin, coated with a thick, oily pus that refused to dissipate no matter how much he rubbed it away. Unlike the rest of his body, the bite wound was disconcertingly numb, as if the chunk of his neck no longer existed. He scratched at it, and pain shrieked through his veins like a bat out of Hell.

Ezekiel vomited violently onto the shore of the bay.

He leaned back on his hands and stared at the sky. "Okay then." He took a deep breath and bellowed across the water. "Palaiologos, you bloodsucking son of a bitch, I'm here for my wife. Get out here and let's settle this, you thieving coward."

The force of the shout winded him terribly, and he had to stop to catch his breath before proceeding with the next, and in his opinion worst, part of his plan. Ezekiel hoped that Palaiologos bucked at the challenge, otherwise he'd be just another corpse floating, bloated in the mire of the swamps of Louisiana. He popped the cork open on the vial and with a final deep and shuddering breath, downed the concoction in a single swallow.

The taste hit him first. He'd ended up face first in murky swamp water before, and he'd eaten grubs and worms when food was hard to find. Throw in the coppery hint of blood and a texture both fizzy and clumpy, and the contents of the vial easily placed as the worst of the three. He placed the back of his hand against his mouth and hoped that he wouldn't burp and have to taste it again, or vomit and ruin everything before it began.

As the taste faded, the pain made itself known. Like the vampire venom, the concoction burned, turning his stomach into a cauldron of flaming liquid that churned and tried to eat its way down through his bowels.

Ezekiel exhaled a puff of smoke and waited. The pain didn't fade. It never would; he'd just have to grin and bear it.

A black boat floated toward the shore. The surface of the water was placid, and Ezekiel couldn't make out the telltale disruption of the water by any oars. The vessel glided across the water in silence, leaving no trace on the black mirror. It bumped against the shore and stopped. The water rocked the boat for the first time, beckoning him to enter.

He did.

2 2

The boat glided across the water just as silently as it had come. Ezekiel hunched over, clinging tightly to himself to stop from shuddering. The pain had tripled since he entered the boat, and he knew he didn't have long. He reached into his pocket opposite the empty vial and pulled out the hand-doll he'd taken from Heloise's strange room.

"Magic mumbo jumbo," he mumbled, turning it around in his hand. The smell had since dissipated, a fact he was immeasurably grateful for. "Okay then…sympathetic. It's already my hand…"

He bit down on his thumb until it bled and smeared a streak of it across the doll's forehead. A rip in his slacks made it easy to tear a piece free and, with difficulty, wrap it around the lower half of the moss-filled figure. Finally, he yanked out a small clump of hairs from the back of his head and pressed them into the seams of the stitched together head.

Something was off. He removed the hairs once more, and using his teeth, tore the left arm from the doll and spat it into the water. The green taste of moss and rotten flesh lingered in his mouth as he replaced the hairs.

"Alright," he held up the doll to eye-level, "I guess you're me now, Ezekiel Blackthorne, one-armed bastard out for revenge."

The tear where the doll's arm had been sealed itself shut, and Ezekiel swore the doll took on his likeness, despite the smooth, featureless surface. He stood the doll up and found that he was standing as well. When he turned the doll left, he turned as well. Every action the doll performed, his body, without thinking, followed suit.

"Perfect." He sat with the doll and waited for the boat to make land.

The island had been farther away than it appeared, to the point that Ezekiel had started to wonder if Palaiologos had trapped him in some endless illusory hell. His concerns shattered as the boat bumped against the black stone shore of the island. The smooth gentleness that had marked the journey ended abruptly, sending him toppling out onto the slick, wet rocks.

Ezekiel struggled to his feet and checked the shallow waters, finding and scooping up his voodoo doll that had fallen out as well. As he wrapped his hand around the doll, an invisible warmth coiled around him. He chuckled to himself as he set out in the direction of the castle.

The plants on the island were different from those on the mainland. Instead of the bald cypress trees and mud-entrenched swamp grass, thick oak trees grew close together out of solid, mostly dry ground. No sunlight filtered down from the canopy of emerald leaves, plunging the forest into an eternal darkness. It was surprisingly warm in the forest, warmer than the chilling air on the shore. The warmth did nothing to soothe the aches that tormented Ezekiel's body.

Ezekiel took wobbling step after wobbling step, watching as the castle in the forested distance grew closer at a painfully slow rate. This close he could make out more details of the vampire's domicile. The walls were made of smooth, lacquered grey and black stone and what seemed to be a faded gold trim. There were no windows, no open portals to let in light of any kind. As he approached, he saw that the surface of the stones only appeared smooth. Cracks and dust marred the individual bricks, and the gold had faded and tarnished, leaving it brown and ugly. The initial grandiose display rotted away into one of crumbling decadence. The forest grew darker as he entered into the ancient structure's oppressive shadow. Ezekiel had never felt so small as it loomed over him, both beckoning and repulsing him.

Six towers like wrought iron spears broke through the canopy of the trees and blocked out any light that attempted to make its way down to the ground. Grass didn't grow here. Ezekiel wondered if it was because the trees took all the light and life from the surroundings, or if the vampire's sickness had started to spread to the forest itself, turning the earth barren and black. His footsteps crunched on the dead ground, shattering a silence devoid even of the normal sounds of natural life.

This was a dead place.

Ezekiel's left leg gave out halfway to the castle. Everything hurt, and he found himself wishing for one of Kate's biting remarks telling him to suck it up and press on. He missed Will's even head, who would have made them set up camp and rest, even here at the enemy's gate. But it was just him, his pain, and a one-way ticket to Hell coursing through his veins.

He pressed on, dragging the leg behind him even as it burned in agony. His second leg betrayed him with only a few steps left to the entry arch: an open gate leading to a stone courtyard. He cracked his jaw on the first stones of the path, tasting bliss in the form of blood and setting his skull ringing. Stone statues of angels and demons engaged in vile acts sneered down at him, their visages twisted in cruel mockery.

"Damn it." He fished the doll from his pocket and moved its individual limbs until he found himself standing once more. An invisible force hoisted him upright. His legs screamed at his weight on them, but he didn't fall back over. He tried to move his legs of his own accord, but they refused. "Fine."

Ezekiel began to walk the doll, turning it so that one leg extended in front of the other and then again with the opposite side. He stretched out his arm in front of him, to move it forward. He felt much like a child might, playing pretend with a toy soldier. His legs moved in a strange, stiff waddle, carrying him through the stone courtyard one agonizing step at a time. The muscles in his legs cramped and trembled as he passed stone gargoyles of grey stone, nude women with skulls for heads, and a grinning depiction of the devil himself. Every statue gloomed above him; their hunched, hungry figures warped in an eternally unsated lust. Ezekiel did his best not to look at them.

A fountain marked the center of the courtyard. It had long since run dry, but the red-brown stains around the rim told him that something other than water had once flowed into its basin. As he rounded it, he saw that it was full of skulls and other bones, cracked and filthy with age. Interspersed with these were fresher, bloody skulls that still in some cases had strips of flesh that clung to them and buzzed with fat, black flies.

Ezekiel set his eyes straight ahead, locking them on the towering dark oak doors. They were cracked and splintered, but still stood, strong and sturdy. The doors swung outward, and the castle entrance yawned a dank, stagnant breath. It smelled of age and decay, like a mausoleum baked under a summer sun.

Darkness beckoned.

Ezekiel crossed the threshold, and the doors slammed shut behind him.

"I so often forget that humans don't have to be invited in." Palaiologos's voice echoed in the massive stone structure. "It really makes you lot seem quite rude, you know?"

Candles flickered to life, lighting a dim path that led to Ezekiel's left and disappeared around a corner. Ezekiel followed them, one shaky step at a time, passing portraits of Palaiologos from different time periods on the walls, and artifacts that seemed to match each image. He turned a corner guarded by a suit of knight's armor and entered into an opulent dining room.

A polished wooden table stretched almost the length of the room, its surface reflecting the firelight in a display of dancing shadows. The table was empty save for a goblet of wine at each end, and a third in the center. Palaiologos sat at one end, and at the other…

"Anna Marie." Ezekiel's throat grew tight, and tears began to form in his eyes. Ten years he hadn't seen her, and now she sat only feet away. He wanted to run to her, to fling his arms around her and squeeze her until his muscles ached from the effort. But he couldn't, instead he just stood, and stared. She looked up from her goblet and gave him a perplexed look.

She turned back to Palaiologos. "Who is this?"

Ezekiel's world shattered. He should have known. Palaiologos had taken control of every other person in his so-called family, why would Anna Marie be any different? His mouth hung open, dry, and wordless. He tried to form words, to tell her who he was, to make her remember, but nothing came out.

Palaiologos watched the war play out on Ezekiel's face with a sly smile. "This is Ezekiel Blackthorne. He and I have had dealings in the past, and he is here to finally settle up."

Anna Marie hummed as she drank from the goblet. "Business." She rose from her chair and gave a short bow, first to Palaiologos and then to Ezekiel. "I'll leave you two be then."

"Anna Marie!" Ezekiel's voice echoed eerily off the dining room walls.

She turned to him with the same even and disinterested expression on her face. "Yes, Ezekiel?"

"Please…" His voice broke. "Please stay."

Anna Marie looked to Palaiologos who watched with bemused interest.

"If you'd like." The vampire waved his hand and Anna Marie returned to her seat.

"If you'd like," she repeated, an echo of her master's voice.

It was Palaiologos who rose this time, moving to stand before the fire. "Anything for that woman." The firelight flickered on his pale skin and set his shadow crawling across the dining room floor. "That's what you told me." He spun around and fixed Ezekiel with an intense stare, his eyes a burnt-orange in the low light. "We tested that, and here you are, short one arm and still fighting." He clapped his hands in a slow, condescending fashion. "I'm honestly impressed."

His eyes danced over Ezekiel as if he was searching for something. They lingered on the voodoo doll in his hand.

Ezekiel's grip tightened.

It didn't matter.

Palaiologos waved his hand, and the doll was ripped from Ezekiel's grasp, soaring into the vampire's hand. Ezekiel himself was dragged across the room, stopping only as he slammed into the table. Wine spilled from Anna Marie's goblet, but she didn't seem to notice.

Ezekiel groaned as agony reintroduced itself to his body, having been lost in the shock of seeing his wife.

Palaiologos admired the doll with an incredulous grin and a grating laugh. "Self-possession? That's true desperation, my friend. Dangerous too." He cocked his head and gave Ezekiel a quizzical look. "Can you even stand?"

"Fuck you." Ezekiel began to sweat.

Palaiologos's eyebrows went up. "I see."

He tossed the doll into the fireplace with a flick of his wrist. Ezekiel's heart froze in his chest as he waited to be engulfed in flames or die in burning agony. At first, nothing happened, but after a few minutes the doll cracked and sputtered in the hearth, and Ezekiel collapsed, his body unable to bear weight any longer.

"Fun thing about sympathetic magic." Palaiologos smirked. "Only lasts while the fulcrum exists. You came all this way to kill me and can't even stand under your own power...what were you thinking?" His grating laugh filled the air, a clawing, aching sound like the scrape of metal on metal.

Ezekiel rolled onto his back and forced himself up into a sitting position, gasping for breath and biting the inside of his cheek to keep the pain from making him scream. "I'm not here to fight. As you can see, I literally can't."

Palaiologos narrowed his eyes in suspicion. "What's happened to you?"

"One of your bastards got me." A wry grin wrinkled his face. "Well, one of Collin's bastards, I guess."

"They are all mine in the end."

Ezekiel shrugged. "Been told the venom is a slow painful death. Seems right since I've been pissing blood since I woke up."

"And yet you still managed to kill both Collin and Prentiss?" Palaiologos's face twisted into a mask of dark fury. "I felt them die, you know."

"You motherfuckers burn real nice." Ezekiel barked out a violent cough, spraying blood onto the floor. "Like dry kindling on a hot ass day. And you'll forgive me if I don't give a shit about what you felt. Or maybe you won't." Ezekiel looked up at Palaiologos. "Doesn't much mean a fuck to me at this point."

Palaiologos stood, glowering, over Ezekiel. "Then why are you here?"

"I came for my wife." Ezekiel jutted his chin at Anna Marie. "Like I said."

Anna Marie kept her head down, but Ezekiel thought her face twitched in the firelight.

Palaiologos looked Ezekiel up and down in disgust. "You're in no condition to take her from me."

Ezekiel's eyes flashed. "You almost sound disappointed."

"I'll admit, in a way, I am."

"Shame there's nothing to be done."

Palaiologos stood in silence, scanning Ezekiel's face. He did his best to remain stoic despite the agonizing pain.

"Since you made it this far, against all odds. I'll give you a boon." A wide grin split the vampire's face. "But be warned, it might be more pain than it's worth."

Ezekiel frowned as Palaiologos whistled. The sharp noise echoed in the castle, bouncing shrilly off of stone and wood before dying in the empty distance. "Girl, get in here!"

A child entered the room, looking around hesitantly before taking a place at Palaiologos's side. Ezekiel recognized the girl's face; it was Elijah's face from the dream world, it was his face from when he was younger. Everything was a perfect reflection of his younger self in female form, except the eyes.

She had Anna Marie's brilliant silver eyes.

"No," Ezekiel said.

"Hello, child." Palaiologos's voice was a saccharine taunt as he wrapped his arm around the girl. He knelt down and pointed to Ezekiel. "Do you see that man?"

The girl gave a quick, shy nod.

"That's your father," Palaiologos said.

The girl's eyes went wide, and she looked from Palaiologos to Ezekiel and back. "But I thought—"

"I said you *belonged* to me," Palaiologos interrupted, "not that I was your father. Now, don't waste too much time arguing with me. He's dying. Do you remember what I told you about dying?"

"It's what happens to people who make you angry."

Palaiologos laughed. "Yes, yes it is. Go on." He flashed Ezekiel a cruel smile as he pushed the girl towards him. "Go say hello."

She stood in front of Ezekiel, who could barely stay in his seated position, and stared at his face. She looked down at her hands and back to him. "You look like me." Her voice was a quiet whisper.

"Yes." Warm tears began to roll down Ezekiel's face as he croaked out the word.

"You're bleeding." The girl stroked his cheek. Her fingers came away red. "Dad—" She stopped, glancing back at Palaiologos. "*He* always says it's a shame to waste good blood, but I don't get it. None of it tastes good."

"Come here." Ezekiel extended his arm and the girl walked closer. Ezekiel pulled her in as close. "I'm sorry I'm so late." He stroked a hand through her coarse hair. "I'm so sorry, Maya."

"Maya?"

"That's what I would have named you," he said. "If I'd been there for you."

"Maya," the girl repeated. "It's pretty."

Maya stood, awkwardly letting him hold her. His arm was limp around her, and he couldn't squeeze her half as tight as he wanted. He pressed his face into her shoulder and did his best to take her all in. Finally, he let her go.

"Go to your mom."

Maya bobbed her head up and down and shuffled over to Anna Marie, who reached down absentmindedly and petted the girl on the head like a person would stroke a cat.

Ezekiel clenched his jaw. His molars cracked as he forced himself to his feet, the pain blurring with the rest of the burning agony that ate away at his body. Every muscle rejected his attempt to stand, straining as though they were being torn apart. His head throbbed, and bloody tears burned and blinded his eyes, painting the world red. He stood.

Palaiologos clapped. "That is impressive. Standing. It's a shame you'll topple over any second."

"You said you wanted to test me." Ezekiel supported himself on the nearest chair. "To see what I'm made of. Well, I got here, despite everything, and I'm still fucking standing. You wanna see what I'm really made of, why don't you come over here? Try and sink those fangs into me." Blood dripped from the corners of his mouth as he grinned. "I bet you couldn't even touch me."

"You're aware that me biting you would not stop you from turning into a vampire unless I wanted it to, so this little ploy of yours…it's pointless. You're still going to die."

"Don't wanna be a goddamn vampire," Ezekiel said. "Just want to kick your ass."

Palaiologos scowled. "If you don't believe me, I'd love to give you just a little bit more despair before you die. And I have grown thirsty, watching you suffer."

Ezekiel didn't have to try to look shocked when Palaiologos appeared right in front of him. A cloud of black mist lingered where he had been standing. His two canines, the sharpest of his serrated teeth, extended until each one was almost an inch long, and he plunged them into Ezekiel's neck.

The burning pain in Ezekiel's veins faded, replaced by liquid ice as the blood was drained from his body. His vision narrowed into a pinpoint tunnel, until the screaming brought him back.

Palaiologos staggered backwards, his eyes wide with horror, mouth open in a ghoulish howl. The network of his veins pulsed black beneath his blue-grey skin. He clapped a hand over his mouth and heaved black blood into his palm. "What is this?" His fist pounded on the dining room table, cracking it in half. "What is wrong with your blood?" He doubled over in pain and retched out a flood of black-brown liquid that shimmered with a weak luminescence on the floor.

Ezekiel offered a weak smile. "I may have had a drink or two before I came."

Palaiologos burst into a cloud of mist, reforming on top of Ezekiel with a hand around his throat. His skin began to smoke, and the ink-black beneath his skin began to spread as his ruined veins ruptured, spilling their contents. "You think you've won?" He tightened his grip. His eyes were red with fury, and black veins pulsed within. "I will rip everything you've ever loved apart." He turned his head and snarled at Anna Marie and Maya. "I can always start over with a new family."

"Hey," Ezekiel said.

Palaiologos whipped back around to face Ezekiel, just in time to receive a spat glob of blood in his eyes. He shrieked and reared back, clutching, and clawing at his face once more until he'd carved his own eyes out of their sockets. Palaiologos seethed and bared his teeth, huffing like a wounded wolf.

"I can still smell every last—" He paused, sniffing the air, confused, just as the rifle crack filled the room. The slug took Palaiologos by surprise and knocked him back, sending him skidding across the floor. He struggled to sit up, looking down at the wound in his chest and touching it with trembling hands. His body, weakened by the potion he drank from Ezekiel's veins, was struggling to maintain its regenerative properties.

"That was my last one." It was Kate's voice.

Six shots rang out, the report of a revolver this time. Roses of dark blood blossomed all across Palaiologos's chest. He clutched at them in shock, then fell still. Tension hung in the air for several moments before Will broke the silence.

"Seven is a good number."

"By the way, he was going to say, 'one of you'." Kate stepped out of a shimmering patch of shadows.

"I was leaning towards 'drop of blood in your veins'," Will replied, appearing by her side.

"Oh, look at you being clever."

"I do try."

"It is honestly never apparent." Kate smirked up at him, then pointed a thumb at Ezekiel. "He looks like he needs a doctor."

Will nodded in agreement, jogged over, kneeling by Ezekiel's side.

"You look like shit."

"I bet shit feels a lot better than I do," Ezekiel replied. He was too exhausted to smile.

"It definitely does."

"How'd you get here?"

"I told you I learned magic," Kate shouted. "Magic portals, like the fireplace."

"Damn." Pain wracked Ezekiel's body as Will helped him into one of the dining room chairs. "Sorry I didn't believe you."

"Traveling like that is terrible." Will shuddered. "Now, what happened to you?"

Ezekiel shook his head, and pointed at Anna Marie and Maya, who hid her face in her mother's bosom. "He got in her head. Help her first."

"But you're—"

Ezekiel gripped Will's arm tight and pulled him close. "Help. My. Family." His grip relaxed, and the arm fell weakly to his side. He slumped into the chair.

Will grimaced but made his way over to Anna Marie. Ezekiel lolled his head to the side to watch. He hoped that he'd be able to see his wife, truly, one last time. Will's words were muffled and unintelligible for the most part, but Ezekiel heard, "I'm sorry, ma'am," followed by the younger soldier striking Anna Marie hard across the face with a loud, wet crack.

"Holy water and a shock," Will looked over to Ezekiel sheepishly, "to break his hold over her."

Anna Marie held the side of her face. A look that mixed shock and hurt lingered there in silence until she finally noticed Ezekiel out of the corner of her eye.

"Ezekiel!" She pushed away from both Will and Maya, and rushed to his side. "What's happened to you? Where are we?"

"Hello again, my love." Ezekiel groaned as she embraced him. "It's been a while."

"Your body." She ran her hands down his chest, feeling the scars that crisscrossed all over him. She looked him in the eyes. "And your face…you're older. How long has it been?"

"Ten years," he said. "Ten very long years. But we're back together. All of us." He beckoned to the girl standing at an awkward distance. "Maya, come here."

Maya shuffled over nervously, placing herself between Ezekiel and Palaiologos.

"Who is—?" Anna Marie's hand went to her stomach. "Ten years? Then,"—she stared at Maya and saw the resemblance—"our daughter."

Ezekiel nodded.

"But I don't remember…anything."

"Start now, then," Ezekiel croaked. "Love her enough for both of us."

Anna Marie frowned. "What are you talking about?"

"Clearly, he's dying." Palaiologos's voice made them all jump. He picked up the dining room chair to his right and hurled it at Kate. It shattered against her with a crack, and she crumpled to the ground.

Will immediately rushed to her side.

"Maya," Ezekiel whispered, "do you trust me?"

"I don't know." Her eyes were wide, darting between each person in the room.

"He's going to hurt all of us if you don't do what I say," Ezekiel said. "You don't want anyone else to be hurt, do you?"

She shook her head. "No."

With his head, Ezekiel motioned to the revolver at his waist. "Slide it out slowly and put it in my hand. Don't let him see."

Maya nodded and did what he said.

Ezekiel smeared his blood on and in the barrel of the gun.

He pressed the gun against Maya, hiding it from the vampire as he smeared his blood on and in the barrel. Her eyes filled with terror.

"Trust me."

Palaiologos pounced, tossing the girl aside. His ravenous expression dropped as he saw the gun, now pointed directly at his head. Ezekiel grinned a bloody smile.

"Girl said you don't like wasting blood." He pulled back the hammer of the revolver with a click. "So have some more of mine."

The gun went off, showering Ezekiel in used powder and black blood as the bullet blew its way through Palaiologos's brain, lacing it with Ezekiel's tainted blood. The veins in his face squirmed beneath his skin like a tangle of coiling snakes. Palaiologos reeled backwards with a howl as Ezekiel squeezed off the second shot, ripping a hole through his throat.

Palaiologos continued to stumble, tripping over a protruding leg of the shattered table and toppling into the roaring flames of the giant hearth.

"Just like kindling," Ezekiel whispered.

Palaiologos didn't scream as he burned; he glared at Ezekiel through the flames, his face twisted into an effigy of hatred. His flesh split and cracked, and all at once, he crumbled into black ash that mixed in with the powdery remains of the fireplace's fuel.

Ezekiel's gun clattered to the floor. "It's over."

Anna Marie rushed back to his side. "What can we do?" She wasn't crying, and Ezekiel was glad for that, but the anguish that deepened the worry lines in her face broke his heart.

"First, get me the hell out of this godforsaken castle."

23

W ill and Anna Marie half-dragged, half-carried Ezekiel out of the castle and back through the dark forest, while Kate and May followed. They laid him down gently at the spot where the black stones of the shore became grass. He stared at the slow lapping of the waves for a minute. The sight that had filled him with dread not an hour ago now filled him with a sense of calm and relaxation.

"You know how long it's been since I truly enjoyed a moment's peace?"

"Ten years is a long time." Will sat down beside him.

Kate and Maya sidled up to his other side.

Ezekiel shook his head. "The past ten have been the worst, but I was still a slave for the first thirty-five years of my life. That's forty-five years of suffering, one way or another. It's been a *very* long time."

Anna Marie knelt down in front of him and took his face in her hands. "Tell me we can fix this."

Ezekiel placed his hands over top of hers. He relished the warmth of her touch, and caressed her skin, making sure not to scrape it with the callouses he'd built up over so long. "I'm done. And there's nothing to be done about it."

Sobs began to wrack his wife's body. She pressed her face into his chest.

"But there is something you can fix." He lifted Anna Marie's head and gestured to Maya. "This girl...our daughter...went ten years without a real mother—"

"Or a real father." Anna Marie's tears ran freely down her face. "She needs you, too."

"Hush now." Ezekiel stroked her hair. "I said you can do two things for me. You've done one, but that one was easy."

"What else?"

"Love her. Raise her. Never let her forget that her father loved both of you so much he struggled for ten years, and fought the devil, just to save you." He took Maya's hand and placed it in Anna Marie's. "Be good for your mama, you hear? I know it'll be hard, but don't hold all this against her. She didn't have a choice in the matter."

Maya nodded.

"I'd tell you both how much you two mean to me, but...actions speak louder than words, and I don't want to muddle the message I've already given." He smiled beneath exhausted eyes. "Just know that I am so happy to see you."

Anna Marie held Maya tight and whispered soothing words, not only for her daughter, but for herself as well.

Ezekiel looked to his right and regarded Will with clouded eyes.

Will's face was grim. "I could try to help you. Maybe if we try a blood transfusion?"

"Don't even think about it, sawbones," Ezekiel warned. "I want to die with all of my remaining limbs intact."

"Right." Will forced a smile. "I know you'd hate me getting emotional, but it's been an honor to have known you, Ezekiel Black-thorne. And your memory will not fade."

"You were right." Ezekiel chuckled. "I do hate you getting emotion-al." He placed a firm hand on Will's shoulder.

"I'll make sure your family is treated well and taken care of."

"Thank you." He pulled out his remaining gun and handed it to

Will. "Now you got the pair. Hold on to them for him, until Maya's old enough".

Kate was in tears. She flung her arms around him in a tight hug, pressing a snot-filled nose into his shirt. Ezekiel resisted the urge to flinch away at the pain. He raised a weak arm and patted her on the back.

"You're gonna be alright, Kate. You're tougher than I ever was at your age."

"God took my brother, and now…the only dad I remember." She shook her head against his chest. "Fuck this, fuck Him, and his stupid plan."

"God didn't take nothing from you, girl. Men and monsters did that."

"If men and monsters are beneath his will, what's the difference?"

"You can put a bullet through men and monsters when they take something from you," Ezekiel said. "God's a bit more stubborn than that."

Kate laughed as she cried. "Right."

Ezekiel patted her back a few more times and then pulled away. "Alright, let me see my wife again."

Anna Marie came back over, leading Maya by the hand. Ezekiel smiled and gestured for the two of them to sit down beside him. He kissed Anna Marie on the cheek, and Maya on the top of her head, then looked out to the black mirror of the bay.

"This is everything I ever wanted." Ezekiel sighed. His last breath was the most peaceful one in his entire life.

EPILOGUE

They buried Ezekiel beneath a large cross on the island in front of Palaiologos's castle, both as a ward against evil and as a reminder of all he accomplished.

Six days later, Will stared down at the two polished revolvers in his hands. They weighed on him, heavy, and wrong, but he slid them into the holsters at his waist as his horse continued on the road. They were escorting Maya and Anna Marie back to Heloise's manor in the hopes that she would be able to provide or find a place for them to stay.

Kate snapped her fingers in front of Will's distant stare. "What's wrong?"

"I didn't carry a weapon on me when the war started," Will said. "Ezekiel gave me one after he lost his hand, but I always assumed I'd give it back. And now…"

"Now you have two," she finished. "At least until Maya comes asking for them."

Will nodded. "It just feels weird."

"Don't think about it too much." Kate patted the rifle hanging from her saddlebag. "I'll make sure you never have to even draw those things."

Will chuckled half-heartedly. He turned to watch Anna Marie riding just ahead of them on Ezekiel's horse. Maya rode in front of her mother. She'd fallen asleep a few hours ago.

Anna Marie hadn't spoken much since Ezekiel died, only saying enough words to agree or disagree with a plan. Her eyes had gone wide when they explained Heloise's situation to her. It took a bit of convincing for her to believe that Heloise did not, as far as they knew, practice black magic, and that she had people's best interest in mind when she worked.

Maya stretched and yawned, waking up. She turned in the saddle to look at Will. "Hey…"

Will rode up alongside Anna Marie and her daughter. "What do you need?"

"What was my dad like?" She stared sheepishly at the passing ground beneath the horse's feet.

"Ezekiel was a good man. He loved you and your mother so much he searched for ten years just to find you."

"Most people would have given up after all that time," Kate added, riding up on Anna Marie's other side, "but your dad never did, even though literally everything was stacked against him." She paused thoughtfully. "In a way, he was kind of like a dad to me too. Which is weird. Will?"

"I guess in a way he was," Will agreed.

Maya nodded. "So, you two…are like my brother and sister?"

Will and Kate shared a look. Kate shrugged.

"Do you want us to be?" Will asked.

"Well…you knew my dad," she said. "Mom did too, but you knew him now…not before." She wrinkled her forehead as she thought. "So, you would be the closest things I have to my dad as he was."

"Then you can think of us as your siblings if you like."

Kate gave a slight, silent nod in agreement.

Maya's face lit up and she looked up at her mother. "I have a brother and sister."

"It seems you do." Anna Marie stroked her daughter's hair and smiled.

The road curved left, and the path leading up to Heloise's manor appeared. Heavy branches leaned over the muddy trail, reaching out vibrant green leaves, like welcoming hands as they rode past. Sunlight filtered down on them from the loose canopy, warming them despite the cooler temperature in the air as night began to fall.

Heloise stood waiting for them at the end of the path, hands on her hips and a disapproving look on her face. She wore a form fitting red dress that seemed to glow in the darkness. "You're late. Had my ass waiting for you a whole extra hour." She turned to Kate. "Didn't I show you the fastest way to get here?"

Kate shrugged. "Will doesn't like portals. Blame him."

"We didn't know we were on a schedule." Will sheepishly rubbed the back of his head. "Sorry."

Heloise huffed. "You need to learn the art of verbal sparring. Then you'll actually be fun to be around. Come along." She waved her hand and began to walk back towards her house.

"Wait," Will said.

Heloise looked over her shoulder and raised an eyebrow.

"Ezekiel didn't make it," he said. "These are—"

"His wife, Anna Marie, and his daughter, Maya," Heloise said, pointing at the two women in order. "And my status as the Voodoo Queen did not change in the few weeks you've been gone." She paused, realizing her mistake. Her attitude shifted and she walked over to where Anna Marie and Maya sat atop Ezekiel's horse. She placed a hand on the animal's side and looked at the two women. "I'm terribly sorry for your loss. If I could have done something…"

"They told me you gave him the thing that killed that…thing," Anna Marie said. "That was more than enough. Thank you."

"Heloise Laveau, at your service." Heloise gave a regal, sweeping bow. "Now, please, follow me."

None of the zombies were working. Instead, they milled about. Some sat in the shade, others simply lingered in one spot, unblinking and unwavering.

Without turning around, Heloise said, "They're all resting."

Will's face flushed at the unwanted insight into his thoughts.

The door to the mansion opened as they rode up to the stairs of the front porch. Albert stood, illuminated in the orange interior light, a stark contrast to the darkness that consumed the sky. He strode down the steps and offered a hand to Anna Marie at her horse's side.

"Allow me," he said.

Anna Marie's mouth hung open in disbelief. She looked from Albert to Will and back.

"It's alright," Will dropped down from his saddle. "He's just like that."

Anna Marie offered her hand to Albert, but he shook his head. "Your daughter first. Don't want her sliding out of the saddle and hurting herself."

"Oh, of course." Anna Marie shifted in the saddle and allowed Maya to lean forward and take Albert's hand. He lifted Maya out of the saddle with ease and placed her gently on the ground. From seemingly nowhere he produced a sweet and tucked it into the little girl's palm with a wink. He turned back to Anna Marie and offered his hand again. Anna Marie took it without hesitation this time and slid out of the saddle, landing on steady feet. Albert released her with a warm smile and made his way over to Kate who sat waiting expectantly.

"No thanks," Kate said, sliding off the saddle herself and giving Albert a smirk. "Just wanted to see if you'd offer to help *all* the ladies."

"It would be rude otherwise," Albert said.

"Yes," Kate said, "it would be."

"What are you all waiting for?" Heloise said, tapping her foot on the threshold of her own front door. "Are you going to come in or not? Bartholomew will come round for the horses."

"Yes, right, sorry," Will said. "We were just—"

Heloise vanished inside her house. Will sighed and followed her. She was reclining in her velvet chaise longue when they all entered, sipping from a steaming china cup. Her outfit had changed from the form-fitting dress to a set of relaxed loungewear. She gestured to a fully prepared tea set when they entered. Will and Kate sat, and Anna Marie and Maya sat between the two of them. Albert went over to his wife's chair and leaned on it with a single hand. Will relished the comfort he'd missed since the last time they'd stopped here. After being on a horse almost constantly for the past several days, he struggled not to sink into a deep sleep right on the couch.

"So, you two need a place to stay?" Heloise asked.

"How did you know that?" Anna Marie asked.

"Knowing things is half of how I make my living, darling." She grinned, then let her face drop. "Just like I know what your next question is going to be."

"They said you can do things,"—Anna Marie looked down at the polished wooden floorboards—"can you...would you bring him back?"

"No." Heloise's tone was sharp and final. Still, she paused as if waiting for an argument, then added, "I can't bring him back. Nor would I if I could."

"But they told me all of your servants—"

"Had a spell placed on them *before* they died. One they consented to, I might add." Heloise took a placid sip from her cup and studied Anna Marie over the rim. "Ezekiel's soul has already moved on, and to drag it back, even if he would consent and want to come back now would...cause problems, to say the least. True necromancy never goes the way you want it to."

"Oh." Anna Marie hung her head. "I'm sorry."

Will put a comforting hand on her shoulder.

"Don't be ashamed," Heloise said. "Almost everyone asks. Everyone loses someone they think they can't live without. But most of them do, it's just a matter of whether or not they dig themselves down into the grave with their lost one. Spiritually I mean, though..." She blinked as if realizing she'd gone off topic. "You're fine, dear."

Maya hadn't taken her eyes off of Heloise since they entered the lounge.

"What's on your mind?" Heloise facing the girl.

"You're really pretty," Maya said.

"Thank you," Heloise said with a sincere smile. "I know." She winked and straightened back up. "You two are welcome to stay here as long as you need...or want. There's plenty of space, and I'm sure Albert would love to have more company while I'm working. Most days he just wanders around at a loss."

Albert leaned down and gave her a peck on the cheek. Her smile brightened in return.

"And the people that work here?" Anna Marie asked. "They won't mind?"

Heloise quirked an eyebrow at Will.

"We told her."

Heloise's smile returned. "Most people wouldn't refer to them as people," she said. "I appreciate the politeness, and I'm sure they will as well."

"Everyone deserves respect," Anna Marie said. "Regardless of their situation."

"Such a less aggressive version of your husband's beliefs," Heloise said. "It's refreshing." She rose from her seat and gestured for them to follow her. Kate was halfway out of her seat when Heloise added, "Will, Kate, you two will stay here for now."

"Well, damn it," Kate dropped back into her seat. "Next time start with that."

"And," Albert added as the three women left the room. "Will you be staying with us long term?"

"No," Will said. He fidgeted. "We have some business left in Baton Rouge to handle."

"A whole nest of those fanged bastards just waiting to run wild." Kate kicked her feet up on a nearby stool and laced her fingers behind her head. "We came across them on the way to Palaiologos's castle. Figured they could all use a good ole fashion ass-whooping."

Will couldn't help laughing. "What she said."

"What do you plan to do with them?" Albert asked, picking up his wife's still steaming tea and taking her seat. He sipped from the cup and lounged in the chair, eyeing them with genuine curiosity.

"We sent notice to General Banks to have a company of soldiers erect a fence of sorts, made of crosses, to keep them in for now..."

"The scrawny Private giving orders to a General." Kate flashed a wolfish grin.

"Corporal." Will scowled. "And it was more of a recommendation. But there is a problem."

"Only for him." Kate's voice flickered with a hint of annoyance. "It's an easy decision."

Will sighed. "Do you have any more tea?"

"Would you prefer something stronger?" Albert asked. He gestured to a cabinet of spirits on the wall to his left. It was well stocked with bottles of all make and shape, some appearing far older than the rest.

"Tea will be fine."

Albert nodded and rose from the chair. He went to the tea cart and poured from an already prepared tea pot, filling two cups with black tea. A spiced aroma with a hint of orange filled the air. "Sugar? Milk?"

"Uh, no," Will said.

"Both," Kate said. "Lots of sugar."

Albert did as they asked and handed them a cup each, before sitting back down in his chair. He nestled in, wiggling until he was comfortable, and then looked at them expectantly. He wore a serene smile that never ceased to unnerve Will.

"We're going to burn the city to the ground," Will said. "I don't like the idea, but...there's so many of them, it's the only effective way to get rid of all of them with the least risk." He sighed and placed his cup to his lips and took a long, slow sip.

"We don't have the best track record with fires." Kate sipped her tea, grimacing at how hot it was. She worked it in her mouth until it cooled enough for her to swallow. "He's nervous."

"But also, it's hard not to still think of them as people, sometimes," Will said, scowling. "They were at one point. And it's not like they chose to become like that, not like Palaiologos did. For most of them, it's not their fault."

"They're dangerous..."

"And it's the best thing we can do for them, right?" Will finished with a heavy sigh. "Put them to rest."

Kate reached over and put a hand on Will's arm. "Think of it like what you did to that lady back when we first set out."

Will scratched his head. "Cauterizing?"

"It doesn't look pretty, but she would have died if you hadn't done it, right?"

"Probably." Will's cup lingered halfway between his saucer and his mouth. "She was losing a lot of blood."

"The vampires are a wound. Healing won't be pretty, but...how many people do you think would die if we didn't stop those ghouls from bleeding out into the world?"

"So many..."

"So many," Kate repeated.

Both of them looked at Albert, who had finished his tea and was smiling at them from the chaise longue. With a slight chuckle, he said, "Well I'm glad I was able to help by doing nothing at all."

Will set his cup and saucer down on the end table to his right and stood up, smoothing his coat as he did. "Speaking of all that, we should probably get ourselves over there sooner rather than later."

"What about Anna Marie and Maya?" Kate asked.

"Let them get settled a bit." Will offered a hand to help her stand. She took it and he pulled her to her feet. "We'll come back to check in once we've wrapped up this whole ordeal." He turned to Albert. "Thank you, and thank your wife again for her hospitality."

Albert raised his cup to them in silent acknowledgment.

As they walked out the door, Kate nudged Will in the ribs and asked, "Since they promised you a promotion, do you think they'll let me be your second in command?"

"I don't think so," Will said. Grinning, he added, "In fact, I'm pretty sure that would *never* happen."

Kate pouted. "Why, because I'm a woman?"

"Because you're just a kid," Will teased.

"I'm gonna shoot you." Kate laughed and punched him in the arm. "Well, I hope you're not expecting me to leave you anytime soon...or follow orders."

"I'd worry you were dying if you suddenly started listening to me."

"Even then, I'd die first," Kate said.

Heloise led Anna Marie down a red carpeted hall lit by golden braziers that burned with yellow fire. They climbed a winding flight of stairs and walked past several rooms until they came to an open door of mahogany wood. The path was disorienting, as if the house's internal logic didn't follow the external appearance.

"Your room," Heloise said at last, gesturing to a heavy wooden door that had recently been varnished. It reflected a good portion of the flickering firelight. The door swung open to reveal a room as opulent as the rest of the manor.

Anna Marie's hands went to her mouth. "This,"—she struggled to form words—"it's bigger than the house we had back when,"—she shook her head firmly—"thank you so much, this kindness is—"

"Not without its cost." There was no menace or darkness in Heloise's voice, just a matter-of-fact tone. "I am a woman of business after all, and dealing with two more people complicates things. As I told Will and Kate, I would be happy to take you in, but there is a stipulation. You understand I cannot just hand out favors for free."

"Of course," Anna Marie bowed her head. "I can work in the fields, or take a job in the city, whatever you need me to—"

"No." Heloise gestured around the house, then brought her hands together in front of her chest. "I have labor. I don't need yours. In fact, I don't need anything from *you*."

"Then what?" Anna Marie searched the hallway in bewilderment.

Heloise pointed a manicured finger down at Maya. "I want her."

Anna Marie pulled Maya closer, enveloping her in a tight hug. The thought of losing the daughter she just learned about filled her with dread. And so close after losing Ezekiel again after ten whole years of separation. She began to cry. Heloise put a gentle hand on her shoulder.

"I don't want to take her from you," she said. "No, I don't really enjoy the presence of children. Not that I dislike them, I just...

Anyway, I will not live forever, and I would prefer someone be ready to take my place. An heiress, you might say."

Anna Marie stifled her tears and relaxed, if only a little bit. "You don't have a daughter of your own to take after you?"

Heloise shook her head. "I can't conceive, and believe me, Albert and I have tried. Magic does always have its risks, and you never quite know what it will give…or take."

The meaning crashed over Anna Marie like a thundering wave. She blinked rapidly and her mouth hung open. "You want Maya…to inherit all of this?"

"Yes." Heloise tapped her foot impatiently. "But there are things she must learn. None of this exists without the perfect blend of reputation and skill. I'll help her develop both of those things."

Anna Marie took a deep breath and looked down at Maya, whose face showed no fear, only curiosity. "You have *my* permission then," she said, "so long as no further harm comes to her."

"No harm will come to your daughter so long as she listens to me," Heloise agreed. "And then nothing will harm her ever again."

Anna Marie nodded. "But she also must agree." She squeezed Maya's shoulder gently. "I won't give you my daughter against her will. If she says no, then we'll leave and trouble you no more."

"That is understandable." She crouched down in front of Maya again, wearing a sympathetic smile. "Were you afraid, living with that vampire?"

"Yes," Maya said in a quiet voice.

"You never want that to happen again, right?"

Maya shook her head.

"I can help you protect yourself, and your mama, if you want."

"How?" Maya frowned.

"Magic," Heloise whispered, wiggling her fingers in front of the girl's face. "A whole world of it."

"I can do magic? Like the vampire man?"

"Ha," Heloise scoffed loudly. "Dimming lights,"—the sconces on the wall flickered out and came back on—"shapeshifting,"—the skin on her hand rippled. The whole appendage morphed into a perfect replica of an alligator head—"and moving things with your mind,"—the door to the room slammed shut and locked itself with a click—"are parlor tricks, sweetie. I mean *real* magic. What do you say?"

"The choice is yours, baby," Anna Marie said. "All yours. And,"—she glanced at Heloise —"if you change your mind, we can leave anytime and figure it out."

Maya thought hard, her forehead wrinkling as she did. "Okay, I'll do it."

Heloise clapped her hands together. "Wonderful. I'll give you some time to settle in, so let's say we get started on Sunday. Good a day as any other. So that's four days from now."

"But first, can I ask a question?"

Heloise paused. "Already? I don't see why not."

"If you're so powerful," Maya asked, her voice small in the large hallway, "why didn't you keep my dad from dying?"

Heloise's face fell.

"Well." She searched for the right words. "One of the things you'll learn…it may be the first thing you learn or the last thing you learn, but everyone learns it…for every single thing that magic lets you do, there are still so many things outside of your control. I couldn't keep your dad from dying because he wasn't *supposed* to be kept from dying. It was his fate."

"Oh…" Maya said. "That's not fair."

"No, it's not," Heloise said. "And that's the hardest lesson to learn."

The End

ACKNOWLEDGMENTS

So many people had a hand in this books birth, and I'm worried that I'll forget somebody, so if you aren't mentioned here and feel like you should be—this is your mention. I appreciate you and what you did to help get me here today. I say this with all the sincerity I can muster and with the hope that you understand that I sometimes forget what I had for breakfast in the morning, let alone all the moving parts of bringing a book to life.

To the names I do remember, I'd like to first and foremost thank Rachel Brune who not only gave *Southern Cross* a chance to find a home with Falstaff Dread, but was also an incredibly supportive and understanding editor/collaborator throughout the entire creation cycle. I'm curious how many "Hey, just checking in," messages I sent, and at what point you started rolling your eyes when you saw them!

Thanks as well to Don Noble, whose cover art graces not only *Touched by Shadows*, but now *Southern Cross* as well. Thank you the people who beta read and offered feedback and dealt with all of my anxiety about the quality of the book: Luke, Lauren, and my wife, Stephanie, thanks for putting up with me ranting and freaking out after just about every chapter.

Thank you to my family, who comes to almost all of my book events and supports my writing with every new announcement and release. To my writing group "Getting Lit with Libations" for making this a less lonely endeavor. And lastly to Austin and Denise Camacho, whose conference Creatures, Crimes, and Creativity is the reason I didn't give up on my dream of writing back in 2018.

ABOUT THE AUTHOR

Vaughn A. Jackson is a Horror Writers' Association affiliated author, editor, and sometimes poet of dark speculative fiction. His work generally falls into one of three categories, Creatures, Kaiju, or Cosmic Horror, and often blends elements of fantasy, science fiction, and horror into one unholy abomination. His published novels include the Kaiju thrillers *Up from the Deep* and *Deepspore: Death Below the Sea*, as well as the cosmic horror novel *Touched by Shadows*. He is also the co-editor of the diverse cosmic horror anthology *Beyond the Bounds of Infinity*. When not writing, he can usually be found hanging with his wife and pets, cracking jokes, and making sure H.P. Lovecraft turns over in his grave.

FRIENDS OF FALSTAFF

Thank You to All our Falstaff Books Patrons, who get extra digital content each month! To be featured here and see what other great rewards we offer, go to www.patreon.com/falstaffbooks.

PATRONS

Dino Hicks
John Hooks
John Kilgallon
Larissa Lichty
Travis & Casey Schilling
Staci-Leigh Santore
Sheryl R. Hayes
Scott Norris
Samuel Montgomery-Blinn
Junkle
Vickie DeSantos
Quincy J. Allen
Allison Charlesworth

THANK YOU
FOR PURCHASING THIS
FALSTAFF BOOK.
YOU ROCK!

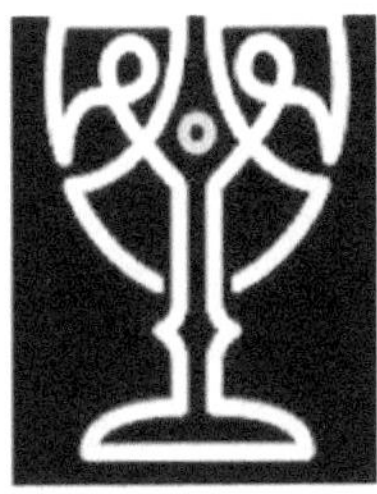

AT FALSTAFF, WE BELIEVE YOU SHOULD READ
WHAT YOU WANT, HOW YOU WANT.
THAT'S WHY EACH PRINT BOOK PURCHASED INCLUDES
THE EBOOK AT NO ADDITIONAL CHARGE!
JUST SCAN THE QR CODE BELOW TO GET YOUR EBOOK!
AND DON'T FORGET TO SIGN UP FOR OUR NEWSLETTER
WHILE YOU'RE THERE, SO YOU DON'T MISS OUT
ON ANY OF OUR AWESOME TITLES!

FOR MORE ABOUT US,
VISIT WWW.FALSTAFFBOOKS.COM